"But I don't understand why. Why me?"

"Because." Something close to anger crossed Sam's face. "Anytime you walk in the room I can't take my eyes off you. Anytime you walk out I have to physically stop myself from following you. I like your bitchiness. I like that you get right in my face. And sweetheart, I adore the way you stand by your criminal of an uncle. You're everything I've ever wanted, May."

"I don't know what to do with that," she whispered, the words pulled from her very soul. "I don't know what to do with *you*."

"Don't you?" he asked and his thumb brushed her nipple. "Maybe you should just kinda stop thinking about it. Just do what feels right."

"That's the problem. I don't think I know right from wrong. I only know who I care for."

"Okay." His hand cupped her breast. "Then care for me, May."

ONCE AND ALWAYS

Elizabeth HOYT

WRITING AS
JULIA HARPER

ONCE AND ALWAYS

FOREVER

NEW YORK   BOSTON

Forever
Hachette Book Group
1290 Avenue of the Americas
New York, NY 10104

www.HachetteBookGroup.com

Printed in the United States of America

First Edition: February 2015
10 9 8 7 6 5 4 3 2 1

OPM

Forever is an imprint of Grand Central Publishing.
The Forever name and logo are trademarks of Hachette Book Group, Inc.

The Hachette Speakers Bureau provides a wide range of authors for speaking events. To find out more, go to www.hachettespeakersbureau.com or call (866) 376-6591.

The publisher is not responsible for websites (or their content) that are not owned by the publisher.

For my brother, Robert McKinnell, who really does own and wear an acorn-brown Resistol cowboy hat and who read an early draft for western Minnesotan accuracy.
Sorry about those scar-inducing sex scenes. :-D

Acknowledgments

Thank you to:

Susannah Taylor for never giving up on this project.

Amy Pierpont, my editor, for making me rewrite this damn book a bamillion zillion times.

And to my Facebook friend, Anne Bornschein, for Otter the Dog's awesome name.

ONCE AND ALWAYS

Chapter One

DAY ONE

Shit. Maisa Burnsey's heartbeat did a little stumble as the familiar police car halted behind her. She pushed up her chunky black glasses. Every damned time she passed through Coot Lake, Minnesota, she got stopped.

In her rearview mirror she watched the tall trooper climb from the squad car. He sauntered toward her Beetle, loose-hipped and long-legged, as if he had all the time in the world. And like the good guy in a black-and-white western, he wore a stupid cowboy hat.

Maisa snorted softly.

He stopped by her car door, his pelvis framed by her window exactly at eye level, as if he was showing off the bulge of his package.

Not that she was looking.

There was an American flag on the left breast of his padded navy uniform jacket, a metal badge on his right, and below that a name tag that read *WEST*. One gloved hand rested on a lean hip, behind a holstered gun. His upper face, obscured by mirrored sunglasses and the cowboy hat, was stern and intimidating. His lips, though, were wide and almost soft, the top just a little fuller than the bottom. The man had a mouth that was beautiful enough to make a woman ache just by looking.

Maisa straightened her spine and glared at him. Okay, she could do this.

He twirled his gloved finger to tell her to roll down the window.

She opened it, letting in the freezing January wind. "What?"

He nodded. "Hey, May."

His voice was deep and gravelly, like he smoked, though she knew for a fact that he didn't.

"*Maisa*," she snapped automatically. She wasn't going to think about the last time he'd called her May. "This is the fourth time you've stopped me here."

"Maybe you should quit speeding." That beautiful mouth quirked. "Or quit running away."

"I'm *not* running away," she lied, poker-faced.

"Darlin', you've been running away from me since last August."

Maisa felt her teeth click together. "*I'm* talking about pulling me over for speeding."

His wide mouth curved. "I'm not."

She breathed deeply. Evenly. God damn it, meditation was supposed to make her *less* angry. "This is entrapment."

"Now," he drawled, his small town accent broadening, "I don't have any fancy un-*ee*-versity learnin', but I'm pretty sure entrapment is if I *falsely* lure you into breaking the law—"

"What do you call a speed trap, then?"

"—*which*, since I didn't *make* you drive well above the speed limit—"

"And that's ridiculous as well." She scowled. "The limit's seventy everywhere else but this stretch of highway."

He shrugged. "Still fifty-five here."

"Well, it shouldn't be. There should be better things for you to do than lie in wait for some poor driver who hasn't noticed that the speed has gone down so you can pounce." She stopped to inhale.

He looked at her. "Like what?"

"What?"

"What should I be doing instead?"

She licked her lips. God damn it. Did he have to stand so close? "Doing your job."

"This *is* my job."

"Following me isn't your job." She could feel the heat mounting her neck with her anger. Oh, to hell with it. "Speeding isn't why you stopped me and you know it. You're harassing me."

There was a pause as if she'd broken some obscure rule in their game. The wind whipped icy snow against her car, making the vehicle sway.

He didn't even flinch, steady as a granite monument to male stubbornness.

"That right? You know, you don't *have* to take this route every month when you drive up from Minneapolis." His voice was terribly gentle, and she had a flash of him straight-armed over her, his mouth wet, his voice a gravel whisper as he'd murmured, *Like that?* And shoved inside of her, quick and hard and confident.

One night. One night last August she'd let him in. It'd been hot and muggy, and her uncle's cabin hadn't had any air-conditioning. She'd booked a room at the Coot Lake Inn and then gone to the only bar in town to have a cold beer. Sam had been there, looking way too sexy in faded jeans and a T-shirt so thin she could see the outline of his nipples when the condensation on his beer bottle had dripped on his chest. He'd bought her another beer and flirted and she'd thought, *Why not?* Why not just one night? So she'd brought him back to her tacky motel room and let him undress her and kiss her and make love to her, and in the morning she'd woken with her heart already beating too fast in panic. She'd dressed without showering, grabbed her bags, and left him there, still asleep on his belly, his wide shoulders bare and erotic in the stark morning light.

It'd been a mistake. One terrible, unforgettable mistake.

She exhaled through her nose, glancing away from him, feeling suddenly sad and vulnerable.

She hated that feeling. "This route is the easiest way to my uncle's house."

"Uh-huh." He didn't even bother to sound like he believed her, which was just insulting. "And me being the cop on duty most of the time along this stretch of highway has nothing to do with it."

"*Yes.*" She was going to chip a tooth if she ground down any harder.

"May—"

"*Maisa.* Look, just give me the goddamned ticket and I'll be on my way."

She could see him shift his weight from one leg to the other out of the corner of her eye. "Your brake light's out."

She swung back. "What?"

He nodded his head at the back of her car. "Right rear."

Maisa started to crane her neck to look before she realized how silly that was. "Oh. I'll get it fixed."

"'Preciate that," he drawled. Did anyone else *drawl* in freaking *Minnesota*? "But I'll have to cite you in the meantime."

"Oh, for God's sake, Sam!"

That got a gloved finger sliding his mirrored glasses down just enough to see the flash of his electric blue eyes. "Well now. Glad to hear you remember my name."

She didn't give herself time to think, just slipped the knife between his ribs, quick and nasty. "Of course I remember, *Sam*. It's not a big deal, you know. You were a good lay, but that's all you were."

For a moment everything seemed to still along the stretch of lonely highway. The land was nearly flat here, rolling farmland broken by small clumps of trees. The wind was relentless, blowing across the prairie in winter. In order to survive it those trees had to be tough, hardy, and tenacious.

Maybe tenacious most of all.

Sam sighed and took off his glasses and she thought obscurely that he'd never hide those eyes if he had any idea what the sight of them did to women. He was thirty-three, but he had lines around his eyes as if he'd been squinting into the sun—like Clint Eastwood looking for the bad guys on the open plains. Except Sam had already found the bad guy and was too stupid—or too bullheaded—to know it.

"You practiced that in front of your bathroom mirror, didn't you," he said, flat.

Of course she had. No way was she letting him in again. Sam West was just too dangerous to her peace of mind—and heart. "Just give me the ticket."

He leaned one arm on the car roof just over her head, bending to look at her through the window. The position put his face close enough to hers that she could smell mint on his breath.

She tried not to breathe, refusing to look at him again. If she could just get away, if he'd just let her go, everything would be okay.

She could freehand a dozen dress designs in one night, she could set a dart so perfectly it'd make any woman's ass look like gold, but she couldn't deal with the emotions Sam West made her feel.

She. Just. Couldn't.

"Listen, May," he said, too near, too damned *intimate*, "I won't give you a ticket this time. Just be—"

The sound of a revving engine came from behind them on the highway.

Sam looked up.

"Fuck," he murmured, and in one graceful movement vaulted onto the hood of her car. He slid spectacularly across the surface on one hip, just as a little red car tore past, so close it rocked the Beetle in its wake. The red car's taillights flashed as it braked for the curve, tires squealing. But the car just kept going straight. It slapped into the packed snow at the outer curve, climbing the embankment, nose skyward, engine squealing before suddenly cutting.

In the silent aftermath Maisa stared, open-mouthed with shock.

Then she remembered Sam. He was no longer on the hood of her car. She couldn't see him anywhere. Panic crowded her chest as she began battling the car door handle.

Oh, God, oh, God, please don't let him be hurt.

Chapter Two

Sam lay flat on his back in freezing snow, watching snow-flakes sail down to land in his eyelashes.

A scowling, feminine face inserted itself into his vision. Maisa Burnsey had a sharp little chin and nose, delicately curved lips, and big brown eyes behind those ugly black glasses. She kept her fine, black hair cut very short. The style made her look kind of innocent and girl-ish at first glance, which was about as far from the truth as could be. She wore a shiny black down jacket and black spike-heeled boots, her hair mostly hidden under a beret—black, natch—pulled jauntily down over one eyebrow. He'd dreamed of her face on lonely nights in his cabin.

Generally in his dreams she'd worn a much more wel-coming expression.

"What are you doing?" May asked. Demanded, really. The woman would never win any awards for her sweet personality.

"Breathing." He sat up gingerly.

"You shouldn't do that," she said, her hands spread and hovering as if she wanted to touch him but was afraid to.

Which was pretty much the problem with their entire relationship.

"Breathe?"

She scowled harder, stamping lines between her eyebrows. The look made him want to put his tongue in her mouth until she forgot to frown. "Get up."

"I'm fine." He keyed his shoulder radio, contacting the Coot Lake police dispatcher. "Hey, Becky."

"Yeah?" Becky Soderholm was in her midfifties and had run Coot Lake's police station since anyone could remember. Probably she'd started in diapers.

"Got a speeder, possible wreck up on 52 just past the 101 mile marker," Sam said. "Damn fool nearly ran me down."

"You're not hurt, are you Sam?" Becky's voice was full on exasperated. "'Cause you know Dylan's off today and Tick is still up at his aunt's in Fergus. Not expected back until tomorrow."

"Nope, just got the wind knocked out of me." Sam stood and shook the snow off his jacket. His right shoulder and hip ached like hell, but he made an effort not to limp. Male pride and all. He took May's arm, ignoring her squawk, and helped her up the bank back to the road. "But I may need an ambulance and a wrecker, depending."

"Depending on what?" Becky snapped.

"If the driver's still alive." They'd reached the highway now. He could see the red compact. It had climbed the hardened mound of snow left by the plows on the opposite side of the highway. The compact's little nose pointed forlornly at the darkening clouds.

Behind him, May muttered under her breath.

A corner of his mouth kicked up. She sounded pissed.

"Get in your car." He said without turning. A semi rocketed by, making the snow whip around his legs. "You can turn on the heat, but don't go anywhere."

"Who're you talking to?" Becky demanded.

"Maisa Burnsey," Sam said as he jogged across the highway.

"Oh, for Christ's sake, Sam," Becky hissed. "How many times are you going to pull that woman over before you give up?"

"Dunno." Sam reached the compact. "Just a sec."

He could hear Becky's impatient grunt by his ear, but he was more concerned with the compact's driver's door opening.

"Don't move, sir."

But the driver wasn't listening. A short, dumpy guy in a bright red windbreaker too thin for the weather tumbled out of the car. He slid on the snow before catching himself with an outstretched hand on the car. He was in his early sixties. His thinning gray hair was slicked straight back from a pasty, soft face that looked like it'd never seen sunlight. Square glasses sat crookedly over an overlarge nose. He had an abrasion on his left cheek and powder from the airbag on his face and chest. Otherwise he seemed fine. 'Course, looks could be deceiving in a crash victim.

"Whoa, there." Sam placed a hand on the guy's upper arm. "Becky, that's an affirmative on the ambulance and we'll need a wrecker, too."

"No ambulance!" The man's voice was high and with a distinct accent. "I do not need an ambulance, you imbecile."

Sam raised an eyebrow, but kept his voice even and calm. "You might have internal injuries."

"No." The guy suddenly clutched at his heart, which

didn't exactly make his case, and sat back down on the tilted driver's seat. "Do I?"

"I don't know. That's why—"

Imbecile Man got up suddenly and staggered to the red compact's back. His windbreaker nearly matched the color of the car.

"Sir," Sam said. "I'd appreciate it if you could sit down until we can get you some help."

The guy was crouched awkwardly, struggling with the trunk.

The radio on his shoulder crackled. "Sam, we've got at least an hour's wait on that ambulance," Becky said. "And a God-only-knows on the wrecker. Cars in ditches every-where, looks like."

Sam keyed the mike. "Okay. I'll take him in myself. And the wrecker can wait until tomorrow, I guess."

"No!" The guy turned so quickly he nearly toppled into the snow. He'd worked his way back around to the driver's side door. "You do not understand! I need... I need to get *this* car to drive." He leaned in to pull some-thing and the trunk popped open.

Sam looked at the compact. It was a Hyundai, maybe an Elantra, with rental license plates. Even if the little car were horizontal, the front bumper was ripped off, the left front corner was crumpled, and that wheel was leaning in as if the axle might be broken.

"Yeah, about that," Sam said. "I don't think you're going anywhere anytime soon."

The guy looked around wildly. A few strands of his sparse hair were standing on end, waving gently in the wind. He was making an odd sound—kind of a whining moan under his breath. Must need to go somewhere quick.

Sam narrowed his eyes. "Let me see your license."

A clear sneer began on Imbecile Man's lips before he suddenly switched tactics. He smiled, revealing stained teeth and said with a pronounced accent, "No problem! No problem, Officer! I shall just go on my way, yes?"

Sam didn't bother replying to that. Just held out his hand and wriggled his fingers.

The guy sighed in defeat and fumbled a wallet out of his pocket. He gave Sam a laminated card.

Sam took it, his brows rising when he saw the State of Nevada emblem. "Long way from home, aren't you?"

"What?"

"Ilya Kasyanov, that right?" Sam waited until Kasyanov nodded. There was something off about the guy— even taking into account that he'd just been in a wreck. "If you won't accept an ambulance, sir, then I can take you into town. Maybe set you up at the Coot Lake Inn."

"Coot Lake?" Kasyanov perked up. "This is Coot Lake?"

Sam raised his eyebrows. Most out-of-towners weren't too thrilled by—or had ever heard of—Coot Lake. It was a small, northwestern Minnesota town and the Crow County seat. Fergus Falls lay a bit to the north and west; Alexandria, a bit to the south; but neither were in Crow County. In winter, Coot Lake had about four thousand residents, give or take. In summer, the population doubled with the onslaught of summer folk heading to their lake cabins.

But in any case, Coot Lake wasn't exactly on the way to anywhere. "Just outside. How about you get into my squad car and I'll run you into town. That is, if you still don't want to go to the hospital?"

"No." The guy immediately shook his head. "No hospital."

He scrambled to the back of the Hyundai's open trunk. There was a black suitcase inside, one of those compact things people took on airplanes.

Sam stepped forward. "Here."

He started to reach inside, but the guy squeaked and grabbed the handle. "Is okay."

"I can see that," Sam said, easy. "Let me help you." He took the guy's elbow, despite the man's instinctive jerk away.

"He needs an ambulance," came a cranky female voice behind them.

Sam turned to look at May. Her cheeks and the tip of her nose had pinkened in the cold, and he wished he could touch her. Just one more time.

She'd been leaning over his shoulder but jerked back and scowled at his movement. "Or something. What?"

"Thought I told you to go to your car," he said mildly.

"It won't start."

"Shit." Sam glanced at the little black Beetle. "Okay. Let me take a look at it."

Her eyebrows winged up her forehead. "Gosh, do you think your testosterone will make it go?"

"Behave, May." Sam guided Kasyanov across the highway and to his squad car.

May trotted behind. "No, really, I bet that's why it wouldn't start for me. Too much estrogen."

The wind was picking up, driving darts of snow into Sam's face. He opened the back door to the squad car and settled Kasyanov in it—sitting bolt upright, clutching his suitcase—and then turned to May, standing between him and her Beetle.

She waved her arms over her head. "Probably you'll just have to squint at my car, all manly and stuff, and *vrooom!*"

He looked at her patiently. "Do you mind?"

She dropped her arms. "What?"

He took a step, bringing their bodies so close together her pink little nose nearly brushed his chest.

She tilted up her chin.

He leaned down until he could smell that sweet scent she wore. Until he could watch her pupils expand and the flush spread up her cheeks. Until he could almost taste the salt on her lips. "Do you want me to try your car. Or not."

He watched the soft skin of her throat move as she swallowed. "Okay."

She held out her keys.

"Coward." Sam took them and stepped around her, careful not to brush against her body.

"Hey!"

He ignored her, walked to the Beetle, and pulled open the door, leaning down to push back the driver's side seat all the way before sitting and inserting the key into the ignition.

Three minutes later he shook his head. "It's not even turning over. Probably your starter. You're going to need that looked at."

May huffed from outside the car. She hadn't sat down beside him, as if she'd thought it was best to keep her distance. "Like I couldn't figure that out for myself."

At least she was smart enough not to mention his hormones—or hers—again.

He got out and locked the Beetle before handing the keys to her. "I'll give you a lift and send a wrecker back

out, but Becky says they're backed up. It may be tomorrow or later before they can get your car in to the garage
in town."

May frowned down at her keys. "I don't have too much
choice, do I?"

"Not really." He turned to walk to his squad car and
then realized she wasn't following. "Well?"

She opened her mouth as if to argue.

He raised his brows.

She snapped her mouth close and pivoted to make her
way to her Beetle. Sam strolled behind her, watching as
she opened her passenger car door to retrieve her purse
before stamping to the trunk of the Beetle. He was right
behind her when she opened it. He grabbed her suitcase
and the smaller, black case with a handle sitting beside it
before she could. The smaller case was surprisingly heavy.

She huffed. "I can carry that."

"Yup." He weighed the smaller case. "What's in this?"

"None of your business," she snapped.

He gave her a look, then turned and led the way back
to his squad car, toting her bags. Everyone seemed to have
one of these black roll-aboard suitcases but him. Must
mean he didn't do much airplane travel—at least not anymore. Not since giving up his former career in the army.

He pushed that thought aside as he put May's suitcases
in the trunk, and then helped May into the front seat.

Sam opened the backseat door and looked at Kasyanov. If the car skidded at all, that suitcase was going to
break the man's nose. "Better let me stow your case in the
trunk. Safer."

He expected an argument, but Kasyanov bit his lip and
released his death grip on the suitcase.

Sam stuck it in the trunk next to May's and slammed the lid shut before getting in the squad car. He checked over his shoulder and then pulled onto 52 carefully. Even with the wind the snow was beginning to pile up, and he didn't want to spin out as well.

"Your uncle's?" he asked May without looking at her. She made the trip up from the cities every couple of weeks or so to stay for the weekend with her uncle, George Johnson. They'd first met on this very stretch of highway when he'd pulled her over for speeding. That'd been almost two years ago.

A lot had happened since then.

"You know that's where I always stay," she said.

He shrugged one shoulder. "You were at the Coot Lake Inn in August."

She blushed at the memory, and Sam felt himself getting hot in an entirely different area. "He doesn't have any air-conditioning. I was going to melt if I didn't get a motel room."

Sam decided it wasn't in his best interest to pursue that line. "Staying long?"

"Through the weekend."

He signaled and turned onto County D. "Then you might like dinner tonight."

"No, I wouldn't."

"Tomorrow night?"

"Nope."

He felt a muscle in his jaw tense. Why did she have to make it so hard? "You sure? Marie's put Rocky Mountain oysters on the menu at the Laughing Loon Café, special. Thought that'd be right up your alley." He glanced at her. "Being a ball buster and all."

She inhaled. "Well, you thought wrong."

And the damnedest thing was that the little hint of hurt in her voice made him want to gather her close and tell her he didn't mean it, not really.

Six months she'd been running away from him, throwing insults and withering scorn like grenades in her wake, and for some reason he couldn't give up the chase. He'd begun to think he was getting off on her cutting words—which was disturbing as hell.

And cutting words were all he'd received these last months.

Before that, though, there'd been that night. One night only. That night she'd whispered words that hadn't left bruises on his skin. Her body had been open and warm and soft beneath his, and she had seemed—this sounded silly, even in his own mind—but she had seemed like *home*.

He'd been chasing that warm home ever since.

"The turn's here," she said, gesturing to the sign for Pelican Road, as bossy as ever.

"Yup." He didn't bother pointing out that he knew where Old George lived. He signaled and turned on Pelican, then slowed, driving carefully. Off the highway and with brush along the road as a windbreak, the snow was beginning to pile up.

Pelican Road ran around the sound side of Lake Moosehead, the bigger of the two lakes bracketing the town. Coot Lake was the smaller lake but had better fishing, though the entire north half of the lake was in the Red Earth Ojibwa Indian Reservation and was marked off with white buoys. In summer, you could catch a mess of sunnies in a morning's fishing on either lake, a walleye if you were lucky.

Beside him, May shifted, and he smelled it—whatever flower scent she used. Maybe just her shampoo, because it wasn't strong, just *there*. Lingering in the heated car. Making him think of August humidity and the damp skin between her breasts.

The squad car was heavy with silence, broken only by Kasyanov, breathing through his mouth.

"There it is," May murmured quietly, as if she felt it, too.

Sam pulled into the drive of a low, red-stained cabin. On the other side of Lake Moosehead new multi-million-dollar "cabins" had been going up for the last twenty years. This side of the lake, though, was weedy with no beach—artificial or otherwise—which meant the cabins were mostly from the forties and fifties. No a/c in summer, and sketchily retrofitted plumbing and heat.

Sam killed the engine and watched the cabin. The lights were out.

"He even home?"

"Yes, of course." She was already struggling with her seatbelt. "There's no need to get out. Just pop the trunk and I'll grab my stuff."

"I can carry them in for you."

"No."

"May—"

"It's *okay*."

Her glare was so fierce that he raised his hands. "Fine."

"Just leave it." For a moment some emotion crossed her face, something more vulnerable than her generally warlike expression.

He ignored the mouth-breathing from the backseat. "You know I'm not going to do that."

Any softness in May's expression was gone so quickly he almost thought he'd imagined it. She shook her head once, and then she was out the car door.

He watched in the rearview mirror as she tramped around to the back of the squad car and retrieved her suitcase and the little black case. She carried them to the cabin and set the cases down before knocking on the front door.

There was a moment's pause, then the door opened and she disappeared inside without a glance backward.

Not that he'd been expecting one.

"Sir?" Kasyanov cleared his throat nervously. "Sir, perhaps we go now?"

"Yeah." Sam put the squad car into reverse. He glanced at Kasyanov as he looked over his shoulder to back from the drive. "Next stop, Coot Lake Inn."

Chapter Three

꧁꧂

Maisa shut her eyes, leaning for a second against the inside of the cabin door, just taking a breath. One frigging mistake half a year ago, and for some reason she just couldn't get past it. Every time she saw Sam it seemed to reopen the wound—made it ooze blood and impossible longing. She swallowed. *Just get over it, damn it!*

Maisa straightened, readying herself for the inevitable grilling from Uncle George.

Except when she opened her eyes the old man was half turned away from her, didn't seem to've even noticed her bizarre entrance at all.

Something was wrong.

It wasn't anything that someone else might've noticed, but Maisa had been studying her *dyadya* since she was a very little girl. She knew when he had a certain squint that he wasn't pleased, that when the right corner of his mouth kicked up he was amused, and when he was tense or nervous his shoulders raised a little and stiffened.

As they were now.

Then, too, there was the cigarette dangling from his lips.

She inhaled as her spine snapped upright.

"I thought you'd quit." She plucked the cigarette out of his mouth as she stomped past him.

"It was only the one, little mama," he said behind her.

"Only one?" She looked pointedly at the cheap glass ashtray beside his big LazyBoy. The ashtray sat on an old metal folding TV table and overflowed with butts and ash. She stubbed out the cigarette she'd taken from him.

The old man shrugged. "Maybe more than one."

He was a tall man, her great-uncle, but in the last couple of years as he'd entered his seventies, his shoulders had begun to stoop and he had a little sloping belly now. His iron-gray hair was as full as ever, though. Dyadya combed it straight back into a pompadour and used pomade to keep it in place. His ears were overlarge for his head, and his eyes drooped down at the corners. Deep wrinkles had imprinted themselves on his weathered face so that he looked like he was perpetually in mourning.

Those sad eyes watched her now without any welcome.

She scanned the main room but saw nothing out of the ordinary. The recliner sat directly in front of the TV, the pink velour worn thin by Dyadya's butt and head. The little kitchen table behind it was piled with old mail and a bowl full of red apples. There was no place to actually sit and eat at the table, which wasn't a problem since Dyadya did most of his dining in the recliner. On the TV table, beside the ashtray, a newer laptop sat with a glowing screen. Over by the simple redbrick fireplace there was a cheap particle-board bookshelf crammed to overflowing with paperbacks. Most were in Russian, but a few American thrillers sat there as well. And on the wall, high up near the ceiling, was the single framed picture: a black-and-white photo of Saint

Basil's Cathedral. The kind that could be bought for a few rubles in any tourist shop in Moscow.

She looked back at Dyadya. "You forgot I was coming."

"I was not expecting you today." He shrugged, not quite an admission.

"I told you two weeks ago that I was coming up this weekend. It's not my fault you don't keep a calendar." She dropped her cases by the green plaid love seat sitting at an angle to the recliner. She shrugged off her jacket and pulled off her beret, letting them fall to the love seat.

"Phtt." Dyadya waved his hand like he was batting a fly. "And who keeps a calendar, I ask you."

"Me, for one."

A faint smile curled Dyadya's wide mouth. "Ah, but you are a woman of business, Masha, mine. I am but an old man. What use is the keeping of time for a man in his last years?"

Maisa's eyes narrowed. Generally Dyadya was pretty pragmatic—not one to bemoan his age. Was there truly a problem with his health? Had his memory begun to go?

She swallowed and crossed to the kitchen. "Well, since you weren't expecting me, do you have anything for supper? My Beetle stalled out on 52, and apparently it'll be tomorrow before it can be towed and looked at. I'll have to take your pickup into town if you need groceries."

Dyadya was trailing her. "But how did you get to my cabin, then?"

She tensed a little, but didn't turn around. "Sam West gave me a lift in his squad car."

"Did he?" His voice sharpened.

A battered soup pot was simmering on the stove. She lifted the lid to distract him.

"You are lucky." Dyadya was at her elbow as she inhaled the fragrant steam. "Borscht. I started it this morning and I think it will be just right for you and me in an hour or so."

"Good." This time Maisa didn't have to fake the smile—she'd loved borscht since childhood, when Dyadya would make it on cold winter days.

She glanced at the frosted kitchen window. This certainly counted.

"You need to get some insulation on the windows in here." She followed Dyadya back into the living room. He rolled as he walked, a man who had been muscular in his youth and still had the long ropy arms of a wrestler. He settled into his recliner and she took the love seat.

Dyadya pulled out his cell phone from his breast pocket and looked at it before putting it away again. "And how was Samuel West?"

"Fine." Maisa shrugged, brushing a bit of lint off her black jeans.

"That is all you can say?" Dyadya tutted. "He is a good man, that West. You could do worse, my Masha."

"*Good.*" The word tasted bitter on her tongue—like a mouthful of regret. "He's a *cop.*"

"And so?"

"*And so* you know the problem with that." She arched her brows at him pointedly. "Do you want me to end up like Mom?"

"Your mother, she was always a romantic." Dyadya said. "And your father—you should pardon my words—is a *durak.*"

"He's an idiot *and* an asshole," Maisa corrected.

She hadn't seen Jonathan Burnsey since the day in the second grade when he'd walked out on his family. And because he'd never married Irina Nozadze—even though Mama had put *his* surname on her birth certificate—there was no divorce and no settlement. Mama should've taken the bastard to court for child support, but Irina Nozadze was a timid, emotionally fragile woman. She'd simply been too frightened to challenge an up-and-coming assistant city attorney for Minneapolis. As a result they'd never had any sort of support—financial or otherwise—from Jonathan. Maisa had taken care of her mother in middle school and high school and had put herself through college, working nights and on the weekends.

Jonathan had been a *good* guy, too—a man who prosecuted criminals for a living. It was precisely because he'd been on the side of good and the law that he'd left her mother. The Nozadze family was most definitely not law-abiding. His association with her mother might have been detrimental to his all-important career.

"Samuel West is not the same as your papa," Dyadya said gently.

"He's a cop and a good man. You said it yourself." Maisa pursed her lips. "He's close enough."

Dyadya picked up the TV remote, fingering it as his brows knit. "You have grown hard, my Masha. I do not know if this is a good thing or a bad thing."

"Maybe it's neither." Dyadya's troubled tone made her chest hurt, but on this she could not waver. Sam came too close to the steel walls guarding her heart. He was much too dangerous to the woman she'd made of herself. "Maybe it just is."

"Perhaps this is so," Dyadya said. "And your mother? How is my niece?"

The change of subject was a relief. She ran her fingers

through her pixie cut, ruffling her fine hair, which had been flattened by the beret. "She's dating some guy she met down at the grocery."

"You don't like him."

She shrugged. "I don't know him, really. He seems all right—better than the car salesman she was dating last summer—but it doesn't matter, does it? He'll leave her in another couple of months, or she'll see someone else she likes better."

Dyadya grunted noncommittally. "And your father?"

Maisa raised her eyebrows. "You know we don't see him. Why do you ask?"

"As a man grows older, sometimes he regrets decisions he made in his youth." Dyadya smoothed his thumb over the edge of the remote where the paint had been worn away from use. The thumbnail was missing on that hand—the right—as was most of his forefinger. "I wondered if your father had discovered that yet."

"No." Maisa's voice was very firm. "And he never will."

"Perhaps." Dyadya tapped the remote against his knee. "Perhaps not."

"You're brooding. What's happened?"

"Nothing, Masha mine," the old man said. "Nothing at all." He tossed the remote into a basket that held old catalogs beside his chair. "But tell me. How is your business? Are you making good money?"

She raised an eyebrow at the unsubtle change of subject. "I'm getting there, Dyadya. I'm planning on a professionally designed website by summer and then I'll be able to set up mail order."

He frowned as if he were about to continue his line of

questioning, and she hastily added, "I brought up Butch to do some work this weekend." She patted the small hard-sided case she'd placed beside her on the love seat. Inside was her favorite portable sewing machine, affectionately nicknamed "Butch" since the moment her mother had paid $2.50 for it at a yard sale.

"I do not understand why you needed four years of college for this." Dyadya pushed his lips out. In Russia, seamstresses had been ill-paid laborers, and Maisa had had trouble convincing him there was a difference between a seamstress and a dress designer who hand-made her creations. Probably it didn't help that she was still working hard to break into the business of made-to-order dresses. "But it is good you like your work."

"You'd prefer I went into the family business?" She gave him an ironic look as she rose.

"No. Do not jest over such a thing." He shook his head slowly like a lugubrious basset hound. "It is very well you never followed my path, as you yourself know."

"I suppose," she conceded, just to get him off the subject. "Here, let me show you what I brought."

Dyadya leaned forward in his recliner as she set the black roll-aboard at his feet. There'd been a sale at Macy's just last week, and when she'd seen the thick wool cardigans she'd thought of Dyadya. He was always complaining that he couldn't find warm enough sweaters for winter.

Maisa unzipped the lid of the suitcase and opened it with a flourish.

But when she looked down, instead of seeing a hand-knit Irish fisherman's sweater, she found a tangle of strange clothes.

"What—?" She wrinkled her nose as she lifted out

an enormous pair of white men's briefs. They were high-waisted and had a hole near the waistband. "This isn't mine."

"And I think this, too, is not yours," Dyadya said quietly. He picked up a ziplock bag from the suitcase.

Maisa squinted at it. There were small pink sparkly things in the bag. "Costume crystals?"

Dyadya brought the bag close to his face and peered at the pink stones. They were in the shapes of little hearts. "Costume. This means fake, yes?"

"Yeah."

Maisa watched, bewildered, as her uncle got up abruptly and went into the kitchen. She heard drawers being pulled open and the sound of rummaging and then Dyadya returned with a jeweler's loupe in one hand and the ziplock bag in the other.

He sat down again and opened the bag, taking out one of the pink gems.

Maisa sat forward. "What—?"

"Hush," he murmured and screwed the loupe into his right eye. Behind Dyadya's recliner was a floor lamp with a swivel head. Dyadya pulled the light close, turned it on, and held the gem between thumb and forefinger, squinting.

He put down the first gem and chose another, peering at it.

By the fifth gem Maisa had lost all patience. "Are you going to tell me what's going on, or do I just have to sit here and guess?"

"Patience, my Masha," Dyadya said calmly as he selected another stone.

"Dyadya!"

He looked up at that, sighed, and took off the loupe. "They are most certainly not costume, these."

She looked between his worried face and the little bag of pink jewels. "Not costume. Then you're saying they're—"

"—diamonds," Dyadya said succinctly. "Perfectly matched pink diamonds of a clarity and color as I have never seen before. These diamonds came from the same mine, I think. And what is more, they have been carved into the shape of a heart, each one." He shook his head, absently picking up a stone to fondle it. "Such a method is extremely wasteful of the stone, thus making it extremely expensive."

"But if they're diamonds..." Maisa blinked, still not completely believing. "Then they must be worth—"

"—millions of dollars," Dyadya said. "I am guessing, but maybe three million."

"Three. Million. *Dollars?*" Maisa squeaked.

"*Da.*" Dyadya nodded thoughtfully. "Someone, I think, is missing this suitcase very badly right now."

Chapter Four

Karl Karlson looked up at the Coot Lake Inn sign. It was the kind that had press-on black letters, some of which had fallen, so the sign read:

OOT LA E I
ee cable & a/ !

Probably the lack of "c" wasn't bothering any potential customers, seeing as it was about seven below at the moment. He slammed the door to his extended-cab pickup and hefted his black suitcase, thumping the back of the truck as he passed. A chorus of cheerful barking answered the thump.

Karl smiled as he opened the door to the tiny Coot Lake Inn lobby.

Norm Blomgren, the Coot Lake Inn proprietor, did not.

"*No*," Norm shouted when he looked up and saw Karl. Norm was a hefty guy, and his shout was kind of forceful, so he staggered back a bit behind the laminate check-in counter, his belly jiggling and his face drawn into an expression that, if Karl didn't know better, he'd mistake for dismay.

Luckily Karl did know better. "Hey, Norm. Long time no see."

He took off his fogged glasses and wiped them on the front of his shirt.

"Not long enough," Norm muttered, because he was a joker, that Norm.

"Say," Karl said, casual-like, as he dropped his suitcase by his feet and leaned on the counter. "You don't happen—"

"No."

"—to have a room for—"

"*No!*"

"—maybe a night or two?"

Norm narrowed his eyes, which, what with his heavy, red cheeks, wasn't such a good look for him. He kind of resembled a horrified hog catching his first sight of the slaughterhouse. Karl didn't tell Norm that, of course, because Karl was a kind person and a good friend besides.

He did crinkle his brow a little to let Norm know that he was kinda taken aback by the proceedings thus far. "Hey, how's the tile in those bathrooms I fixed up for you? They sure looked good when I finished, didn't they?"

"That was last summer," Norm said, jutting his chin out. Now he looked like a *hostile* horrified hog. "And I *paid* you for that work. And let you stay here on the house while you did it. *And* you mooched off my kitchen!"

Well, that just hurt. Karl let Norm know this because communication was important in any relationship, even between bros. He'd read that in a *Cosmo* in the checkout line at Mack's Speedy, right under the article about "5 Moves

Your Man Will Never Expect," which had been quite illuminating. "Hey, that hurts, Norm. I shared my chili—"

"God-awful *farting*—"

"—every night while—"

"Stole those tomatoes—"

"—I was working on those baths—"

"—right out of *my* garden—"

"—and it was tasty, too." Karl finished triumphantly, because he was on pretty firm ground here. No one made chili as good as his. "Hey, I could cook for you again while I'm here. You still got that half a pig you bought from Al? 'Cause I make an awesome pulled pork. Secret recipe handed down from my great-grandfather."

Norm looked suspicious. "Your great-grandfather made pulled pork on the reservation?"

Karl drew himself up. "Pulled pork is a proud Ojibwa tradition. We taught it to you white folk, you know."

"That's what you said about hacky sack when we played it in junior high."

"My great-*great*-grandfather's hacky sack ball," Karl began patiently, because sometimes Norm didn't understand the finer points of Ojibwa history.

The office door blowing open interrupted him.

Sam West strolled in, stomping snow from his Sorels. He had an older guy with him, sort of short and tubby with a nervous, unhealthy face behind crooked glasses. Sam held a black suitcase in one hand. He had the other on the guy's elbow. It was just resting there, but Karl knew Sam's grip was strong due to a misunderstanding some years back involving a sweet yellow Corvette, a case of Budweiser, and three live ducks. Doubtful if Tubby Guy could break away.

Not that he was trying. No, he was staring around Norm's little check-in office like he expected killer ninjas to jump out from behind Norm's one fake potted plant.

"Norm," Sam said, putting down the suitcase. He took off his hat, hitting it against his jeans to knock the snow off it, and jerked his chin at Karl. "Hey, Karl."

"Hey, Sam." Karl carefully did not look down at his own black suitcase. Nope. He'd learned that kind of tell could send an eagle-eyed lawman like Sam into an investigative frenzy, which might be very awkward given the contents of said suitcase. Instead, Karl settled in more comfortably at the counter. This looked like it might be interesting, and it wasn't like his conversation with Norm had been headed in a positive direction. "Who's this?"

Sam smiled slow and amicable, but Karl knew that smile and knew Sam wasn't completely relaxed in the stranger's presence. "This is Ilya Kasyanov, who just went into a snow bank up on Highway 52."

"Oh, man." Karl shook his head in sympathy. "I've done that before."

"And not even in winter," Sam drawled.

Karl ignored that. "Ilya? Hey, are you Russian? 'Cause—"

But at that point Sam tripped over his own feet or something and drove his elbow into Karl's side, knocking over the two suitcases in the process.

"Oof," said Karl, wondering if he still had intact ribs. "What—?"

Sam gave him a glare so scary that Karl immediately got the point: *Ixnay on the Ussianray.*

"Sorry," Sam said, not looking sorry at all. He righted

the suitcases, and then turned to Norm. "Do you have a room for Ilya here tonight?"

Norm brightened. Fact was, even though the Coot Lake Inn was the only motel in town, it didn't do a whole lot of business, despite Karl's awesome improvements to the bathrooms in numbers 21, 23, 25, and 9.

"Yup," Norm said, busily setting out the paper registration form and a pen. "Got a nice one out front. Has a bathroom just renovated, too."

"Purple and black tile," Karl put in to help. "Custom work."

"Okay, yeah," Ilya said, and there was a faint but pretty distinct Russian accent there, if Karl knew his non–Coot Lake, non-Ojibwa reservation accents. And he did. "I'll take the room." He pronounced *room* as "rhoooom," like he was gargling a bunch of extra consonants and vowels at the back of his throat. "But only for one night, yes? I leave in morning, quick."

Sam lifted an eyebrow, which was kind of a neat trick that Karl had once spent an entire afternoon trying to do in a mirror, sadly without success. "Blizzard's only going to get worse. Might think about staying a couple of days."

Kasyanov looked alarmed, his sad-dog eyes widening. "But . . . but my car must be fixed. I pay well."

"Sure, you can pay well and your car might be fixed," Sam said easily, "but that doesn't guarantee you'll be able to drive on two feet of snow."

"Heard it was going to be three," Karl put in.

Norm scoffed. "Two and a half max. It never gets to three no matter how much the weather guy on four jumps around." He turned to the Russian. "We got cable, though, and Marie at the Laughing Loon Café will deliver if you order over twenty bucks of food. You'll be fine for three or four days."

Kasyanov had been swinging his head back and forth like a cat following a feather toy. Now he made a dying whale sound. "*Days?*"

Sam looked at him, squinting a little. "Yeah. You got some place to go?"

See, the way Karl figured it, *everyone* has a place to go, so he was slightly surprised when the guy rolled over and started backpedaling. "No...ah, no. I am fine here in Loon Lake." He smiled, showing yellowed teeth. The smile was totally unconvincing and kind of gross to boot.

"Coot Lake," Norm corrected, but not meanly, because after all the guy, yellow teeth or not, was a paying customer. "Here." He pushed the registration form at Kasyanov.

Ilya sighed and picked up the pen.

Sam turned to Karl. "What're you doing here?"

"Well, Norm's helping me out with a place to stay—"

"Am not," Norm muttered, but then got distracted by Kasyanov filling out his form.

"Something wrong with your trailer?" Sam asked.

"You could say that." Karl had a real nice mobile home up on the Red Earth Ojibwa Reservation. Only forty years old with almost real wood paneling in the den/living room/dining room/office. "Water pipes froze."

Norm looked up just then, and with a heavy sigh reached for a room key and shoved it across the counter with a grunt. Karl nodded and took it.

Sam winced. "Ouch."

"Yeah," Karl said. "But what with the meeting of the Crow County Mighty Mushers this weekend, it's just as well. I can be in town with—"

"Wait. Wait." Sam held up his hand in a stop sign. Sometimes Sam had trouble coming out of his cop man mode. "Your crazy musher friends are arriving in town?"

"Sure." Karl had been trying to get Sam into the dog-sledding club for years. "You could come by and check it out. We're going to sled around Moosehead Lake, have a few brewskis, and then maybe do a loop up by County M before coming back into town."

"How many?"

"Miles?" Karl blew out a breath, estimating. "Oh, at least fifty. But the way the snow's coming down—"

"No, not miles. *Mushers*."

"Uh." Karl shrugged. "Well, normally we'd have at least twenty, twenty-five people, but with this weather? Maybe fifteen or so all told. Depends on whether Doug Engelstad has recovered from those two broken legs, I guess. And his cousin, Stu Engelstad, was threatening to move to Alaska 'cause he says it's too warm here—"

The Russian choked a bit for no reason that Karl could see.

"Which I can totally get, but really, there aren't many girls in Alaska, so I wouldn't myself. Not"—Karl interrupted himself thoughtfully—"that Stu seems that interested in girls. Or guys. Or, really, *humans*—"

"Karl." Sam had a real even voice, usually, but sometimes when he was a might cranky it came out sharplike. "Does Doc Meijers know about your meet?"

Karl's forehead crinkled, confused. "No. Why would he?"

"So maybe you could get a *permit* from the police chief to invite fifteen drunken mushers and all their dogs to town and then chase them around Moosehead Lake?" Sam said, his tone kind of getting loud at the end.

"Oh, hey," Karl said. "Do we need a permit for that?"

"*How* much?" the Russian yelped at the same time.

Karl was sympathetic. Sometimes Norm had a tendency to gouge. He *was* the only motel in town.

Sam turned to the counter and Karl bent quickly to grab his suitcase. He picked it up and then hesitated. Both suitcases were black; both looked exactly alike. Was it...?

He glanced up to find Sam staring at him. "Something the matter, Karl?"

"Nope. Nothing at all," Karl grinned a grin of outstanding blandness and tightened his grip on his suitcase. "Imma just show myself out."

Sam narrowed his eyes, Karl was already hustling out the lobby door. He didn't want to stick around to find out about dogsledding permits. And besides, Norm was busy enough without showing him to his room.

Karl knew the way anyway.

Chapter Five

"*How* many dogs?" Doc Meijers barked.

Six hours later Doc and Sam sat in Ed's bar, a checkerboard on the table between them, Sam's acorn-brown Resistol cowboy hat on the seat beside him. It was crowded tonight, despite the weather, and Sam had to lean forward across the battered wood table to be heard. "Well, figure fifteen mushers with eight to ten dogs each..."

He shrugged, sitting back in the booth. Doc could do the math well enough himself.

The Coot Lake police chief was in his early sixties and had a bit of a paunch and the sort of well-weathered, scowling face that frightened everyone but very small children who hadn't the brain cells to know any better yet. Little kids loved Doc Meijers.

Doc muttered something, but the jukebox started up with Carrie Underwood's "Before He Cheats" and his words were lost in the wave of feminine hostility.

"Yup," Sam replied because he was pretty sure he knew the gist of what Doc had said.

Carrie complained about restroom cologne—which, as it happened, Ed made sure to keep in stock—and Sam drank Sam Adams and watched Doc bitch to himself as he captured two of Sam's men.

By the time the song had wound down, so had Doc.

To a degree, anyway. "Goddamn fool, that Karlson," he shouted into the sudden lull in sound.

Fortunately, Ed's was the kind of dive where no one looked up. Ed had taken the former VFW post—fake wood paneling and all—run a counter across the back, bought some secondhand tables and chairs, mounted a stuffed bobcat on the back wall, and called it a day. No one knew what the bobcat was for—wasn't like there were any live ones locally. Sam had always figured the bobcat was Ed's idea of decoration. Either that or he'd gotten it free.

Ed's was the only place open past eight on a Friday night in Coot Lake, so if you didn't want to drive a ways—and who wanted to in a blizzard?—Ed's was it. Right now there was a table of women of a certain age to the side of the room. Becky the dispatcher was one of the women. She'd recently got a new dye job that was an eye-popping purplish red, even in the bar's dim lighting. When asked, everyone said it looked real good on her—especially when Becky gave them the squint-eye. The ladies were sharing a plate of Ed's microwaved nachos and a pitcher of beer, and they looked scarier than anyone else in the room.

That was saying something, because a bunch of big guys in plaid and Sorels were at a back booth—probably some of Karl's musher friends. Tick, one of the two other Coot Lake policemen besides Sam, had returned from his aunt's in Fergus. Tick had the night shift, though he was taking his dinner break right now. He was leaning his skinny ass on a stool at the bar, talking away to a bored-looking Ed as he ate his greasy burger-and-fries dinner. Tick had recently grown a soul patch below his bottom lip and seemed pretty proud of it, despite Doc muttering that it looked like a spider had died on his chin.

The final member of the Coot Lake police force, Dylan Rorsky, was off duty and on what passed for a dance floor at Ed's, along with Haley Anne, one of the waitresses at the Laughing Loon Café. Dylan was only twenty-three, with a face so fresh and unlined it made Sam feel ancient—especially with what Dylan was doing with Haley Anne on the dance floor. Haley Anne wasn't even a year out of high school. She had pink streaks in her dark hair and a ring through her bottom lip that bobbled when she smiled. Sam was trying hard not to look too long in their direction, because last time he had he'd been kinda scarred.

"You'd think after that last fiasco," Doc said, still harping on the mushers, "Karl would've thought ahead to getting a permit."

"Not sure Karl does much thinking ahead." Sam jumped one of Doc's men and took it off the board.

"Say that again." Doc grunted moodily and took a sip of his Schell's—the only beer Ed kept on tap. He nudged one of his pieces forward. "And he's not the only one. Didya know Tick confiscated a whole bunch of firecrackers from some teenagers last week and just yesterday was asking if he could set them off in the municipal parking lot?"

Sam winced. "He's not so bad."

"And Dylan." Doc shook his head as if the youngest member of the Coot Lake police force had only days to live. "That girl he's with is a menace. Only a matter of time before Dylan forgets the condom and we wind up with a shotgun wedding."

Sam shrugged. "He could do worse than Haley Anne."

The outer door opened, blowing in freezing wind and snow and May Burnsey.

Sam randomly moved a piece.

Doc grunted and took his only king. He didn't bother looking over his shoulder at the door when he asked, "That Maisa Burnsey just came in?"

Nothing he could reply would gain him anything but embarrassment, so Sam took another sip of his beer. She'd made it very clear that she didn't want to see him tonight. Only a jerk would assume she'd come in just for him.

May was stomping her boots, looking around the room. She caught sight of him and even across the room he could see her eyes narrow. Sam nodded at her. She started weaving through the tables, and it kind of looked like she might be headed in his direction, but as she passed the group of middle-aged ladies Becky caught her. May leaned down to say something.

"I heard you stopped Maisa this afternoon," Doc rumbled.

"Becky gossips too much."

Doc raised a pointed eyebrow.

"She was speeding." Sam checked, but he was pretty sure he didn't sound defensive.

"Son," Doc said, using his heavy paternal voice, so Sam must've been off on his self-assessment. "That woman isn't for you."

Sam raised his Sam Adams to his lips rather than say something he might regret later.

May had shed her jacket. She wore a soft sweater that outlined and cupped her breasts. Every man in the room—excepting Doc, who still hadn't turned—had his eyes on her.

"She's city." Doc looked at him significantly. "And she's George Johnson's niece—and you know darn well what George is."

Sam winced, thinking of the crude tattoos Old George sported on both hands. Each knuckle—the ones he had left anyway—had a Cyrillic letter and a symbol of some kind. There were ornate crosses, strange Xs, skulls, and half circles that looked like moons—and those were only on the parts of his body they could see. God only knew what he hid beneath his clothes. Tats were pretty popular nowadays, but generally not the kind that George sported.

The kind that meant he either was or had been Russian mafiya.

"We have no proof," Sam said low, because even though the jukebox had started into Styx—Ed's musical tastes were kind of all over the board—he didn't want to be overheard. "For all we know Old George was a victim of communist Russia and spent time in the gulag."

"Then what's he doing with a last name like *Johnson*?" Doc grunted and pushed one of his men into the last row on Sam's side of the board. "King me. Bet on it—he's in hiding from something or someone."

Sam grimaced—both because he was losing the checkers game and because this wasn't the first time they'd discussed Old George, his Russian accent, his mafiya tats, and his odd choice of retirement place. Hardly anyone moved to Coot Lake unless they had some kind of tie to the community. It wasn't like Coot Lake was on the Most Scenic Small Towns list.

He glanced up and found May watching him. She hastily looked away, smiling at one of the women at the table. Someone had found a chair for her and she was sipping a half-full plastic cup of beer. What was she up to?

"You gonna move?" Doc growled.

"Sure." Sam took another of Doc's men, making the older man scowl. "Did Becky happen to mention the wreck up on 52?"

"Guy went into the ditch?" Doc asked without really asking. "Becky said it happened right in front of you."

"Yup. Definitely speeding. Nearly took me out when he went by. But," Sam said hastily as Doc opened his mouth, "that's not why I brought it up."

"Then why?"

"The driver had a Russian accent."

Doc jumped four of Sam's men, starting with the one that Sam had just moved and effectively ended the game.

"Well, shit," Sam said, staring down at the ruins of his defenses.

Doc shook his head and began gathering pieces. "I've told you once, I've told you a thousand times: Can't get too attached to your pieces. Sometimes you gotta sacrifice a man. You play afraid and you'll never win any game."

Sam flinched at the thought of sacrificing a man. He took a sip of beer to cover.

Doc eyed him, but didn't ask. He never did, which Sam appreciated. He glanced at the ladies' table, but May was determinedly looking away from him.

Tick zipped up his parka, waved farewell to the room at large, and left, presumably to tend to the wrecks up on 52.

The jukebox started playing something slow Sam didn't recognize. One of the mushers broke from the pack, the others catcalling and slapping him on the back. He started toward May.

Well, that just wasn't happening.

"'Scuse me." Sam drained his beer bottle and stood.

Doc muttered something behind him, but Sam ignored him.

He had his sights set on an ornery little brunette.

Chapter Six

Maisa bit her lip, watching Sam bear down on her out of the corner of her eye. It'd seemed like a good idea earlier when she'd left Dyadya's cabin with the excuse that she needed to pick up a few things in town. She'd go to Ed's—where everyone would be on a Friday night—and find out what Sam knew about the guy who'd crashed his car. She wasn't about to approach the stranger by herself—for all she knew he was some kind of mob courier—but she had to at least try to discover what was going on. Dyadya had smiled and gently deflected all her questions, acting suspiciously innocent before declaring that she shouldn't worry, the whole matter would be resolved in the morning.

Maisa snorted softly to herself. Yeah, and the Russian mob had suddenly become a charitable club.

"Hey," a male voice said by her elbow.

She turned quickly, but she already knew it was the wrong male voice. A huge guy with an untrimmed beard and scuffed Sorels stood there, looking shy.

She smiled at him and then froze when he smiled back.

Flakes of chewing tobacco were stuck to his front teeth. "Wanna, y'know, da—"

"Sorry, bud, she's already taken." Sam appeared next to the guy, and although he was over six foot, Tobacco Boy was easily a head taller.

And also, he'd lost his smile. "Listen, asshole—"

"Ah. Ah." Sam shook his head. "Watch the language in front of the ladies."

"Damned straight." Becky belched.

"May?" Sam held out his hand and although his voice held the polite question, his posture sure didn't.

She narrowed her eyes a moment. If she didn't need him for information, she might be tempted to go with the other guy, tobacco-stained teeth or not, just to show Sam.

But she did need him, so she placed her hand in his, rising. She smiled apologetically at the big man. "Maybe another time."

He might've replied, but Sam was already dragging her to what passed for a dance floor in Coot Lake.

"Do you mind?" she hissed as he turned her and drew her much too close.

One corner of his mouth quirked up and stayed there as he placed his big hands on her waist and began swaying gently.

She huffed and put her palms on his shoulders. He was wearing a denim shirt so warn and faded that the fabric was like suede. She couldn't help but surreptitiously circle her fingertips, her eyelids half lowering. Soft, soft fabric over warm, hard muscles. If she let her head sway forward just a little she'd bet she could smell his shaving gel. He used something corny, cheap, and all-American, like Old Spice.

Perfect.

"How'd you get into town?" His voice was a quiet rumble beneath the gentle croon of Bonnie Raitt.

"Dyadya's pickup." She caught his brows lowering and added, "He's got snow tires on, you know he does."

He shook his head. "Snow tires don't mean a damn if it starts to ice or the snow's too deep." But his voice was still low. He knew it was too cold for the roads to ice over tonight. She had another hour or so before the pile up of snow got dangerous for driving.

His hands slipped down a little—nearly, but not quite settling on her rear.

She was so tempted to lay her head against his worn denim shirt and just forget about mysterious pink heart diamonds for the night.

The jukebox hiccupped and a new song started: Pink imploring "Please Don't Leave Me."

That song always made her tear up for some reason. She fought the feeling, pulling back a little from his embrace. "Did you have any more wrecks to take care of this afternoon?"

He tilted his head, studying her, and she was reminded once again that Sam West might be a small-town man, but his intelligence was anything but small. "A few people skidded off the road, but no major wrecks."

"That's good."

"Yup." He bent his head and murmured in her ear, "How long you stayin' this time?"

She swallowed drily. "Just the weekend. Like usual."

"Too bad," he whispered, his hips brushing against hers. "I'd like to see more of you."

"What for? Sex?"

For some reason her hostile tone made his mouth

twitch in amusement. "That, too. Mostly, though, I want to get to know you."

"What for?" She found she'd gripped his shirt in her fingers and she carefully smoothed it out, frowning at the wrinkles. "It's not like we have anything in common."

"Oh, I think we do," he said, confident as always, his voice deep and seductive.

"Like what?" she demanded.

He shrugged, his big shoulders moving under her hands. "You care. I do, too."

"Care?" She laughed incredulously, feeling vulnerable, almost pained. "What gave you the idea I care?"

"Because," he said tenderly, "you stopped to talk to Becky though you didn't want to, apologized to that musher with the bad breath, and asked about the people on the roads tonight."

"Yeah, well, maybe I have an ulterior motive."

He looked straight at her with blazing blue eyes, no lies, no sidestepping. "Do you?"

"I..." She shook her head—partly at his naïveté, partly at herself. What was she doing? She'd come here to get information, not to fall into Sam West's too-honest blue eyes. He'd never had to swim that muddy gray stream between right and wrong. "No. You're a fool if you think we have anything in common."

"Now how can you say that when you don't even know me?" he asked, slow and hard.

She stumbled, maybe because she wasn't used to that tone from him, maybe because he was right.

He just kept on talking in that gravelly voice. "You don't know what I eat for breakfast, what my favorite baseball team is, if I snore at night. You don't know what

I think about in the middle of the night. What I'm afraid of. What I'd die for. Hell, woman, you haven't even tried, have you? You scratched my surface and stopped right there."

"Maybe I don't want to," she hissed low and defiant and not a little shaken. Was she really as shallow as that?

"You want to, all right," he said, a kind of flaming anger behind those blue eyes.

Maisa wondered vaguely if she should be frightened. But they were in the middle of *Ed's*, for God's sake. Sam wouldn't do anything here.

Would he? Suddenly she realized that she had *no idea* what he was going to do next. He was right—she didn't know him.

He bowed his head to hers, a tender gesture, but his words were anything but tender. "Something's just holding you back. Spent most of last fall trying to figure it out, you know. Thought it might be the small-town thing or the no-college thing or the blue-collar thing, but that's not any of those at all, is it? It's something else, and May, if you think I'm going to rest or give up without finding out everything that makes you tick in that sweet little head of yours, well, you'd better think again."

She wanted to wrench herself from his arms, run away and hide, but she still needed that information.

Or maybe that was just what she was telling herself.

"Come on," he said low, his voice like smoke, insidious and unavoidable, almost taunting. "Tell me what you're doing here tonight in my arms, May."

"What if it has nothing to do with you?" she spat. "What if I'm just here for information?"

"Yeah? Like what?" His mouth twisted again, but this

time it was bitter. She hated that she'd put that cynical look on his face. "I'm an open book, right? That's what you think, isn't it."

And for the first time she faltered. *Was* Sam West an open book? He must be. He was a small-town cop, never been to college. What more could there possibly be?

For a moment the room tilted ever so slightly to the left. What if everything she thought she knew was wrong? What if Sam West was a man she wanted—no, *needed*— to know?

Then she stomped that uncertainty right down. *Dyadya* might be in trouble. She needed to focus and find out what Sam knew about the man in the car crash this afternoon.

Maisa steeled herself and met his gaze with a confident half smile on her lips. "Where did you put him? That guy in the accident?"

"He's at the Coot Lake Inn," he said easily, as if the information was nothing. As if he was telling her that snow was white. She hated herself for using him. But then he tilted his head closer, whispering as if imparting a secret. "Why d'you ask, May?"

And suddenly she couldn't catch her breath. She panted, looking up at him, wishing they were in an empty room—hell, a dark corner would do. She wanted to strip off his baby-soft shirt and feel the hard muscles beneath. Wanted to forget this stupid game she was playing.

"I think," he said quietly as the jukebox changed again. The beat was all wrong—a pounding pulse—but he ignored it, continuing to hold her close. "I think Old George has some questions, doesn't he? And he's using you, sweet May, as his hunting dog to scare the pheasants."

"Dyadya wouldn't use me," she said breathlessly. "Did you just call me a bitch?"

"'Course not." His hands had slipped slyly down and now he cupped her ass frankly as he pulled her against him, insinuating a long leg between hers.

"Stop it!" she hissed.

"What?" His blue eyes were wide and innocent while his lean thigh pushed against the V of her legs.

Oh. Oh, just there.

For a moment she lost the thread of the conversation. Forgot that she needed to keep alert. She pushed against his shoulders, but it was like trying to move granite. Not to mention her hips had begun to undulate against his leg, which wasn't exactly helping her case.

She glared at him, trying to ignore the heat pooling low in her belly. "Half the town's here."

His lips twitched. "Yup."

"Including your boss."

"Uh-huh." He lifted her a bit so that she was standing on her tiptoes, most of her weight balanced on his leg. She could feel the hard ridge of his erection pressing into her stomach.

"Sam." Embarrassingly, his name came out a breathless whine. "You're a cop!"

"I'm off duty." He chuckled then, the vibration traveling through his body and hitting her where they touched: breasts and belly and the juncture of her thighs. "Why're you using me, May?"

"I... I don't—"

"Bullshit," he murmured gently. An endearment. "You already said you didn't come here for me. Either Old George needs the information or you do."

How could he think to ask questions when she could feel his big body hard against her? She wanted to get mad. Wanted to pull away and stomp out.

He shifted his thigh again, and she only just suppressed a moan.

He bent his head to hers. "Which is it?"

"I...I..."

"May."

"I..." She swallowed, gathering her wits. "I'm the one—"

"The one what?" he whispered against the side of her face. He took her earlobe between his teeth and bit.

For a second everything whited out.

She ducked her face into his chest, her panting breaths humid against the denim shirt. "I'm the one who needs you."

His hand tightened against her hips, and she immediately realized her mistake. She pressed her hands against his chest. "Needs your *information*."

One of his hands left her bottom as he set her gently back on her feet. "Why?"

She was silent.

"Why, May?"

She shook her head, still recovering but determined that she wasn't going to talk anymore. This whole night had been a very bad idea.

She felt his fingers threading her hair. "I'd love to kiss you right now, but I have the feeling it'd be a while before you talked to me again if I did. That right?"

She nodded vigorously, her face still hidden.

"Then why don't I get your coat? That snow's not getting any thinner on the ground, and I'd like it if you made it home tonight."

Grown-up women didn't hide forever, even if they might've had a rather intimate encounter in the middle of a bar dance floor. Maisa took a deep breath and raised her head, hoping she wasn't as flushed and sweaty as she felt. "Okay."

His wide mouth curved and he bent to brush it against her temple. "That there doesn't count as a kiss. I just want you to know."

"I know," she said. "And it doesn't matter anyway." She pulled away from him and stood on her own. It felt a bit like peeling a layer of skin off, but she did it anyway. "I doubt I'll be seeing you again this trip up."

He frowned at that. "Look, May . . ."

She aimed a smile in his general direction. "I'd better be going, remember? Roads will only be getting worse."

She turned without waiting for his reply and strode to the table where she'd left her jacket. She didn't stop for more than a few words with the ladies sitting there, and then she was pulling the door open.

The snow hit her with an icy blast, and if there'd been any lingering haziness, it was blown clean away. Sam West wasn't a viable option.

Maisa made a mental note to herself: *Stay away from the man.*

Chapter Seven

"That looked like it went well," Doc said as Sam slid back into his seat.

Sam didn't bother replying. Partly because he was trying to sit comfortably with a hard-on trapped in his jeans, partly because there really wasn't anything to say to Doc. One moment May had been all soft sweetness in his arms, the next she'd blown him off.

He sighed and wished he'd stopped for another beer before sitting down again.

"What'd she want?" Doc asked. No one had ever said the old man wasn't sharp.

Sam looked at him a beat, then reached over and snagged Doc's glass of beer, draining the last of the Schell's. It was warm. "She wanted to know about the guy wrecked his car in front of us this afternoon."

Doc grunted. "The driver of your wreck say anything about Old George?"

"Nope. When I told him he'd need to stay the night to see his car fixed—a rental, by the way—he didn't say anything about George. Which you think he would've, if he knew him." Sam shrugged. "I even took May by her uncle's place and no peep out of the back."

"What do you mean, you took Maisa?"

"Her car stalled when I pulled it over."

Doc grunted at that, frowning at his beer. "You get the driver's name?"

"Ilya Kasyanov."

"You had time to run him through the system?"

"Yup."

"And?"

Sam shrugged. "Nothing. Lives in Las Vegas, has no priors on him."

"He work at a casino?"

"Nope. He's a private accountant of some kind."

Doc leaned forward. "If he's so innocent, then why'd Maisa Burnsey ask about him?"

"You know damn well May isn't involved in anything illegal."

"Do I?"

"George may—or may not—have ties to the mafiya, but May sure as hell doesn't," Sam drawled, eyes narrowed. "Seems kinda wrong to hold a person's relatives against them."

"Is it? Aw, I know all that PC crap"—Doc swatted the *PC crap* with his hand—"but really, a woman's family means a lot. A man doesn't just marry the woman, he marries her family, her friends. Do you even know who Maisa Burnsey's friends are?"

Sam didn't, so he ignored that. "Who said anything about marriage?"

Doc gave him the Idiot Look. "Son, I know damn well when a man's got the bit between his teeth. You just made a damned-fool spectacle of yourself on the dance floor. I think Dylan was taking notes. You've been chasing Maisa Burnsey for months now. If that woman ever stands still long enough, you'll have the ring on her finger and a rented powder blue tux on so fast she won't even have time to plan the goddamned flower arrangements."

Sam chuckled at that, but it had an edge. "Yeah, well, doesn't look like she'll be standing still anytime soon."

"Just as well." Doc paused to take a swig of his beer. "I know you're not from Coot Lake originally, but you *belong* here, Sam. People like you. Heck, even *Becky* likes you, and you know that woman is harder'n stone. If you—"

"Doc...," Sam began, hoping to forestall the usual lecture from the police chief.

But Doc leaned forward, suddenly intent. "No, damn it, Sam, just listen a minute."

Sam frowned but inclined his head.

Doc blew out a breath. "I know I'm a stubborn old bastard, seems like I'll stick around forever, but my blood pressure's high and my cholesterol is all to shit."

Sam knit his brows, worried. This was the first he'd heard of any problem with Doc's health.

"No"—Doc held up his palms—"I'm not sayin' I'm going to keel over anytime soon. My dad lived into his eighties and managed to drive Mom and us kids near around the bend before he finally gave in and kicked the bucket. I'm just saying that sometime I'm going to have to be replaced. Hell, I'd like to retire someday. Do some fishing on a weekday, maybe take some old gal dancin'."

A corner of Sam's mouth lifted. "Some old gal like Becky?"

Doc shook his head, though his own mouth was twitching. "I'm not speaking out of turn."

"Don't suppose you have to." Sam glanced out of the corner of his eye at Becky's table. She was trying too hard not to look at them. He'd always thought Becky'd be up for it if Doc ever made his move.

"Don't suppose I do." Doc sighed again and turned serious. "But Sam, my point is you have the potential to help this town. To be more than a patrol cop."

"I like being a patrol cop," Sam said, easy, twirling the neck of the empty Sam Adams.

"Catching speeders up on 52?" Doc cocked an eyebrow. "That really what you want to be doing for the rest of your life?"

"What if it is?"

Doc lowered his head like an old bull and hit him, stubborn and dangerous. "I don't know what happened over there in Afghanistan, but whatever it was wasn't worth you giving up the rest of your life."

Sam jerked his chin up, refusing to acknowledge the hit. His former army career was something he didn't want to think about or discuss—with Doc or anyone else.

Slowly he set his bottle of beer down.

"Don't give me that look," Doc snapped. "I know something happened. You still smiled when you got back, but you'd lost your drive. Lost your focus. You gotta get it back, Sam. I miss the boy I knew when your dad brought you to visit."

"That was twenty years ago," Sam said, flat.

Doc and his dad had been in Vietnam together, but while Doc had gotten out as soon as his tour was over, Dad had been career army. It'd just been him and Dad growing up—his mom had left the family when Sam had been little. They'd lived all over, he and Dad, both in the U.S. and abroad, but at least once a year they'd come visit Doc and go fishing for crappies. Doc had taught him how to put his first worm on a hook. When Sam was eighteen, he'd gone into the army. Figured he'd have the same life as his old man—live and die the army—because that was just what his father had done: had a full career, made colonel, retired, and dropped dead of a heart attack not a month later. Wasn't a bad life. He was hoping for the same—maybe with a longer retirement.

Except it hadn't worked out that way.

"Doesn't matter," Doc said. "You were the same, boy and man, until that third tour in Afghanistan."

Sam was quiet. There was no way he was going to talk about this with Doc.

The police chief must've understood him. He brushed Afghanistan and all its horror away with a wave of his hand. "All you need is a couple of classes up at the university over in Morris and you'll have your degree. I can recommend you for assistant chief of police, and then when—"

Sam was already shaking his head, getting kind of angry now. Doc just wouldn't stop *pushing*. "I'm not going to do that."

Doc stared, shoulders bunched, eyes narrow, and slowly pulled his lips in. "Damn it, son—"

"And I'm not your son," Sam said, hard.

Doc broke their stare first, looking away, and for a moment Sam felt a soul-deep regret. He hated this, hated arguing with Doc, hated disappointing the old man. But it was better than the alternative.

"Fine." Doc tipped his beer mug, swallowing the last of the glass before banging it back down again. "But you'd better stay away from Maisa Burnsey."

"Yeah," Sam replied, feeling tired, "I'm not about to do that, either."

Chapter Eight

❧

Dzhaba Beridze, unaffectionately nicknamed "Jabba the Hutt," leaned against the Mercedes SUV stopped by the side of the road and watched as Nicky walked toward him, silhouetted in the headlights of the SUV behind him. He exhaled a plume of Cuban cigarillo smoke. Nicky looked nervous. But then many of Jabba's men were nervous around him.

They had cause.

Nicky stopped a cautious three feet away.

Jabba flicked the stubble of ash from his cigarillo. "Well?"

"Ilya Kasyanov was supposed to fly from Las Vegas to Minneapolis, Minnesota. He would've made a connection there to Amsterdam."

"But?"

"There was a storm, sir. His plane was diverted to Fargo."

"Where the fuck is Fargo?"

Nicky's Adam's apple bobbled in his thick throat. "North Dakota. Sir."

"And?"

"He rented a car."

Jabba brought the cigarillo to his lips and drew acidic smoke into his mouth. It had been a wearying few days for him, beginning with his arrest by the *mudak* FBI. Fortunately, his incarceration had been short-lived due to the fact that the sole witness, a man named Anzori the Rat, had been found dead the next morning. Well, in truth, it was Anzori's *head* and *torso* that had been found. The remainder of Anzori was missing. But the part of Anzori that *was* there had been rather creatively displayed: he'd been mounted on the hood of the car belonging to the FBI agents who had arrested Jabba. And in case anyone was confused about the message sent, Anzori's tongue had been cut out and nailed to his forehead.

It would have been a satisfactory ending to a disruptive incident were it not for the discovery that Jabba had made when he'd arrived back at his Las Vegas office. His accountant of over a decade, Ilya Kasyanov, had taken the opportunity of his arrest to open his safe and steal something very precious. This had been a surprise to Jabba. In all the years he had known Kasyanov, the accountant had been nothing but a coward. Apparently Kasyanov had been under the delusion that Jabba would be out of the way long enough for him to flee the country.

Instead, he was in a car somewhere in the upper Midwest.

Jabba opened his mouth and breathed smoke. Two other Mercedes SUVs were parked behind the one he leaned against. Dark shapes stood by the last SUV— Sasha, Rocky, and Ivan, waiting. None of the remaining seven men had bothered getting out of the trucks. Above, the Nebraska night sky was filled with stars.

Nicky shifted nervously.

Jabba's gaze flicked to him. "You know where he is headed, yes?"

Nicky started shaking.

Jabba sighed wearily.

Many, many years ago he had lived in Moscow in a flat so small there had been only room for a single, narrow bed. He had shared it with his mother, a woman who perhaps had been once pretty, though he did not remember her so. At night she brought home men and he'd go sit in the hallway, waiting and listening as they fucked her. When she'd earned enough or when she was simply too tired to go on, he would return to crawl into the stinking bed and lie beside her. One night the man with her had stabbed her and that was the end of his mother. Mama had worn a plastic pink heart around her neck on a cheap chain.

Her murderer had taken it. Why, Jabba had never known. Certainly it was not worth pawning. Perhaps it had been merely a whim of her murderer. Why not? He'd already taken her sex and her life. Why not take her pink plastic heart as well?

But Jabba had resented the theft. He did not like things being taken from him. And many, many years later, after he'd grown to manhood, after he'd found his mother's murderer and made him bleed, after he'd become rich, and all around him feared him, then he'd acquired his own pink hearts.

His were diamonds, not plastic. Perfectly matched pink diamonds, graduated for a necklace, the largest a full five carats. Diamonds that had been cut from the earth from the same mine in Russia. Men had died bringing them to the surface. Jabba liked to think of those deaths when he ran his diamonds through his fingers. The pink looked like blood dissolved in water.

Jabba stuck his cigarillo in his mouth and reached back to take the gun out of the waistband of his jeans.

Nicky started to kneel, but had only bent one leg when Jabba pistol-whipped him across the face.

Nicky fell backward into the frozen grass beside the road, his hands clutched to his face, blood streaming from between his fingers.

Jabba tucked the gun back into his waistband and toed out his cigarillo.

When he looked up, Ivan's face was white and Sasha had his lips pursed. Sasha jerked his head at Ivan, who hurried over to help Nicky up.

"This rental car, it will have the GPS. You will use your contacts to learn all you can about the GPS and the rental car, and then you will find the accountant," Jabba said as he opened the door to the SUV he traveled in. He glanced back at Nicky. "Find him, or next time I will not be so sweet."

Chapter Nine

DAY TWO

Maisa woke shivering. She wasn't a morning person even at the best of times, and having spent the night on the foldout bed in Dyadya's couch she wasn't particularly rested.

And that didn't even take into account that the cabin was *freezing*.

"Turn up the heat!" she yelled, pulling the blanket over her head.

There was no reply, which she didn't even notice for a couple of minutes.

The blanket tickled her nose. Maisa sighed in exasperation and peeked out from beneath her cave. The room was light, so it was morning, but she didn't see Dyadya. The old man liked to rise practically at the crack of dawn, and usually he was up well before Maisa woke. She could easily see into the kitchen from the couch and it was empty—even the coffeemaker wasn't on. Dyadya liked his hot tea, but he kept an old Mr. Coffee on the counter for when she came to visit.

Maisa frowned. Maybe her uncle was beginning to take it easy as he aged. Or maybe he wasn't feeling well.

Vague worry made her wrap the blanket around her shoulders, put on her glasses, and get up. She yelped when her bare feet hit the cold floorboards. Swearing under her breath she tiptoed to the little bathroom next to the kitchen. Empty. She peeked in Dyadya's bedroom. His bed was already neatly made. Huh. The cabin was tiny. All that was left was another bedroom that had long ago been turned into a storage area—boxes, old electronics, bric-a-brac piled to the ceiling. Even so, a quick look proved Dyadya wasn't there. Her breath misted in front of her face as she stood there blankly.

It was really hard to think without coffee.

A sudden pounding at the front door made Maisa jump, then she smiled in relief.

"Did you lock yourself out?" she called as she pulled open the door.

Powdery snow drifted across the threshold, pulled inward by the wake of the door. Outside everything had turned white—sky, ground, trees. Everything but Sam West, standing square on the thin concrete step, weight on one hip, hands shoved in the pockets of his parka, cowboy hat tilted over his eyes. Sam blazed in Technicolor.

For a moment she simply stared, as if his sudden appearance had made every thought vanish from her brain.

His electric blue eyes flicked up and down her body and she felt like every nerve had been zapped. Her brain kicked in, flailing in panic, and she was suddenly aware of two things. One, behind her, next to the foldout couch, was a suitcase that contained a fortune in diamonds. And two, she was wearing only a thin black sweater and pink panties under the blanket. Her pajamas had been in her suitcase—the one *not* holding diamonds.

She wasn't entirely sure which realization was the more disturbing.

Maisa licked her lips. "What?" Her voice came out a raspy croak. Oh, lovely.

"Good morning to you, too, May." A slow smile curved the corner of his lips and her gaze fixated on it helplessly. Jesus. Did the man's every move have to reek of sex?

He stepped toward her and her eyes snapped up in alarm. "What? What?"

"Mind if I come in?"

Well *of course* she did, but she couldn't figure out if it would be suspicious to deny him entry—or *more* suspicious to invite him in, given her antipathy. And as it turned out, it didn't really matter anyway: Sam was advancing toward her, obviously intent on entering with or without her permission.

She moved before he could touch her and wordlessly pulled the door open wider. Then she abandoned the door altogether and turned to walk back into the house. Not an admission of defeat—a strategic retreat.

"George home?" She heard the door slam behind him. "I see his truck's gone."

"Nope." She went straight into the kitchen and rummaged in the cupboard for the store-brand coffee Dyadya insisted was just the same as any name brand. He was utterly wrong, but she'd learned to live with bland coffee when she visited. At least it would be hot. And caffeinated.

She needed her brain working with Sam in the house.

"Your heat's out." His voice was closer and she saw out of the corner of her eye that he was lounging in the kitchen doorway. Despite the cold he'd half-unzipped his navy parka, revealing a light blue chamois shirt, the top button undone. She could see the base of his neck, looking strong and kind of like it wanted to be licked.

Not that she *was* looking.

Memories of last night's debacle on the dance floor came flooding back. In the light of morning some of her life choices were glaringly poor.

Which didn't stop her from clenching with desire.

Caffeine.

"Uh-huh," she muttered in reply as she filled the glass carafe from the sink, studiously keeping her eyes on her hands. He wasn't near her, but she still felt crowded in the galley kitchen, his big body barring the way out.

He sighed. "Know where George is?"

"Nope."

"Know when he'll be back?"

"Nope." She concentrated very carefully on measuring coffee. After she'd returned from town last night she'd found Dyadya waiting up for her. He'd plied her with hot borscht and assured her once again that the weather would be better in the morning, they could make plans, go together, it would all be fine, and probably there had only been a very small mix-up. The diamonds? Oh no, he doubted very much that they were stolen.

Lying old coot. Where the hell was he?

Sam shifted and she was aware of every single molecule of air separating their bodies. "May. Was your uncle here last night?"

"Yes." Maisa's hand trembled just a bit. Ground coffee dusted the counter.

She ignored it as she ignored the man standing beside

her. She could hear him breathing, slow and even. Patient and waiting. There wasn't any reason for him to stay now. He'd come for George, apparently, not her, and George wasn't here.

And she was being a bitch.

For a moment she wondered if he was going to finally break. If her hostility and one-word answers would drive him over the edge into walking out and leaving her.

Giving her up.

But he merely took a deep breath, his broad chest expanding, and let it out slowly. She'd never seen Sam West lose it—not even on *that* night. He used his cool, his ease, like other men used the threat of physical power: as a stone wall to keep everyone off. He was contained, controlled, but not tightly wound. The opposite, in fact. He was so loose-limbed, so damned *relaxed*, you might be fooled into thinking he hadn't a care in the world. That he himself didn't care.

Except she knew better. Once or twice—and last night—she'd thought she'd seen the ragged edges of his control. She'd always had the suspicion that Sam kept his deeper emotions well hidden precisely because they were so strong. Maybe even *volatile*. She shivered a little, and almost dropped the blanket at the thought—that under all that damned cool, there was a heaving miasma of white-hot heat.

That thought really, really shouldn't have made her mouth go dry.

Maisa slammed the basket in the coffeemaker harder than necessary and hit the On button.

Damn Sam West and her own libido anyway.

The coffeemaker sat there, mute and with no green light.

She turned the power button off and back on again. Nothing happened.

"Your electricity's out," Sam drawled, oblivious to rejection, hatred, and something very like fear. "I told George he ought to get a backup generator."

She looked at him finally. He'd opened the refrigerator door and was peering into the dark interior.

She felt really, really frustrated. "Well, shit."

He shut the fridge door. "You'd better come to my cabin."

"No." She pouted at the dead coffeemaker. "Dyadya can deal with the stupid electricity when he returns. I'll be fine until then."

"It's freezing in here, May."

"I can build a fire in the fireplace."

"You'll suffocate yourself if you do," he said, the gentleness in his voice making her want to throw something. "That chimney hasn't been used for years. Doubt it'll draw—it's probably blocked with bird nests and such."

"I can..." Her forehead wrinkled as she thought, pulling the blanket tighter around her shoulders. Her toes were beginning to ache from the cold linoleum. "I can put on my coat."

He chuckled, his breath blowing across the fine hairs at her nape, and she realized that he'd snuck up on her while she wasn't looking, her defenses down because of frozen toes and lack of caffeine.

"May," he whispered, too close and too kind, "I came over because the storm dumped about a foot of snow last night and more's coming today. You're not going to get anyone out to fix your power today—or even tomorrow.

You'll be frozen before George comes back from wher-
ever he ran off to. Come home with me."

"No."

His mouth tightened and she held her breath, wondering if this was finally it. Would he let it out, all those feelings he kept inside? She had to be driving him to the very
edge of his control.

But he just reached out with one hand. She watched
it approach and saw it: a tiny tremor, a small crack in
his enormous defenses, and something in her crowed in
triumph.

He brushed a strand of hair off her forehead and she
felt that minuscule tremor—the only physical symptom
of what she was doing to him. "You're coming with me,
May. I'm not letting you stay here out of stubborn fear."

That made her chin jerk, dislodging his fingers from
her face. She glared. "I'm not afraid."

He leaned close and his mouth was no longer kind or
gentle. "You're shit-scared out of your skin, sweetheart."

"I—" She had a comeback, a really nasty one, too, but
she was having trouble remembering it.

And then he stepped even closer, the slick material
of his parka brushing up against the fuzz of the blanket
she clutched over her heart. "You want me to prove it to
you?"

No. Oh, no, she didn't want that, thank you. Except…
maybe she really did.

Her glare was made less effective by the sudden shiver
that wracked her body. Still, she gave it her best. "I can't
just leave."

His smile was slow and nearly sweet. *Nearly* being the
operative word. "I've got coffee."

Chapter Ten

❧

Sam watched as May's face scrunched into a scowl at the mention of coffee. She turned and shot a glare of pure spite at the dead coffeemaker. Probably there was something very wrong with him that the look made his cock twitch.

"Dyadya expects me to be here," she said, her voice almost a growl, which only interested his dick more. "What if he comes back and finds me gone?"

Sam shrugged. He had her now, he knew. It was just a matter of letting her pride find a way to give in. "So write a note."

Her eyes slid away for a second. "I doubt he'll be very long. I won't freeze waiting for him."

"It's fifteen below, last I looked," he said with a hard smile. God, did she argue with everyone like this or just him? "Without heat, this cabin'll get very cold very fast. George has never upgraded the insulation and the windows are single-paned. I'm giving you fifteen minutes and then I'm just putting you over my shoulder."

He was kind of hoping that she'd resist some more.

She huffed. "Fine. Just let me get dressed."

He allowed his eyes to trail down her blanketed form to her small, reddened toes flexing on the worn linoleum floor. She'd painted her toenails black. They were awful cute. "Sure. Fifteen minutes."

When he looked up he caught it: the slight softening of her shoulders, the heat in her dark eyes, a tiny tremble to the fingers clutching the blanket. May wanted him just as badly as he wanted her, and they both knew it.

In the next moment she blinked and it was gone. She shot a glower over her shoulder for good measure before marching out of the kitchen, back straight, slim shoulders level. The red blanket swished behind her. She stopped by the couch and the blanket slid away from one thigh.

"Do you mind?"

He glanced up to find her glaring over her shoulder at him. Probably best to let her think she was still in charge.

Sam shrugged and turned his back to the open doorway. George's kitchen was tiny. The tin cabinets were white enameled, the counters so old they were edged in chrome, tiny green squiggles wriggling over the lighter green background. The coffeemaker stood forlornly in a corner and the walls were bare, not even a calendar to add a touch of decoration.

Behind him, May cursed softly and something rustled.

He shifted, his shoulders bunching as he fought the urge to look.

More rustling.

This shouldn't be turning him on.

"Okay."

He pivoted at the word to see May, dressed and with her parka and beret on, the handle of her black suitcase clutched in one hand, the smaller case in the other.

He nodded. "Ready?"

She rolled her eyes and stomped to the door. "You know you can just drop me off at the motel."

"Filled up yesterday," he lied without remorse.

She shot him a suspicious look. "Maybe someone checked out today."

"Doubt it." He gave her a friendly smile as he opened the door. "Roads are pretty much shut down."

"Then how're we going to get to your cabin?"

"Same way I got here." He nodded at his red Chevy extended-cab Silverado. It was outfitted with a power snow blade across the front.

"Of course you have a snow plow on your truck," she said, as if it were an outlandish toy instead of damn near a necessity in a Minnesota winter.

"Comes in handy," he replied, grabbing her suitcase out of her hand before she could try to haul it into the truck by herself.

Her eyes widened at his movement and she clutched the remaining case to her chest.

He snorted. Damn woman couldn't even let him load her suitcase without a fuss.

A shovel-wide path had been cleared through the snow to the drive, probably by George. Sam led the way down the front walk, ignoring the muttering behind him. He put the suitcase behind the driver's seat and climbed in, leaning over to unlock the passenger door. Any other woman he'd've offered to help into the high seat, but May needed to think this was all her idea when she got into his truck.

He started the engine to get the heat going but waited as she settled herself and buckled in, the smaller, square case on her lap. Then he glanced over his shoulder and backed from the drive. "You left a note?"

"I said I would," she muttered like a little kid.

"Good." He put the truck in drive and lowered the plow blade, rumbling down the road. She was soft and warm and here beside him, and he was beginning to think that if he just *kept* her by his side they could work this out. "Got any idea where George might've gone?"

She didn't answer at once, and for a moment he thought she might've not heard him. Then he glanced out of the corner of his eye and saw she had her bottom lip caught between her teeth.

She seemed to notice his gaze at the same time, letting go of her lip. "No. I have no idea why he took off."

He nodded, tapping a forefinger against the steering wheel. She was probably lying. Disappointing, sure, but he didn't take it too personal. May was the kind of secretive woman who lied as a matter of habit.

Which kind of made sense if her uncle really was hiding from the Russian mob.

But she hadn't seemed to recognize Kasyanov yesterday. Sam frowned, stopping carefully at the stop sign before 52. He lifted the blade and then turned onto the highway.

It was deserted.

Had May known Kasyanov and hidden it from him—or was Kasyanov's arrival accidental?

"You know, I've never seen anyone else visit Old George."

She stiffened at that comment, as though he'd poked into something private instead of making an offhand observation. The woman's fences were built in odd, unexpected places.

"So?"

He kept his eyes on the road this time, not wanting to spook her. "So, I dunno. Are you his only relative?"

"No."

He waited.

She blew out an exasperated breath. "There's my mom. You know that."

"Actually, I didn't," he said quietly. "You've never talked about your family before."

She shrugged. "There's not much to talk about. It's just my mom and me and Dyadya."

"She's his sister?"

"Niece." May wrinkled her nose. "My grandmother was Dyadya's sister. She died before I was born, though. Back in Russia."

She darted a suspicious look at him as if she'd said too much. Truth was, she'd never mentioned her Russian heritage, even though Old George had a strong enough accent Sam'd have to be an idiot not to guess. Not to mention the tattoos.

He didn't know whether to be amused or insulted.

"Uh-huh." He signaled and turned into the back lane that led to his cabin. "Your mom lives in Minnesota?"

"Yes. In Saint Paul."

A real bit of information. He carefully kept himself from smiling. "How come she doesn't come up to see George?"

She sighed, rubbing a hand against the black jeans she wore. He remembered that glimpse of pink panty he's seen when she'd first opened the door to the cabin, the smooth, soft length of thigh. He'd never seen her in anything but black. Even that night her lingerie had been black. Was her bra pink as well? Was she even wearing a bra?

He reached over to turn down the heat.

"They don't really get along," May said. "Mama argues with him when they get together. Then Dyadya gets sarcastic, she gets weepy, and it kind of goes downhill from there."

He nodded. "And he never goes to visit her, does he? He never travels at all."

She blinked and straightened and he knew at once that he'd made an error.

"Why're you asking so many questions about my uncle?"

"Because he's *your* uncle, May. Because I'm interested in you. Everything about you."

Her eyes widened. What? This was news to her? "You shouldn't be."

"Yeah." He snorted, looking back at the road. "That's what everyone tells me."

He expected a sharp reply. A slice from that blade she called a tongue. But her side of the truck remained quiet.

"So . . ." He took a deep breath. "You seeing anyone?"

"What?" He wasn't looking, but he felt her whiplash turn toward him. "No! Why would you think—?"

"You've never said."

There was a moment of silence. Then: "I haven't seen anybody since last August."

"Good." Something in his chest loosened. He chanced a glance at her. She was scowling, biting her lip like a little girl. "Before that?"

She shrugged one shoulder. "It's been a while. There

was a guy in college. We saw each other for a bit after we both graduated, but then he moved to Washington for a job."

"State or D.C.?"

"State." She blew out an exasperated breath. "What can that possibly matter?"

"Everything," he said quietly. "I said I wanted to know everything about you and I meant *everything*."

He could feel her staring at him. "Why? What have I ever done to attract you, Sam?"

"Breathe," he said, and it was true. "First time I saw you, simmering because I'd pulled you over for speeding, I wanted you. Then you began telling me all the ways I was wrong and how I ought to do my job." He shrugged. "I wanted to grab you and kiss you and make all those clever arguments completely fly out of your mind."

"That's..." He glanced over to see her face had reddened with a blush. "That's the stupidest thing I've ever heard."

"Yeah, it kind of is, isn't it?" He signaled and turned into his lane. "But it's the truth. And I gotta tell you, it's only got worse since."

"So if I stop arguing with you, you'll stop chasing me, right?" Was that a touch of sadness in her voice?

"Hate to disappoint you," he drawled, "but no. You stop arguing and we'll finally be able to get going."

Sam turned into his drive, bumping down the winding stretch to his lake cabin. He pulled to a stop and switched off the truck.

He looked at her, the scrunch of his parka on the seat loud in the silence. She was staring straight ahead, a little thoughtful wrinkle between her brows. "Here we are."

Chapter Eleven

Maisa stared out the windshield of the big red pickup and realized that she'd never seen Sam's house. That one night last August they'd spent in her motel room at the Coot Lake Inn—he'd never taken her here before. Maisa winced, amending the thought: she'd never *let* him take her here. It seemed a bit obscene somehow—that she'd had the man's tongue in her mouth, his *penis* inside of her, but until this very moment, she'd had no idea where he lived. She really didn't know Sam West at all.

That...that was an oddly disturbing thought. She was used to him chasing her, used to his cowboy hat and electric blue eyes. She felt as if, somehow, inside her, she did know him, but the reality was right in front of her. She didn't. And she never would if she kept pushing him away.

Well, that was what she wanted, wasn't it? He wasn't for her—she'd already decided that. It'd been a logical, considered decision, and if it gave her a twinge of regret, or of...loneliness...just thinking about it, well she should just ignore it.

Maisa frowned fiercely. Now was not the time to start doing an in-depth analysis of her life choices.

"Coming?" Sam was already out the driver's side door and reaching back for the suitcase.

"Yeah." She scrambled down from the high seat, the smaller black case heavy and awkward.

Sam's cabin was solid looking—a dark brown shingle two-story, nice, but nothing fancy. A bit like Sam himself.

Maisa shook herself. She had to focus. She needed to get the suitcase away from Sam and make sure he had no way to find out what was inside.

He was tramping up his neatly shoveled walk, carrying the suitcase as if it weighed nothing at all. Maisa hurried after him, trying to remember if she'd noticed a difference in weight yesterday before she'd opened it. Diamonds were heavy, but the gems were no more than a handful, all told.

A fabulous, expensive handful.

Damn, she needed coffee bad. She needed to *think*.

Sam mounted the steps and juggled the suitcase, switching hands as he inserted his keys in the bright red front door.

There was a scrabbling and something coughed behind the door.

Maisa froze, eyeing it with alarm.

Sam opened the door and glanced at her. His eyes sparked with amusement at her stiff form. "Don't worry. He doesn't bite. Usually."

She narrowed her eyes, but followed him inside.

Immediately a short little furball hurtled at Sam's legs, barking wildly. He squatted to catch the thing as her glasses fogged, blinding her. Maisa set down her case and took the glasses off to wipe them with a tissue as she glanced around.

She didn't know what she'd been expecting, but it wasn't this. The front door opened into a large, vaulted room, bright even with the overcast sky outside. With the sun out, it'd be blazing. The floor was dark wood, refinished to a high gloss and left bare. The walls were painted white and mostly bare as well, save for sports equipment hung here and there: fishing rods, a fishing net, what looked like an old rifle, and crossed wooden snowshoes. To the left, an enormous fieldstone fireplace took up most of the wall. Straight ahead was an open kitchen, stainless-steel appliances, a light gray granite counter, and dark wood cabinets. In the middle stood a butcher-block island with two stools. Behind the kitchen an entire wall of glass overlooked the lake. A couple of mission style wooden chairs with leather cushions faced the lake. And to the right, up high, was a wide, open, railed loft, obviously Sam's bedroom, although she couldn't see the bed from where she stood.

The whole place, taken together, was stark but calm. Beautiful, in fact.

Maisa glanced at Sam and saw that he'd been watching her examine his home. She blinked, feeling her cheeks heat.

Then she took a good look at the animal at his feet. "That's the weirdest-looking dog I've ever seen," she blurted in wonder.

The shaggy gray dog was on its back, legs in the air, as Sam went back to rubbing its belly. It was maybe average length for a medium-small dog, but its legs were too short. Add to that, wiry, shaggy fur, an overlarge head, and drooping ears, and the whole was just ugly.

"Yeah, I know," Sam said with affection, pulling gently

at the hanging ears. The dog's big eyes gazed up in adoration and its tongue lolled to the side.

"What is it?"

Sam shrugged, still squatting easily, still rubbing the stupid dog with his stupid long fingers. "Some kind of pedigreed terrier breed."

Maisa glanced irritably at him. "How do you know that, but don't know the breed?"

He finally looked at her, his eyes hardening. "Because Otter the Dog is a hand-me-down from an ex-girlfriend. When Rachel moved to her new apartment, they didn't allow pets."

"Oh."

Now the dog was looking at her, too, and his expression was no longer adoring. Wonderful. Sam's dog hated her. Sam's ex-girlfriend's dog. *Not* that it mattered that he'd had a girlfriend—or that they'd been close enough that he'd adopted her dog.

A sudden thought hit her: how long had Rachel been an *ex*-girlfriend? Because Sam had been pulling her over for speeding for at least *two* years. "How long have you had Otter?"

"Otter the Dog." For some reason her question made his eyes soften. He straightened, suddenly too close to her. "Two and a half years."

"Oh." Great. The damn dog had reduced her to monosyllables. She glanced away from him. "Mind if I take a shower?"

"Sure."

He took off his hat, shrugged off his coat, and hung them both on a wooden peg next to the front door. There was a row of pegs mounted on a dark board over a wide bench set against the wall. Below that was an old hook holding several keys on key rings.

He turned and held out his hand to her.

She opened her mouth, shut it, and took off her black puffy jacket and beret.

"Thanks," he said, dry as desert sand.

He hung up her coat next to his.

Maisa looked at the polished wood floor and then her heeled boots. She sat on the bench and tugged them off, setting them side by side on a mat to the side of the door. Sam toed off his own big boots before picking up the suitcase. He strode past her, his shoulder brushing her arm, making her shiver in animal reaction.

The dog hopped up and followed Sam, and she noticed that his tail was stupid as well—much too long for his body and extravagantly feathered. Scowling, Maisa brought up the rear.

There were two doors beneath the loft, and Sam opened the nearest. Inside she saw what was obviously a spare room. A few cardboard boxes piled on top of a futon, a particleboard desk with a dust-covered computer, and odds and ends stacked here and there.

"Sorry for the mess," Sam said as he began moving the boxes. "I use this as my office. Sometimes. The futon isn't too bad, though." He glanced at her over his shoulder and must've caught her wince. "Unless"—he deliberately straightened—"you'd rather sleep in my bed upstairs? I can take the futon instead."

"No, this is fine. What about Dyadya, though? You said his heat wouldn't be on anytime soon."

He stopped and looked at her. "Did you tell him in that note to come here?"

"Yes."

"Good." He turned back to the boxes. "Then he can take one of the chairs in the kitchen when he gets here—they're pretty comfortable."

She frowned. Dyadya was in his seventies. "No, I'll take the chair and he can have the futon."

"Suit yourself."

She moved forward and picked up a box to move off the bed. It was open and she found herself staring down at a curling photo of a bunch of men in desert army fatigues. She set the box on the desk without thinking, peering at the photo.

"Is this you?"

"What?" He glanced over and something in his face seemed to close.

He reached for the photo, but she snatched it up before he could. There were five men in the photo, loosely standing as if captured after a day of work—or whatever one called being at war. For it was obvious from the background that the photo hadn't been taken in the U.S. It was some foreign place, somewhere with sand and rocks and very little vegetation for a human to survive on.

She looked up. "Is this Iraq?"

His mouth thinned. "Afghanistan."

"You were in the war?"

He didn't answer, simply turning away to stack boxes.

She examined the photo. In it, Sam was wearing a helmet, his arm draped over a slightly shorter, stockier man with sunburned cheeks and red stubble. The shorter man grinned, while Sam had half his mouth cocked up. Two of the other three men were sitting, arms draped wearily over knees while the fifth man was half turned away from the camera, a water bottle tilted to his lips.

"How long were you there?" she asked and somehow her voice had gentled against her will.

"Three years."

"That's..." She considered her words, choosing them carefully. "Isn't that a long time?"

"I was career."

She frowned. She knew very little about the military— her own family tended to be on the opposite side of things, generally—but even she knew he was much too young to have retired. Had something happened in Afghanistan? She winced at her own naïveté. Of course something had happened to Sam. No one returned from war the same.

Gently, she placed the photo back in the top of the box. There were questions she wanted to ask, but that would only lead to more intimacy and that she simply couldn't afford. It was none of her business anyway. She'd given up the right to Sam's secrets when she'd made it plain that she didn't want anything further from him than that one night of sex.

She frowned, feeling vaguely melancholy, and then realized that the room had grown silent.

When she looked up he was watching her, his blue eyes shuttered. "Okay? Do you need anything else? I'll go get you some clean towels."

"No." She ran her hand through her hair. "Th...this is great."

Sam nodded and left. The dog gave her a pitying glance before following.

Maisa repressed the urge to stick her tongue out at the mutt. *Great?* She sounded like a peppy cheerleader.

So Sam had a few secrets. Didn't everyone? Except, of course, she wasn't interested in everyone's secrets—just Sam's. The realization made her pause. Well, *that* was inconvenient. If she were smart, she'd leave the thing alone. Leave the *man* alone. He was just too dangerous to her peace of mind—among other things.

Somehow she had a feeling she wasn't that smart.

She scowled, turning to the black suitcase. Time to get with it, coffee or no coffee. Maybe she could hide the diamonds somewhere. At least make sure they weren't right on top if anyone else opened the suitcase. She reached around, feeling for the small zipper tab, but something seemed to be stuck. She bent over the little suitcase, peering at the corner, and saw a strip of ragged masking tape covering the zipper. In neat block letters, written in black marker it said, *BOMB. DO NOT OPEN.*

"Oh, Dyadya," she whispered. "What have you done?"

Chapter Twelve

Sam had his hands full of towels when he nearly walked into May.

She stopped short, just outside his spare room door, her eyes wide, her pupils dilated.

He looked down at her. Half an inch more, maybe not even that, and she'd be in his arms, soft breasts pressed into his chest. He inhaled and smelled woman. Smelled May. He'd never had a chance to lick her neck that night, see if she tasted sweet or salty. Find out if he could make her moan without even touching her below the waist.

He wasn't an egotistical man, but he was pretty sure he could.

She slammed the spare room door closed behind her and shifted as if barring his way.

Sam raised his eyebrows.

May's big brown eyes were kind of squinty. "Are those for me?"

"Yup." He handed them to her and looked from her to the spare room door. Unless she'd somehow found an old porno magazine in his boxes, he couldn't figure out what would spook her in there. The photo she'd held earlier was innocent enough—if you didn't know the fates of the men in it.

"Sam?"

She was looking at him with worry now, her brows slightly knit.

Sam shook his head, exhaling hard. Afghanistan and what had happened there was in the past. It had nothing to do with May. "Don't you want some clean clothes?"

She dropped the towels. They both squatted at the same time to retrieve them.

"May?"

"Are you saying I stink?" she asked with a half smile like it was supposed to be a joke, but there was worry in her eyes.

"Uh…" He examined her. Something was up, but for the life of him he couldn't tell what. "No."

Her face softened suddenly as she straightened. "Sorry. That was…" She blew out a breath. "I'm really not terribly civilized before I've had my coffee."

"Then I'd better get making you some," he said slowly.

"Thank you." She took a deep breath and smiled. It wasn't a very natural smile. "Shower?"

He debated challenging her, but maybe she really would be easier with coffee.

"The shower's on the upper floor," he said, leading the way. "There's a bathroom downstairs off the kitchen, but it only has a toilet and sink. I've been meaning to knock out the back closet wall, install a shower stall, but I guess I haven't gotten around to it yet."

"Sam?"

He stopped at the top of the stairs. He was probably putting May to sleep with all this information.

She smiled, though, one of her rare, sweet smiles with no hint of sarcasm or malice, her soft pink lips curving gently, and laid her hand on his arm. "It's nice, Sam, your house. It's very nice."

He had to clear his throat before he could speak. "Thanks."

She took the towels and shut the bathroom door.

He waited until he heard the shower running before loping down the stairs. Otter was lying in the middle of the entryway floor—Otter wasn't much for movement unless he had to. He watched as Sam opened the door to the spare bedroom and peered inside. The room looked exactly like he'd left it only moments before: old cardboard boxes on the desk, suitcase by the futon. He went to the desk and looked in the box she'd carried. Zippy, Enrico, King, and Frisbee, and his own stupid, too-young face stared back, stuck in time. He closed the box and set it on the floor behind the desk.

He looked around the room again, but didn't see anything out of place. He'd have to fold down the futon and make it if Old George was sleeping here tonight, but it was still morning. Plenty of time for that later.

Sam went into the kitchen and started making a fresh pot of coffee.

Fifteen minutes later he heard May's footsteps down the stairs.

Otter, sitting hopefully by Sam's feet, glanced at her but didn't move.

Sam reached over to the coffeemaker and poured May a cup. "I didn't know if you took cream or sugar."

He pivoted to slide the mug across the island that sat square in the middle of his kitchen.

May was standing uncertainly on the other side of the island. Her short, dark hair was slicked back like a seal, those too-severe black glasses perched on her nose. Without makeup, her hair still wet, she looked very young.

She'd picked up the smaller black case and now she gestured with it. "I forgot to put this in your guest room."

He raised an eyebrow. "What's in it anyway?"

She hesitated, standing there like a little girl lost, and he was sure she wouldn't answer. But then she came to the island and set the case carefully down. "Butch."

Butch?

She frowned down at her mug. "Cream."

"In the fridge." He pointed with his chin, putting his curiosity on hold.

She went over and opened the door. "It's two percent."

"Yeah?" He couldn't tell if she wanted more or less milk fat.

"I like half and half." She stuck out her bottom lip as she poured milk into her coffee.

"Sorry." He stirred the eggs, making a mental note to get a carton of cream for her.

She drifted over, cradling her mug, and peered into the pan on the stove. "Are you making me breakfast?"

"Yup."

"You don't—"

He turned and popped a strawberry in her open mouth. "Unless you'd rather I gave it to Otter."

Her eyes widened a second before she swallowed the strawberry. "What a weird name for a dog." She retreated behind the island and sat on one of the stools.

"Yup."

He heard the latches on the case pop behind him

and turned in time to see May lift an old black sewing machine out of the case. Gold painted filigree decorated the side, swirling around the word SINGER.

He raised his brows. "Butch is a sewing machine?"

"Yup." She smoothed her hand over the black enamel lovingly. "He's my travel machine. I've got a Bernina and a digital Singer at home, but Butch is kind of special. He was my first sewing machine. Mama got him from a yard sale for me when I was thirteen. I learned to sew on him."

"And now you travel with him."

"Of course." She looked at him oddly, and he knew he was missing something. "For my business."

"Which is?"

"Oh." She blinked and for a moment she looked the most vulnerable he'd ever seen her. "I guess I never told you. I design and sew dresses. I'm on Etsy and I've got my own website and a couple part-time seamstresses, but I'm hoping in the next year to hire them full time."

She stopped suddenly, her narrow little face pink with excitement.

Sam couldn't help but smile in return. Imagine that: his May sewed clothes. Somehow he'd never thought she did anything so domestic for a living.

Not that he was stupid enough to share that thought.

"What kind of dresses?" He took a sip of his own coffee—black and unsweetened—and put a tiny slice of cheese on the counter in front of her.

She looked down at it, puzzled. "Retro styles. You know—full skirts and tight bodices, although I do pencil skirts as well. Everything is originally designed and I sew to order: I have the customer measure very specifically and sew the dress to fit her."

"Uh-huh." He reached for plates from the cupboard. "You're doing good business?"

"Yeah. Retro styles are very in vogue at the moment."

"And you did this all by yourself?"

She thrust her chin out. "Yes, I did. I got a small bank loan, worked nights waitressing, and built the business up until I could quit waitressing."

"That's great." Sam said softly. He glanced over. She was poking at the cheese. He nodded at Otter. "He likes cheese."

He turned the scrambled eggs out onto the plates, added toast to both—two pieces for him, one for her—and brought them both to the island.

May was now holding the cheese between her forefinger and thumb.

Otter, sensing a patsy, was already sitting patiently by her feet.

Sam put the bowl of washed strawberries between them on the island, along with the honey, butter, and a jar of strawberry jam already sitting there, and pulled up a stool at the corner across from her.

May still held the cheese. Otter was beginning to drool. She scowled at him. "What do I do?"

He took another sip of coffee, considering. "Well, you could keep holding it up above his nose like you are now and eventually he'll just melt through the floor. Or you could drop it."

She dropped it and Otter's jaws snapped shut on the cheese like a shark on a penguin. Or whatever sharks ate.

May squeaked.

Sam hid a smirk and forked up some eggs.

"These are good," she said after another minute. She'd

tried the eggs and was putting honey on her toast, no butter.

"Thanks." He glanced up at her, wondering. "You never told me why you came into Ed's last night."

Her knife paused for a fraction of a second before she carefully laid it across the edge of her plate. "There's not much else open late in Coot Lake."

"Mm." He took another sip of coffee. "I think you were looking for me."

She glanced up at him over her toast. "Ego."

He shrugged. "Normally I might agree with you, but you did have some very pointed questions."

She was silent, crunching her toast.

Otter whined and shuffled closer to May's knee.

"If you're in trouble," he said, "I'll help you. You just need to tell me."

She shook her head.

"Even if it's your uncle." His voice hardened a bit with the thought of Old George dragging May into something. "I'll help."

She pursed her lips, pushing her eggs into a neat triangle at the side of her plate.

Sam's jaw firmed. She was avoiding whatever it was, and he was tempted to shake it out of her. But that wouldn't work on May. She'd just clam up tighter. He had to be patient and wait for her to trust him.

"Who were those guys in that photo, Sam?"

He stared at her, so taken aback that his mind went blank for a moment. He never talked about this—not even with Doc.

Sam blinked and stared down at his own plate. But then again he'd been pushing her to let him in, tell her something about herself. Seemed only fair for her to want the same in return.

He got up and refilled his mug, half expecting her to ask again. But she was smart, his May. She just waited patiently.

He sat and looked at her. "They were guys in my unit. Zippy, Enrico, King, and Frisbee."

She smiled. "Those couldn't have been their real names."

His shoulders relaxed a little. "No, we all had nicknames."

"What was yours?"

He shook his head.

"Come on." She leaned closer, her lips twitching, teasing him.

God, she was seductive. "No way. Zippy was like one of those yappy little dogs that trot everywhere. He was kind of hyper, probably one of those kids, when he was younger, that popped Ritalin all the time. Enrico's real name was Samuel. I have no idea how he got the name Enrico. King had a crown tattooed to his bicep, and Frisbee—"

"—liked to play Frisbee?"

He nodded, taking a sip of coffee.

"How long ago was this?"

He shrugged, his shoulders tightening again. "Six years."

"They were friends?"

He blinked, staring down at his coffee. "I guess."

"What does that mean?" Her head was cocked in question.

"Friendship in a place like that, it isn't a matter of like

and dislike or even having things in common. It's just…"
He shoved an unsteady hand through his hair. He really,
really didn't want to talk about this. Ever. But he took a
breath and looked at her. "It's a matter of being there, sur-
viving. Depending on one another. Here in the States? Me
and those guys wouldn't have wanted to spend more than
a couple of hours together. There? We were closer than
brothers."

She nodded. "Thank you."

He frowned. "For what?"

"For telling me that." She forked up some eggs and
then paused staring at them. "Eggs and toast."

"Huh?"

"What you eat for breakfast." She waved the fork.
"Now I know." Her smile was sweet.

He took a slow sip of his coffee, watching her over the
rim until she began to blush. "I guess you do."

She swallowed and gestured to Otter. "He's looking at
me again."

He glanced at the dog. Otter had his head on May's
knee under the eternal dog hope that he was going to get
an entire plate of eggs and toast. "He wants another treat."

May frowned down at his dog.

"Doesn't mean you have to give it to him," he
pointed out.

May took a drink of her coffee. "You have a nice view
of the lake."

He eyed her over his mug. She'd never struck him as
the small-talk type.

She pushed her eggs around her plate for a moment and
then set down her fork. "I'm worried about Dyadya."

"Any reason why?"

"He left before I woke up." She waved a hand at the lake. "The roads are blocked."

"And yet he got out this morning," Sam said, mild. "He probably ran into town for cream or something. You left a note telling him where you are. He'll show up soon."

May picked up a piece of egg and dropped it on Otter. The dog got it before it hit the ground, swallowed, and immediately went back to watching her like a starving hawk.

May split her toast in two and then again in fourths. "It's just..."

Otter put his paws up on her knee. Sam nudged him down with the toe of his shoe.

"He's old," May finished, and absently gave one of her toast quarters to the dog. She looked up at him, all her usual defenses down. "He didn't take his cell phone, Sam. I'm worried."

"Okay." He shoved the last of his toast into his mouth and picked up their plates, putting them in the sink. "Let's go."

When he turned, she was watching him with a look of wonder. "Just like that?"

He walked to her and held out his hand. "You said you were worried."

She blinked as if puzzled, but all she said was, "Oh."

And then she put her hand in his.

Chapter Thirteen

The tubby little Russian guy was giving Karl the stink-eye again.

Karl was having his weekly breakfast with Molly Jasper at the Laughing Loon Café, which was a delight—even if it was right next to George Johnson and the aforementioned tubby Russian guy, sharing a square table. George had walked in with a black roll-aboard suitcase, which was really quite a coincidence since not only did Tubby Russian have an identical suitcase with him, but Karl did as well.

Black roll-aboards were obviously the fashion accessory of choice in Coot Lake this morning.

Karl could feel sweat gathering under his arms. Maybe he should've left the suitcase in the dog truck. At the same time he had this really weird urge to check the contents of his suitcase. That was just crazy, though. He'd packed his suitcase full yesterday morning before setting off to the Coot Lake Inn, and nothing inside would've changed since then.

Would it?

Karl glanced up in time to see Tubby Russian giving

him a look so evil it was a wonder Karl didn't go up in smoke right there. What the heck was the matter with the guy?

"Karl!"

Karl's head jerked and he looked across the table at Molly Jasper. He always had a moment when he first saw Molly, when he felt like he'd taken a punch to the gut. Molly's hair was pulled back into some kind of twisty thing, shiny and dark and thick. Her cheeks were round and the light brown of toffee. Her eyes were deep brown like the mud at the bottom of Moosehead Lake. And her mouth was a light pink, wide and soft and sweet.

Well, sometimes. At the moment, Molly's mouth was pinched and hard as she opened her lips to speak to him. "Are you listening to me at all?"

"'Course I am." Karl smiled winningly.

For some reason that just made Molly frown harder. "You need to find a real job."

"I have a job. It's kinda real."

"No." She shook her head slowly, making the light glint on her shiny hair. "Fixing things once in a while isn't a job."

Karl was pretty sure it was, but he offered another point instead. "I sled, too."

"Which doesn't pay." Molly laid her hands on the Formica table. They were pretty little hands, with dainty fingers and dimples on the knuckles, but they were also strong hands. Karl had seen those hands write tickets for illegal fishing, haul traps with spitting raccoons around, and pat fry bread dough gently but firmly into shape. "You were so smart in school, Karl. I don't know why you didn't try for college."

Karl looked at her, a bit appalled. Molly had gone to the U in the Cities—and he was damned proud of her for it—but Molly had been valedictorian of their class. College would've been god-awful for him. The only thing he'd liked about school was the girls and the chance to play hockey. Oh, and that taxidermy class old Mr. Shultz had taught. Stinky but fun. He kinda doubted they taught taxidermy at the U.

"Army was time enough away from the rez," he said, being diplomatic. "Got to see Germany and Korea and then come home. I don't really want to leave Minnesota or Crow County again." He thought about that a second and then amended. "Well, not unless you want to visit Anchorage. I've always wanted to race the Iditarod and I know you like whales..."

He stretched a sly fingertip over the tabletop to stroke her dimpled knuckles, but her hand recoiled like a snail withdrawing into a shell.

Karl sighed and glanced around the café. The crowd was sparse today on account of all that snow last night and the warning of yet more to come. Most folks were probably holed up at home, not willing to battle the roads. But Karl would've tunneled through a mountain of snow to get to his weekly breakfast with Molly. She'd moved off the rez about a year back, to a small apartment in town, though Karl still couldn't quite figure out why—everyone they knew was on the rez, and besides, the trailer she'd been living in hadn't been *that* bad. The heat had worked most of the time.

The bell over the door tinkled as a tall guy in a navy anorak blew in, stomping powdery white snow on the already sodden mat.

Karl looked back at Molly. She was frowning into her coffee now, two deep lines drawn between her brows. He wished he could make those lines disappear. For a wild moment he thought about telling her about the money he was making—darn good money, even Molly would think so—but the method was just a shade—

There was an exclamation from the table next to theirs and suddenly all three black suitcases were on the floor.

"Ah, I am sorry, my friend," the tubby Russian said loudly. He bent to pick up one of the suitcases.

George reached over and took the other end of the suitcase. "That is mine, I think."

"Your pardon, but it is mine." The Russian was smiling through gritted teeth.

Karl looked between them and then at the other two suitcases still on the floor. His eyes narrowed. "Is that my suitcase, dude?"

"No, I think this is yours," the Russian said and shoved one of the suitcases on the floor over toward Karl.

Ooohhh, no he wasn't going to be fooled that easily. Karl grabbed the third suitcase. "Actually, I'm pretty sure *this* one is."

He grinned triumphantly as the Russian's right eyelid began to tick.

"Then this suitcase is yours, Ilya my friend," George said, pulling the suitcase they fought over out of the Russian's hands and shoving the last suitcase at him.

For a moment all three men eyed each other and their suitcases.

"You should look to make sure," Molly said.

Karl gulped. "No, that's okay." He pushed the suitcase under his feet.

Ilya clutched his own suitcase protectively to his chest. "Ms. Jasper."

Karl looked up. The guy from the door had come over. He had one of those deep, resonant voices that sounded good on movie trailers but were kind of silly in real life. He'd thrown back his hood, and Karl could see now that he was an Indian, his skin a deep hickory brown that might've been enhanced from a tanning bed. Also, he'd had the good fortune to get the high-cheekboned Indian genes as opposed to the round-face-and-possible-adult-onset-diabetes gene.

The fucker.

"Who're you?" Karl said, pushing up his glasses aggressively.

"Oh, please call me Molly," Molly said at the same time.

Karl narrowed his eyes suspiciously. Molly's face had gone soft and her voice was all *simpery*.

The guy pulled off a lined leather glove and stuck out his right hand at him. "Gerard Walkingtall, Native Rights Council."

Karl took the hand and squeezed. Soft, but the guy did have a good grip. Walkingtall? *Really?* Figured. Most of the Ojibwa Karl knew had either white names or names like Big Wind Blowing. Not quite as sexy as Walkingtall. "Cherokee?"

Walkingtall's eyes widened and he smiled, revealing straight, white teeth, like a picket fence Karl had once seen in a grade-school storybook. "How'd you know?"

Karl shrugged, grinning himself. His teeth might not be perfectly straight or perfectly white, but they were all there. "Lucky guess."

Molly shot him a look. "Gerard is here to make sure the dig up on the rez is okay."

Walkingtall slid into the booth next to her without even asking and leaned forward across the table. "The white man has stolen enough from us already without stealing our people's bones and grave goods as well."

"Really." Karl sat back, arms folded across his chest. If he shoved his fists under his upper arms, it almost looked like he had biceps. "I heard the dig is over fifteen hundred years old. That's not Ojibwa."

Walkingtall stared hard, a little frown on his severe lips. He looked like he was posing for a monument to Dead Indians Everywhere as he intoned, "All our people are as one."

"Tell that to the Dakota," Karl muttered.

"Huh?" Walkingtall looked blank.

"This?" Karl made a broad, sweeping arm movement, and did *not* knock over his water glass. Score. "Used to be Sioux land." He dropped his arm, sitting straight. "Until the Ojibwa came along and kicked their asses into the Dakota badlands. Booya!"

Molly glared at him. What? She knew their history same as him.

"Only because the white man had pushed the Ojibwa west," Walkingtall said.

Haley Anne hustled over, eyeing Walkingtall curiously. Between him and the Russian they were having a run on strangers in Coot Lake. "Coffee?"

Walkingtall looked at her. "Do you have herbal tea?"

"Um…" Haley Anne chewed her gum thoughtfully. "I think maybe Earl Grey?"

"That's not herbal," Walkingtall informed her like a pompous…ass.

"Yeah?" Haley Anne replied, looking bored.

Walkingtall sighed. "Just water, please."

"'Kay. Anything to eat?"

"Yes. An egg white omelet, spinach and mushrooms, no cheese."

Haley Anne scribbled on her notepad. "White or wheat?"

"Neither."

She looked up. "Cornbread?"

Walkingtall shook his head.

"Biscuit?" Haley Anne tried.

"No—"

She looked doubtful. "We might have an English muffin in the back."

"I don't eat carbohydrates, thank you," Walkingtall replied without even a trace of a smile.

Haley Anne just shrugged and turned to Molly. "Watcha want, hon?"

Molly slid a nervous glance at Walkingtall. "Um ... I'll just have a poached egg. And a bowl of oatmeal."

"Brown sugar?"

"Yes, please." She looked apologetic.

Karl snorted and when Haley Anne turned to him, he said, "A big stack of blueberry pancakes, lots of butter and lots of syrup."

"Sure thing." Haley Anne winked at him and pivoted off to head to the kitchen.

"Our ancestors preferred a diet of meat and what bounty the earth provided," Walkingtall said. "Much of the white man's food has led to health problems in our people. Alcohol. High fructose corn syrup. Dairy products."

Karl double-checked. Molly couldn't be taking this moron seriously? But she was nodding straight-faced.

"Oh, for fuck's sake," Karl muttered under his breath.

"Karl!" Molly hissed.

"I beg your pardon?" The other man turned and Karl saw that his hair was slicked back into a thick single braid.

Most men's braids had a tendency to look like a drowned rat's tail. But Walkingtall's braid didn't look like a rat tail. It looked sleek and manly and actually kind of cool. Karl ran a hand through his own buzz cut, wondering if he maybe should grow it out, before he realized what he was doing and dropped his hand.

He scowled. Figured Walkingtall would even have good hair.

Walkingtall had turned to Molly and was expounding on...buffalo jerky? Oh, for God's sakes. If the other guy had even seen a buffalo up close, Karl would eat his...shoe.

"So you probably need to get back to the rez," Karl interrupted. Molly made an irritated face, so he tried to look earnest and encouraging. "Get right on that dig."

"It's winter," Walkingtall replied as Haley Anne set a glass of ice water next to him. "The dig has been suspended since October."

"No kidding," Karl said. "So why're you here if there's no digging going on?"

Molly leaned across the table, her breasts nearly going in her coffee, which, for a moment, distracted Karl from her words. "Gerard thinks someone is stealing from the site. Digging up and selling our culture, our history, our people's *soul* on eBay."

"eBay?" Karl took a sip of his coffee, carefully *not*

glancing at the suitcase by his feet. His eyes widened in what he hoped looked like innocent horror. "What could they sell on eBay?"

"Arrowheads," Walkingtall intoned like Darth Vader after smoking a pack of Camels. "Somebody is selling arrowheads to *collectors*"—he spat the word, making Karl cover his coffee cup—"on eBay."

"Golly," Karl said. "Who would do that?"

This time he couldn't help it—his gaze went to his battered black suitcase. The one nearly full of carefully, meticulously made *fake* arrowheads. 'Course, the people he sold them to on eBay didn't know they were fake. And obviously both Molly and Walkingtall didn't know, either.

Now if only Karl could keep it that way.

Chapter Fourteen

Sam's hand was warm and strong and entirely too right.

Maisa thought about pulling her hand from his grip. It was what she should do, certainly, but he was already tugging her to the front door, the silly little dog trotting along behind them.

She *did* have to find her uncle, and somehow in the last hour or so, she'd begun to trust Sam to do it. Maybe it was the cabin—homely and obviously cared for—maybe it was the silly little dog he seemed to adore, or maybe it was that photo of Sam and his fellow soldiers. There was something about that photo. She'd heard it in his voice as he'd told her about King, Enrico, Frisbee, and Zippy. His voice had almost been vulnerable when he'd spoken about his friends. That was an odd notion: that Sam might be vulnerable in any way. And yet she was beginning to see that there was much more to the man than she'd first thought.

She'd been almost hilariously mistaken about him. He was much, much more than a simple man. The question now was: Did she want to delve further? No, that wasn't right. She *did* want to find out more about Sam. Having once discovered that there were unplumbed depths to the man, she couldn't help but want to find out more, keep digging until she had all his secrets in her hands. But was that *smart*?

Maisa smiled wryly to herself. Had she'd ever been smart about Sam?

Sam let go of her hand long enough for both of them to get their winter gear on before leading her out the door. The terrier hopped down the front step, his tail wagging madly.

"Do we have to take the dog?"

Sam didn't break his stride. Neither did the terrier. "Nope."

She scowled, skipping a step to try and catch up. "Then why is he coming?"

"Because he likes the ride." Sam opened the passenger door to his truck and boosted the little dog in. Great. The mutt was riding on the same side as she was. Sam glanced over his shoulder with a cockeyed grin as if he'd heard her mental grumbling. "And his name is Otter."

"Otter. Right," she muttered as she neared the truck, feet dragging. "Otter the *Dog*."

"Yep," he said, and before she caught on to what he was about to do, placed his palm firmly on *her* bottom and boosted her into the truck as well.

Maisa landed with a rather winded "Oof."

Otter glanced at her sideways with what looked like scorn.

Wonderful.

She tried to smooth out her face as they both watched Sam tromp around the front of the truck and get in the driver's side. He turned on the engine, put the truck in reverse, and turned, laying his right arm along the back of the seat to watch behind as he backed out of the drive. Otter immediately scrambled onto her lap and put both stubby paws on the passenger-side windowsill.

She raised her hands and glanced at Sam, wide-eyed.

A corner of his mouth lifted. "He likes watching out the window." He quirked his eyebrow at her hands, still hovering over Otter, as he turned back around. "Not a dog person?"

"What was your first clue?" She frowned down at the little body on her lap. He smelled vaguely of fish, and he was heavier than he looked. Also, his paws were wet. "I've never been around dogs."

"Not even when you were growing up?"

"No."

"A cat, then."

She shook her head. "No pets."

He glanced at her as he pulled out onto the county road. "Allergic?"

"No." Now she sounded—and felt—defensive. "Mom and I moved a lot."

He was silent as he concentrated on maneuvering the big truck onto the highway. The road still wasn't plowed. A lot of the snow had blown off the highway, but some was packed down right where the lane met the main road.

Sam shifted down and bumped over the mound. "What about your dad?"

She shrugged. Otter slid just then, one of his back paws scrabbling on her leg, and she caught him around the middle to steady him so he wouldn't fall to the floor of the truck. His fur wasn't soft. Instead it was wiry and kind of oily, but the body underneath was warm. The little dog didn't seem to notice that she'd placed her hands on him, still staring intently out the window, so close his breath had fogged the glass.

"My father wasn't around," she answered absently.

"Your mother divorced him?"

"No. He left us." Her words were bitter, the memory like fresh bile, hot and acidic.

Sam didn't say anything.

Oddly, his silence spurred her to continue. "My father was ashamed of us—of what we were. I remember hardly anything of him. Just bits and pieces. His voice arguing with my mother. The time he slammed the door as he left and Mama threw a mug against the wall and it shattered. Dyadya yelling at him. They had horrible fights..." She trailed off and her fingers tightened on the little dog's gray fur.

She tried not to think too much about Jonathan. She usually pushed any memories, any stray thoughts, from her brain as soon as they occurred, but now, strangely, she remembered the watch he'd worn on his wrist—old and gold and with an actual watch face, the second hand softly, inevitably, ticking. He'd once held it to her ear when she'd been very young to let her hear and count the beats.

"Nothing nice?" Sam asked, interrupting memories that surged past her walls, and Otter turned to look at her as if he asked the question, too.

She smiled, but it wasn't happy. "He took me to the zoo once, the little one at Como Lake in Saint Paul, and bought me a Popsicle, but it was hot and I threw up. It was bright red on the hot asphalt and I could tell he was embarrassed."

Embarrassed of her.

So embarrassed he'd made damned sure to tear their family apart.

His hand tightened on the wheel, but he offered no stupid words of sympathy. Some hurts were so old that belated Band-Aids couldn't heal them. The only hope was that they would scar and eventually fade.

She felt something soft and warm and looked down to see that Otter was licking her hand. She stroked his head. The fur on his forehead was wiry, but his ears were surprisingly soft.

"That's why he's so important, you see," she told Otter's silky ears. "My uncle. He was there when Jonathan wasn't. At my fifth-grade school play. To make borscht for me on Saturday nights when Mama had a date with some loser. He brought me with him when he went to the Russian café to drink tea with his friends. I'd have a teacake and a glass of sweet tea and listen when they'd talk in Russian. Dyadya was there." She finally looked at Sam and saw that his face held no pity, only interest. "Jonathan wasn't."

Sam nodded, not looking at her. "You're close."

"Yes."

Otter sighed heavily and collapsed into her lap. Maybe the unvarying snowy scenery out the window had finally bored him.

"You don't have any brothers or sisters?"

"No."

"Neither do I."

She glanced away, feeling the heat rise in her cheeks. She'd never asked him about his family. That felt suddenly wrong. "No relatives?"

"Nope."

"What about the police chief?" She frowned. "Doc, right?"

He looked amused. "Right about Doc being the police chief, wrong about him being related. He was a friend of my dad's. No relation at all."

"Was?"

"Dad's gone."

She opened her mouth to tell him she was sorry when she remembered: he hadn't when she'd told him about her father. They were past polite, meaningless condolences.

"But...did you grow up here?"

He shrugged. "Dad was in the army. Originally from Texas, but his people are mostly gone. I grew up all over."

"Your mother?"

A corner of his mouth kicked up, but not in amusement. "Kind of like your dad."

"Oh," she said softly, feeling a kinship. "So you're by yourself."

"You're gonna hurt Otter the Dog's feelings."

She smiled at that, stroking the little dog's wiry fur. "I was only out of the state when I went to college in Madison."

He nodded. "George said you had a degree in accounting."

She winced. She guessed she really hadn't spoken much about herself if he'd had to question her uncle to find out what she'd majored in. She cleared her throat. "Where'd you go?"

"What?"

"To school?"

"You mean college." He shook his head. "Army, remember?"

"No ROTC?"

"Nope."

"Why not?" she asked before she could stop herself. It really wasn't any of her business. She scowled. "You're smart enough."

"Thanks." His tone was so dry she winced. "Never saw the need."

"Humph." She sank lower in the truck seat. "I'd think it would help with your career."

He smiled as he signaled and turned. "I'm a small-town cop, May. Not exactly a high-powered *career*."

"But..." She frowned, moving restlessly. "You want to move up in the department, don't you?"

He shook his head and laughed.

"What?" she asked indignantly. It hadn't been that stupid a question.

"You sound just like Doc," he said. "He's always pushing me to get a degree, take a leadership position in the police department, that sort of stuff."

"So why don't you?"

His mouth tightened. "Things don't go so well when I'm in charge. The town's better off where I am."

She noticed that he didn't say *he* was better off where he was. What did he mean by "things" not going so well? What exactly had happened in Afghanistan?

Maisa opened her mouth to ask, but one look at his shuttered face made her think twice. It wasn't any of her business anyway what Sam did with his life. It wasn't as if she cared one way or the other.

She took a deep breath, pushing away the sadness that thought brought, and said lightly, "So out of all the world you decided to settle in Coot Lake, Minnesota."

"I'm not exactly the only one," he said softly, casually. Too casually. "Your uncle retired up here even though, as far as I can figure, he didn't know anyone here before he came. Kind of odd that he'd move up here when there isn't a Russian for miles around."

She looked at him.

He turned his head to pin her with those laser blue eyes. "In fact, the only other Russian I've seen since Old George got here was that guy yesterday."

She'd been lulled by the musty warmth of the car heater, the heavy weight of Otter, and most of all by Sam's carefully light voice.

She blinked stupidly. "What?"

He nodded as if her astonishment had confirmed something and looked back at the road. "The guy in the red car. Didn't you notice the accent when I drove you both to town?"

She straightened. Otter grumbled as he was disturbed and had to move his head to a new position on her arm. She thought frantically. The oily little man whose suitcase she'd wound up with. He'd worn a red windbreaker . . . and that was all she'd remembered of him.

"He didn't speak while I was in the car," she said sharply.

He nodded again. "His name is Ilya Kasyanov. Russian, I bet, and I can't help wondering what he's doing in Coot Lake when the only other Russian here is your uncle."

The pink diamonds. Dyadya's unwelcoming face. Dyadya disappearing without a note this morning. The bomb in the suitcase. *Oh, God.*

The mafiya had found Dyadya.

Chapter Fifteen

There was fear in May's face, and Sam hated it. May should always wear the confident smirk that he was used to. The flame in her big brown eyes that said she was about to try and cut him down a notch. The combative feminine spark. That was the expression she should have on her witchy little face: defiance and fire and daring. Not fear.

Never fear.

Sam tightened his hands on the steering wheel, keeping his eyes on the road. It was slow going—the snow on the highway was compacted in places, but in others it had iced over, creating dangerously slick patches. God only knew how Old George had managed to get out of his drive.

When they caught up with him, Sam was going to have a talk with the old man. Let him know it wasn't cool to put himself in danger when it bothered May. But before that, he was going to have to weasel out of her exactly what was going on.

"You didn't know him? Ilya Kasyanov?" he asked to clarify.

She shook her head. Her brows were knit as she

absently stroked Otter's back. The terrier was snoring on her lap, and Sam just hoped he didn't fart in his sleep. Otter packed powerful ammunition.

"Never seen him before?" he pressed. "Your uncle ever mention his name?"

"No, Sam." She sounded almost irritated, but not quite and the difference worried the hell out of him.

"Talk to me, May," he said, not letting any gentleness into his voice. Now was not the time to let his feelings for her get in the way of finding out the situation. "What's going on?"

She shook her head, not saying anything, but her face was white.

The *Welcome to Coot Lake* sign flashed by on the right, adorned with the emblems of the Knights of Columbus, the Veterans of Foreign Wars, and the American Legion.

Sam slowed at the town speed limit and blew out a breath, thinking. "Kasyanov didn't have any tattoos that I could see."

He felt more than saw May's quick look.

He waited a beat, then went on, "Of course I suppose not everyone is tattooed in that crowd."

"I don't know what you mean," she said far too quickly. Poor May. She was better at offense than defense.

"No?" He turned the wheel to pull into one of the diagonal parking spots before the Laughing Loon Café. The stripes couldn't be seen beneath the snow, but everyone knew where they were. There were only two cars parked in front: Haley Anne's silver hatchback, and a bright red Jeep with out-of-state plates next to an older snowmobile. He put the Silverado into park and glanced at her. "The Russian mob? George has a Russian accent,

Russian mafiya prison tattoos, and he showed up out of nowhere ten years ago. Either he's working for the mob now—which seems kind of unlikely, since we're not in a teeming crime center—or he's in hiding, maybe witness protection. Which is it, May?"

Her soft pink lips parted, her face shocked. He flashed on her wearing that look last August, her head thrown back, her eyes closed, fine strands of hair stuck to her temples with sweat as he entered her.

He smiled at her. Hard. "Not much point in holding out on me, sweetheart."

She inhaled, looking around. "I don't...how do you know about mafiya tattoos?"

That was just insulting. "I *am* a cop, Maisa."

"Okay." She swallowed audibly, clutching at Otter's fur like he was a teddy bear. "It's...He's not in witness protection."

He turned off the truck and waited.

"You're right—he was in the mafiya. First in Russia and then here." She jerked her chin up, meeting his eyes defiantly. *There*. There was the May he knew. "He worked for a powerful *pakhan*—like a Russian godfather. The *pakhan*'s name was—is—Gigo Meskhi."

Sam frowned. "Meskhi doesn't sound like a Russian name."

"It isn't." She shrugged. "My mother and Dyadya are from Georgia."

Sam's brows rose. He knew that Georgia had been within the former Soviet Union, but that was about it. "Different names?"

She half smiled. "Different language—though most speak Russian as well."

"Do you?"

"Speak Georgian?" She shook her head. "No. I don't speak Russian, either, though I know a few phrases. That's about it. I wish I'd learned as a child, but both Dyadya and Mama were adamant that I speak English at home. They grew up under the communists and they wanted to leave that world behind—especially Dyadya. He was in the gulags. He doesn't talk about it, but they were terrible, I know."

Sam nodded. He'd heard pretty bad things about the Russian judicial system. "What happened with Meskhi?"

May inhaled as if bracing herself. "Ten years ago Dyadya was forced to testify against Meskhi."

"Forced?"

"Forced by my father."

"*What?*"

Her mouth twisted. "My father is Jonathan Burnsey. He's a prosecutor now, but at the time he was an ambitious assistant city attorney with information about crimes Dyadya had committed. My father gave my uncle no choice. Dyadya's testimony put Meskhi away in prison for life." Her fingers clenched hard on Otter's fur. "I think...I think Dyadya did it for me."

Sam watched as Otter turned his head and licked May's fingers. "Why do you think that?"

She uncurled her fingers from Otter's fur and began to stroke him. "Because there was no reason for him to do it otherwise. My father might've forced the issue, but Dyadya could've gone into hiding or fled the country. Meskhi may have threatened me and Mama, I don't know." She looked at him and she'd let down the shields that normally hid her eyes. She looked afraid, confused, maybe a little lost. "In any case, I think Dyadya saw it as the only way to keep us from Meskhi's influence. He has no family other than us, you see. Dyadya never married, and the rest of his family is gone."

Her family as well, he thought. She lived in a very small world, his May.

She took a breath and concentrated on her hands, as if she were talking to Otter. "Meskhi is a very dangerous man. Dyadya had to go into hiding even before the trial was over."

"But you said he's not in the witness protection program."

May smiled cynically. "He doesn't trust the government."

Of course he didn't. Sam frowned, thinking. Outside, the streets were deserted. Most people would stay home on a day like today—no point in going out and getting stuck in the snow. "Who knows he lives here?"

"Just me and Mama."

He looked at her sharply. "But you've been coming up here for two years."

She looked stubborn. "I've told no one. Our last name isn't the same as his, and anyway he changed his name."

"He should've left you and your mother and never made contact again."

Her eyes widened, outraged, but Sam hadn't the time for her sensibilities. George Whatever-His-Real-Name-Was was a fool. Simply staying in touch with May and her mother put them all at risk.

Letting May visit him here in Coot Lake was an act of suicide.

"So Kasyanov might be a Russian hit man," he said.

Her head jerked up, her eyes widening. "He didn't seem like—"

He looked at her. "A good hit man wouldn't."

All the color drained from her face. "Oh, God, Dyadya."

"Was he at all nervous yesterday?"

She broke eye contact with him. "No. Well, maybe a little."

His own eyes narrowed. "May, now isn't the time to keep secrets from me."

She pursed her lips and glared at him. "I'm telling the truth. He'd made borscht like he does for company..." Her voice trailed away.

"May?"

"He was expecting him," she whispered. "I thought the borscht was for me, but he was surprised when he opened the door and saw me. He'd forgotten I was coming."

Sam sighed, took off his hat, ran his hand through his hair and resettled the hat. "Okay. He must know Kasyanov, then, right?"

"I..." She bit her lip. "I don't know."

He watched her a moment more, wishing he could trust her to tell him everything. That was the problem, though, wasn't it? May *didn't* trust him. She wouldn't open herself fully to him, wouldn't let him in to find out who she was. To let him help her.

And it might get her or her uncle killed.

Sam made up his mind. "Let's go find your uncle."

He pushed opened the truck door and got out.

He rounded the hood to find her hesitating at the passenger-side door. "What about Otter?"

He shrugged. "He's fine in the truck."

"Won't he get cold?"

"He's got fur." He took her elbow, sharp and delicate

even through the padding of her shiny black down jacket. "Come on. Let's see if George just went to breakfast."

It was beginning to look less and less like Old George's disappearance was that simple, but they might as well start with the easiest explanation and work out from there. George's battered blue Ford pickup wasn't parked out front, but there was always the possibility he'd parked somewhere inconspicuous.

Sam glanced at May. Her head was down-bent as she watched her footing on the narrow, cleared path to the café's front door. He could see only the black cap of her hair. She liked holding all her secrets close to her vest, but she was going to have to reveal them to him if George was in trouble. If she was in danger.

And he might not have the time for patience.

He opened the door for her, the little bell jingling overhead. Haley Anne was sweeping the floor while Jim Gustafson nursed a cup of coffee in the corner. Jim was the only customer. He sat with his year-round John Deere bill cap pulled low over thin hair in need of a cut. Jim was a bachelor farmer, mostly retired now, with the vaguely neglected air of a man without a woman at home to tell him when he needed grooming.

Sam nodded at the man as they walked to Haley Anne.

"Want a table, Sam?" the waitress asked, setting aside her broom. She eyed May.

"That's all right, Haley Anne," Sam said easily. "We were just wondering if you'd seen George this morning."

"Sure." Haley Anne looked back at her broom as if debating whether to work or talk. Gossip won out. "He was in with a round little guy, kind of squirrelly. They ate breakfast together."

Ilya Kasyanov. It had to be. Sam glanced at May, but if she was surprised her uncle had had breakfast with the other Russian, she hid it.

He turned back to Haley Anne, now poking hopefully at the tip jar near the cash register. "When did George leave?"

Haley Anne gave up on the nearly empty tip jar and frowned. "Uh...like, half an hour ago? Maybe more?" She shook her head. "The café cleared out at about the same time. I didn't really notice."

"Twenty minutes," came a voice made raspy from disuse.

Sam looked at Jim. "You sure, Jim?"

The farmer nodded at the big front window in front of him. "They left a bit before those black SUVs went through town, and that was fifteen minutes back. Says so on the First Bank clock right there."

Sam swiveled. The old First Bank clock was kitty-corner across the street, directly in Jim's line of sight.

Then a thought struck. He swung back at Jim. "*What* SUVs?"

Jim looked at him. "Three of 'em, 'zactly alike, one after the other. Going through town."

"Kind of weird, huh?" Haley Anne piped up. "I mean, the roads are pretty bad. Haven't had anyone but locals in this morning—'cept for the squirrelly guy. Oh, and a friend of Molly Jasper's, but he left with Molly and Karl. Black SUVs sound like something out of a movie."

"Government spies," Jim said darkly.

Or Russian mafiya.

May was obviously way ahead of him. Her face was white and she was already heading to the door.

"And the weirdest thing?" Jim said behind them. "They were headed south."

South was away from the interstate. Sam pivoted and strode after Maisa. Not much was south of town.

Except the Coot Lake Inn and Ilya Kasyanov.

Chapter Sixteen

Five minutes later Sam accelerated onto the frontage road that led to the Coot Lake Inn, his tires churning through deep snow. The clouds had opened up again, the predicted second snowfall already starting. Pretty soon the roads were going to be impassible. That meant any backup he might need would be slow to arrive.

Assuming it arrived at all.

He reached over and flipped open the glove compartment, taking out his police radio and keying the mike one-handed.

Nothing.

Sam tried a couple of frequencies before giving up and shoving the radio back into the glove compartment.

He took out his cell phone and tossed it on May's lap beside Otter. "Call the police station. Tell Doc we might have a situation."

He switched on the wipers, watching grimly as they merely smeared the snow around the windshield. The snow was thawing and then immediately freezing to the glass, creating an opaque film nearly impossible to see through.

Beside him, May lowered his phone and stared at it.

"May?" He didn't take his eyes from the road. "What's going on?"

"You don't have a signal." She was already rummaging in the pockets of her black coat. She took out her phone and fiddled with it a moment before looking up. "I don't, either. Both phones are out."

Well, shit.

There was a blue lump in the snow on the right side of the highway. A pickup, facing them. Someone had skidded all the way across the highway and into the bank.

As they passed he saw that the front windshield was completely gone.

"That's Dyadya's truck!" May swiveled to look back just as he had the same realization.

Sam braked hard, then put the Silverado into reverse. He threw an arm across May's seat back and stomped on the accelerator, reversing fast until they were parallel to the wreck.

Someone was struggling out of the passenger-side door. The driver's side was embedded in the snow bank.

There were bullet holes in the grill of the truck.

Sam glanced up and down the frontage road. Empty. He reached for the Beretta under his front seat. "Stay here."

But May had already shoved Otter onto the floor and was out the other door.

"Damn it, May." It made his nerves crackle, her out in the open. Sam held the Beretta nose down by his thigh as he got out.

"You must help us!" Ilya was scrambling from the wreck, his eyes wild, glass shards in his hair.

"Where's my uncle?" May demanded, fierce and low.

"I am here, Masha, mine." George appeared at the passenger-side door, bright red blood trailing down the right side of his face.

Sam slogged through the snow to him and took George's arm with his free hand. The blood appeared to be from a small cut at George's hairline. "You okay?"

"Yes, yes."

Sam steadied him as George maneuvered down the bank. "What happened?"

George glanced at the Beretta and then gave him a heavy-lidded look. Sam knew immediately he wasn't going to hear the whole truth—or maybe even any of it. "We have run into old friends. We had a...disagreement."

Sam looked up in time to see a black SUV rounding the curve a half mile away. It roared as the driver accelerated.

Not good.

"They have automatic weapons!" Ilya babbled, wading through the snow to Sam's pickup. "We must go! He's insane, this is well known."

"*Who's* insane?" Sam demanded as he hustled the two men to his truck. "In the truck, May."

Neither man replied, although Ilya whimpered.

Down the road the SUV skidded and rammed into the packed snow by the side of the highway. The engine suddenly stilled.

"We need the suitcases," George said, as Sam pushed him into the back of the Silverado.

"No time," Sam muttered, eyeing the stalled SUV. He needed to get May out of here.

But George stopped dead in his tracks. "The suitcases."

He jerked his chin at Ilya who, even in his panicked state, turned and hustled back to the old man's truck.

Sam stared at George. "What's in those suitcases that's worth more than your life—and May's?"

A gleam of amusement lit in the older man's eyes. "Nothing is worth more than my Masha's life, Officer West, I assure you. But if one wants to bargain with the Devil, it is best to sit down at his table with his favorite vodka."

Sam watched as Ilya struggled with the two black suitcases. What was in them? What was the "vodka"?

And who the hell was the Devil?

Down the road, the SUV revved its engine.

Well, fuck.

Sam pushed George into the back of his truck. Ilya came panting up with the suitcases. Sam grabbed the suitcases and tossed them in the Silverado. "Get in."

His pickup was facing the SUV, which was spinning its wheels. Sam climbed in the truck, sticking the Beretta securely between his legs before putting the Silverado into drive and making a U-turn.

He stomped the accelerator, peeling out.

Or trying to.

The snow was flying nearly horizontally now, hitting the windshield and crusting. Even with the wind it was accumulating. The truck bumped over something, skidded, and for a god-awful moment looked like it would go directly into the ditch. Adrenaline spiked along his veins, sharp and acid. Then the wheels caught and Sam began feeding the accelerator more cautiously. He heard a shot and looked in the rearview mirror.

The black SUV was climbing his ass.

He swerved into the oncoming left lane and tapped the brake, letting the SUV shoot past before accelerating again.

"What're you doing?" May demanded, hanging on to the grip over her door. Her face was chalk white. On the floorboards near her feet, Otter crouched, panting heavily.

He didn't bother replying. Just steadily applied the gas, his grip firm on the wheel. Ahead, the SUV's driver had gotten angry. The driver slammed on the brakes, fishtailing before straightening. Sam pulled up beside him, still in the left lane, and immediately tapped the brake.

Just as the SUV made a violent swerve into them. The Silverado was a fraction too slow. The back bumper of the SUV clipped his right front headlight.

Sam swerved. Corrected. Steadied. Kept on the road.

The SUV wasn't so fortunate. It went into a spin, skidding 180 degrees around until it was actually facing them.

Still sliding backward down the road.

The driver's eyes were wide through his windshield, his grip on the steering wheel straight-armed and clenched.

Sam showed his teeth at the asshole and picked up May's left hand, placing it on the steering wheel. "Take the wheel, sweetheart."

"What—?"

He took his gun, rolled down the window, and leaned out. The wind bit into his cheeks, snapped against his eyes.

"Sam!"

The Silverado jerked to the right.

Sam grabbed the door. "Keep her steady, May. It's important." He inhaled, and re-aimed, squinting against the icy snow.

Gripping the Beretta with both hands he emptied the clip into the front of the black SUV.

Immediately, he ducked back inside, grabbed the wheel from May, and began applying pressure to the brake.

Up ahead the SUV jumped as if goosed and flipped, rolling over in midair before disappearing into the ditch. There was a muffled *whump*.

Sam slowed and then, with the road clear, picked up speed again. As they drove past there was movement in the SUV.

"Jesus," May whispered, turning back around, white-faced and wide-eyed. Otter crawled into her lap, leaning against her chest and drooling in anxiety. She petted him absently.

Sam's fingers trembled ever so slightly on the steering wheel. Adrenaline letdown.

"That," George said from the backseat, "was very good driving. And shooting."

Sam glanced in the rearview and saw the old man watching him steadily.

For a moment he held the older man's eyes. There'd been *three* SUVs, according to Jim. George—and, by extension, May—wasn't out of danger yet.

He needed to find a safe house.

And then he meant to find out what the fuck was going on.

Chapter Seventeen

Jabba Beridze crawled on his hands and knees from the wreckage of his SUV. He had not crawled anywhere for anyone for decades. The side of his face was numb.

He stood and looked down the road. The red truck was gone.

He looked back at the SUV. Ivan was pulling Viktor from the front seat. Viktor screamed. His arm was twisted, bone protruding from his sleeve.

"Leave him," Jabba said to Ivan, but Ivan paid no attention.

There was the sound of engines in the distance. His other two SUVs were nearing. One had become stuck in the snow back at the motel parking lot, blocking the other from leaving.

A fuckup. A royal fuckup.

Jabba sneered as he looked down and pulled a piece of glass from his left palm.

Nicky was struggling from the backseat of the crashed SUV.

"I said leave him." Jabba drew his gun and shot Viktor between the eyes.

Viktor's head jerked back and he fell to the snow as Ivan's hands opened. Ivan looked up at Jabba and backed up a step.

The two remaining SUVs pulled to a stop beside the wreckage. Sasha climbed down from the one in front.

He glanced at Viktor, powdered with snow, and lifted his brows. "Hard to hide a body, Boss."

"We leave for Budapest when this is over." Jabba watched as the snow melted into the round hole in Viktor's forehead. It had begun to tinge pink. Soon, as Viktor's corpse cooled, the wound would ice over. "What trash we leave behind will be gathered by others."

Sasha's face was impassive. "The SUV is totaled. Ilya did this?"

"No. It was an American in a red truck," Jabba said thoughtfully. "He helped both the accountant and the other one—George Rapava."

Sasha looked at him. "Rapava? The Rapava who put your uncle in prison?"

"Yes." Jabba tilted back his head to the falling snow and spread wide his arms, eyes closed. He inhaled, cold air searing his lungs. "It is my lucky day."

When he opened his eyes, Sasha was silently watching him, waiting for orders.

As it should be.

Jabba nodded, moving toward Sasha's SUV. "I drive with you, then."

"Where to?" Sasha asked.

"To the little shit town," Jabba said as he entered the SUV. "I will set fire to it and burn it from the earth."

Chapter Eighteen

Maisa clutched Otter to her chest and wondered if she was in shock. The terrier's little body was trembling all over and he was panting worriedly. She petted him with hands that shook, trying to comfort both him and herself. She knew what Dyadya was—what he'd done in the past, the people he'd associated with, why he'd had to go into hiding—but it had never touched her own life so violently.

She'd never even heard a gun fired in real life before.

She took a deep breath, looking at Sam. He faced straight ahead, watching the road, his blue eyes flicking to the rearview mirror, the side mirrors, and back again. His expression was calm but his lips were thinned, and there were new lines on either side of his mouth. He'd shot at an SUV full of people with a sort of deadly calm that should frighten her, she knew. He hadn't even been breathing fast. It struck her suddenly that he might've done this before.

Shot at people.

Killed people.

Jesus. The reality of Sam was so far away from what

she'd initially thought it was almost funny. He wasn't the all-white good guy she'd pegged him for. He had dark, murky-gray depths that ought to have her inching away from him.

Instead she found herself leaning toward him. Sam knew what to do. He could keep her safe. There was a part of her that wanted that from him—wanted it deeply. Wanted only to curl up close to him and let him protect her.

Not to mention that calm, capable violence was sort of a turn-on.

Maisa swallowed and looked down at poor Otter. She didn't have only herself to think about. There was Dyadya, too. Sam was not her uncle's friend.

He might be their enemy.

She had to keep a clear head. Fend for herself and her family, small though it was. Not let herself get drunk on testosterone fumes. "Where are we going?"

"To my cabin," Sam said. She was right: he did know what to do. He glanced in the rearview mirror and she knew he was watching Dyadya. "Do they know where you live?"

"This I do not know." She didn't turn, but she imagined her uncle's elaborate shrug. "Perhaps my house is no longer safe."

"Hiding...hiding will not save us," Ilya moaned. "He will find me and cut off my balls. It is what he does."

Maisa turned to stare in horror at the little man in the backseat. He was huddled in the corner, as if trying to hide.

"*Who?*" Sam demanded.

"Jabba Beridze."

"The mobster?" Maisa saw Sam's hands tighten on the wheel. "He's Vegas, isn't he? What's he doing in Minnesota? Why's he after you?"

"I . . . I . . ."

Sam slowed the truck abruptly. "If you want me to help you, Ilya, I need to know what's going on."

"I have something he wants," the pudgy little man blurted.

The diamonds, Maisa thought. Was that was what was in the black suitcase Dyadya insisted be taken from his truck wreckage? Had he put the diamonds in a different suitcase and left her with one containing a bomb? But if so, what was in the *second* suitcase taken from their truck?

"It is not safe for me," Ilya insisted. "Beridze will not stop until he has what he wants. Until I am dead. He is mad. I must leave."

Sam snorted. "Good luck with that. Even if you could find a truck to buy or rent, the roads are probably already closed. Doubt anyone will be going in or out of town."

"Then I am already dead," Ilya moaned.

"Not yet you aren't." Sam turned into the lane that led to his cabin. Otter perked up, presumably at the prospect of home.

"What will you do?" Dyadya asked.

Sam pulled into his drive and turned to Maisa. "You and George should be safe here. They didn't follow us and they have no idea who I am." He was already out of the truck door when she realized he was planning on dumping them.

Maisa opened the passenger-side door and Otter

jumped down as if abandoning ship. She scrambled after, the wind catching her breath as she called anxiously to Sam. "Where are you going?"

He was wrestling the two suitcases from the back. Dyadya was already on the doorstep. "I'm taking Ilya to the police station. We can protect him there and I can get backup."

"But you can't leave," she said stupidly, her mind stuck on the fact that he might be going back into danger.

"Listen, you'll be safe here," he said. "Ilya's the one they're after. I'll take him into town, that'll take the danger away from you—and your uncle."

"It's not *me* I'm worried about," she hissed at him low. For some reason her eyes were watering. "It's *you*."

"Yeah?" He paused, looking at her, his blue eyes boring right to her soul. "Good."

Her heart clenched. "Sam—"

"I'm a cop, May. I'll be fine."

"But…" He was right—of course he was—but she hated to let him out of her sight.

He was tall and muscled and knew how to shoot a gun from a moving vehicle, but he was only a man after all. Only flesh and blood.

Flesh could break. Blood could bleed.

She turned abruptly, making her way to the front door. Otter was already there, front paws against the wood, impatient to get inside to the warmth and shelter.

She was, too, but she paused and let Dyadya walk ahead. Let Sam open the door and set the suitcases inside, disappearing briefly before he reemerged, loading his gun.

Still she hesitated, even as her uncle's voice faded as

he walked inside with the dog. When she entered, Sam would leave. He would have no reason for staying.

She scowled. It didn't matter. He'd been a one-night fling six months ago. She'd been drinking, she barely remembered that night, truly.

All that was long past—*in* the past. They had no future together, only a present.

Oh, God, even *she* didn't believe her protests anymore.

He was in front of her suddenly, his ridiculous cowboy hat pulled low on his brow against the wind.

"You're so stupid," she snapped, teeth chattering. There was ice forming on her eyelashes, but she glared at him anyway. The watering of her eyes was from the wind, nothing more. "This isn't your fight. They aren't even your people. You're a small-town cop, nothing more. That's what you yourself said."

"Hush," he said, and his mouth was on hers, hot and alive, his tongue thrusting into her mouth as if he had every right. As if she hadn't just eviscerated him with her sharp words.

Stupid, *stupid* man.

She clutched at his heavy Minnesota coat and opened herself, kissing him back angrily. He tasted of pine and snow and the winter wind, and she hated him suddenly with a passion she never even knew she had.

It wasn't fair that it had to be this man. It simply wasn't *fair*.

He pulled back and used one gloved hand to pull her black beret over her ears, the gesture so tender she wanted to scream. "Go inside, May, and lock the doors. Try the landline. I doubt it's still working—the lines have probably blown down—but if it is, call Doc first. Tell him what's going on, then call the next county. Maybe they can get someone through to us."

Then he was striding toward his truck, tall and broad shouldered and brave and every woman's dream.

No. That wasn't right. *Her* dream. Maisa's dream.

She was so fucking screwed.

Chapter Nineteen

Karl Karlson pulled his pickup into the parking lot of the Coot Lake Inn and stared. It'd only been two hours since he'd left this morning to go to breakfast, but in that time apparently World War Three: Alien Invasion had broken out. The snow was all churned up, three of the motel room windows were shot out, and Norm's check-in door had a wobbly line of bullet holes across it.

What the actual fuck?

Even his dogs seemed to sense something wasn't right: they'd stopped barking as he'd pulled in. Now, though, there was a familiar yip from Cookie, his lead dog, in the back, and an answering bark from two of the dog trucks parked to the side of the lot. A pause and then the full chorus started.

Norm's head poked out around the bullet-hole-riddled lobby door.

Karl climbed down from his truck and slammed the door.

Norm flinched and turned wide eyes toward him. His hair was sticking up all over and there were white flecks in it like crumbled drywall. "Is it over?"

"Is *what* over?" Karl asked.

Molly's forest-green Red Earth Ojibwa Indian Reservation Natural Resources truck pulled in beside his and Molly rolled down her window. "What's going on?"

"I dunno." Karl shrugged and turned to Norm.

Who was still looking spooked. "Bunch of yahoos, yelling and shooting. Sounded like automatic gunfire."

Karl's jaw dropped. "For real?"

"Realz, man." Stu Engelstad emerged from the back of his custom truck bed, slapping his hands on his thick, jeans-clad thighs. "Three SUVs, bunch of assholes in each, don't know how many shots fired. Went peeling out of here not five minutes past."

The passenger side of Molly's truck opened and Walkingtall got out. The idiot hadn't been able to back his sedan out of the Laughing Loon parking lot after breakfast, and Molly'd offered him a lift back to the motel. Apparently the guy couldn't ride in Karl's truck, because he was allergic to dogs. Who the hell was allergic to dogs? Karl half suspected Walkingtall had made up the allergy so he could ride with Molly. *Dick.*

Now the idiot held up a cell phone, doing an impression of the Statue of Liberty—if the Statue of Liberty was an Indian guy, had a cell, and was frowning at it. "I've got no signal."

"None of the dogs were hurt, though, thank God," Stu said, getting down to the important stuff. "Motherfuckers were shooting at anything that moved."

"Does anyone have cell phone reception?" Walkingtall asked, waving his cell.

"Jesus," Karl said again. He looked around, but except for the snow and Walkingtall still poking his phone in the air, nothing seemed to be moving. "Who do you think it was? Meth cookers?"

They'd had a real problem with meth dealers on the rez about three years back, although Karl had heard that the worst of the druggies had been sorted out.

"They were asking about the Russian," Norm said. "Just before they took off."

"The Russian?" Karl's eyes widened. "What, that little tubby guy? *That* Russian?"

"That was Old George's truck they were chasing, wasn't it?" Stu turned to Norm. "Isn't he Russian?"

"Doesn't anyone have a phone that works?" Walking-tall asked plaintively.

Everyone looked at him in surprise, even Molly, still in her truck.

Norm shook his head. "Landline's dead in the office. Power lines must've been blown down by the storm."

Stu was peering at his own battered cell phone. "No bars." He shrugged and pocketed the phone. "Cell towers are probably down as well—will be for a couple of days at least. Who you got to call anyway?"

"The *police*?" Walkingtall replied in clear exasperation.

"Station's not a mile down the road in the center of Main," Norm said helpfully. Walkingtall was a paying customer, after all, and Norm liked to say he was in the hospitality business. "But I expect Doc and Sam have figured out by now that there's strangers running around town shooting the crap out of things."

"But...but...," Walkingtall sputtered. "We can't call for help. What'll we do if they come *back*?"

Molly sighed and got out of her truck, kind of hopping

off the running board—Molly had short legs. She walked back to the covered bed and unlocked the tailgate.

Stu spat into the snow and reached into the cab of his truck. "Son, if they come back, we'll be ready for 'em."

He brought out his compound bow as Molly straightened and racked her shotgun.

Karl grinned at Walkingtall's appalled face and said in his best Mexican accent, "Badges? We don' need no stinkin' badges."

Chapter Twenty

May would be safe at his cabin. Sam clenched his jaw and reminded himself of that fact. There was no reason for this Beridze guy to look there. He didn't even know who Sam was. Sam's job was to get Ilya to safety, alert Doc to what was going on, and secure the town. That was it. He had an entire community to take care of, not just one fiery woman.

Even if her eyes had been full of tears for him.

The problem was that George was a wild card. He tightened his grip on the wheel at the thought. Had George kept in touch with the mob this whole time? Had he called or talked to them since they'd hit town?

Could George somehow have let the Russians know where he—and May—were now?

Sam made himself slow as he hit the highway. The snow was building here, slick and compacted. He shifted down, going no more than twenty.

"How many were there?" he asked the silent man beside him.

Ilya's face was slippery with sweat, his complexion a sickly yellowish white. His chunky glasses sat crookedly on his face, and there was a crack in one lens. "I . . . I don't know. There is Beridze and he had the three big black trucks."

Two SUVs now. Say four men per vehicle, that was twelve men, including Beridze. Of course that was only an estimate. He could have more or less. Some could have been wounded or killed by the crash.

Either way though, the Coot Lake police force was most likely outnumbered. Way outnumbered.

They needed backup.

After half an hour more of crawling along the road, the visibility getting ever poorer, Sam pulled into town. Main Street was practically deserted now. Haley Anne's little silver hatchback was still outside the Laughing Loon, nearly covered in snow. She'd probably been picked up from work by her mother, who had a four-by-four and lived closer to town—unless Dylan had picked her up. That was another thing: they needed Dylan and Tick back in town. Both were on duty today, but Doc had probably sent them out to deal with the snow and people getting stuck.

There was a little parking lot around back of the cinderblock municipal building, and Sam parked there. No point in advertising their presence if the Russians happened to cruise through town.

He hustled Ilya into the building, one hand on the man's upper arm, the other holding his drawn Beretta down by his thigh. He let the back door slam shut behind him and locked it.

Inside, was a small reception room with two plastic chairs, a plastic table, and a plastic plant. To the left was a counter. Usually a receptionist sat there. Today, the counter was abandoned. Everyone had probably gone home at noon while they still could. Beside the counter was a set of wide stairs leading to the upper floor and the police department. Sam crossed the room and flipped the lock on the front door before leading Ilya upstairs.

The entire upper floor—what there was of it—was the police station: a big desk for Doc, a couple of smaller ones shared by Sam, Dylan, and Tick, a free-standing barred cell with a toilet and cot in case they had to bring in any drunk-and-disorderlies for the night, and Becky's dispatch station. There was a row of windows to the north, over-looking Main, and a smaller row to the south, overlook-ing the municipal parking lot. The entire room could be crossed in five strides.

When he entered the room, Doc was leaning over Becky's shoulder. Becky was at her dispatch station, muttering under her breath and stabbing buttons like she wanted to disembowel the radio.

"Nothing?" Doc asked.

Their dispatcher scowled. "Lots of static. The storm must've knocked down the tower."

"Well, shit," Doc said, straightening. "We got no way to communicate with Tick or Dylan. Just have to hope those boys have enough brain cells to realize the situation and come in on their own." He looked at Sam, eyes nar-rowing at his drawn gun. "Thought it was your day off, Sam. What's up?"

"We got a situation. Russian mafiya boss named Jabba Beridze and his goons, three vehicles—black SUVs—though probably one is out of commission. They shot up the Coot Lake motel." Sam shoved Ilya gently into a chair. "According to Ilya Kasyanov here. Found him and

George Johnson in George's wrecked pickup. Was helping them when we were chased and fired on by one of the SUVs. Lost them up on County W when they skidded out and I shot the grill and their front tires. Put May and George in my cabin and brought Ilya here."

"Well, heck, Sam," Doc said. "Good thing you weren't on duty."

"Take it the radio's not working?" Sam nodded at Becky's station. "I couldn't get anything from my handheld earlier."

Becky looked disgusted. "Radio's kaput."

"The phones out?" Sam glanced at the old rotary dial sitting on Doc's desk.

"Yup." Doc already had his cell out, fiddling with it. "My cell isn't doing anything. Becky, you have a different carrier. How's your's?"

Becky shook her head. "It's been out since noon."

"So we're on our own," Doc said thoughtfully.

"Oh, God, oh, God," Ilya moaned quietly, rocking back and forth in his chair.

"Nothing to worry about," Doc said. He unhooked a bunch of keys from his belt and went to the gun cabinet. "Either those boys are already gone, or if they're smart at all they've gone to ground until the weather clears."

Sam nodded. "Okay. So we just sit tight, you think?"

"'Spect so," Doc murmured, taking down a shotgun and handing it to Sam. "Ammo's in the second drawer down, right side, underneath those firecrackers Tick seized last week."

He tossed the keys and Sam caught them on the way to Doc's desk. He pulled open the drawer and shoved shotgun shells in his pocket, then took a handful and gave

them to Doc. "I'm going to check back on May at my
cabin—"

Someone pounded on the front door.

Ilya shrieked and ducked.

Becky looked up, eyes narrowed.

Both Sam and Doc raised their weapons.

"Il-ya!" sang an accented voice from below outside.
The wind made the sound faint and eerie. "Il-ya! I've
come for your testicles."

Chapter Twenty-One

"What possessed you to put a *bomb* in my suitcase?" Maisa hissed at her uncle as soon as the door to Sam's house closed.

She plucked Sam's phone from the wall and listened, but there was no tone. *Damn it.* She slammed the phone back in its cradle, trying not to think about Sam going into town all by himself. The other policemen would be there, wouldn't they?

Wouldn't they?

When she swung on Dyadya, all jangling nerves, she saw he was squatting, making clucking noises at Otter the Dog as if he hadn't a care in the world. As if he hadn't just been in a shoot-out with insane mafiya thugs, a car accident, and—*oh, yeah*—left her literally holding a *bomb*.

Otter sniffed at Dyadya's hand and then licked his fingers, confirming Maisa's low opinion of the dog's intellect. "Dyadya!"

He rose, shrugging. "I did not want anyone to tamper with the suitcase and I did not want to leave you defenseless while I saw to the diamonds. I am sorry to have frightened you, my Masha."

"Oh, for God's sake!" She saw with a pang that the blood on his face had smeared. "Sit down."

She stalked over to the door nearest the kitchen, discovering the little bathroom Sam had told her about this morning.

That seemed a very long time ago now.

"And what about those other suitcases, then?" she shouted as she rummaged under the tiny sink. "The ones you and Ilya had. Do they have bombs, too?"

Spare TP and the toilet cleaner, nothing else. She slammed the cabinet door shut. Damn it, Sam was a cop—he had to have a first-aid kit around here somewhere. No, no. She didn't want to think about Sam right now.

She went back into the kitchen to find Dyadya feeding the leftover eggs from breakfast to Otter. She set her hands on her hips. "Well?"

"Ah, as to that, I have a small confession." Dyadya looked almost embarrassed. "I took the diamond suitcase and left you with one of my own."

"With a bomb in it."

Dyadya actually winced. "No."

She stared. "*No?*"

"I lied. There is no bomb in the suitcase you have." He shrugged sheepishly. "I do not have the materials to make a bomb, you see."

Maisa threw her hands in the air and stomped to Sam's kitchen cabinets. "Why in the world would you put a note on the suitcase saying there was a bomb inside?"

"Because, Masha mine," he sighed behind her, "this Jabba Beridze that Ilya flees from, he is a very powerful man, a very insane man, a very evil man. I did not know the diamonds Ilya carried were his, but I suspected they were trouble, so I tried to lure trouble away from my home. I took the diamonds and met Ilya to find out what disaster he had brought to me, but I wanted to leave you with a weapon."

She turned from a cabinet full of canned soup and looked at him.

He glanced up and gave her a sad smile. "Even if that weapon was a false one."

Maisa shook her head and shut the upper cabinet. She leaned down to check the cabinets under the counter. "So you've met him before? Beridze?"

"He is the nephew of Gigo Meskhi."

She stared at the first-aid kit she'd finally found on the bottom cabinet next to the sink. "Oh, *Dyadya*."

"Is not good," he agreed.

Maisa grabbed the white plastic box and came over to the kitchen island where Dyadya sat at a stool. "Does he know about you?"

Her uncle gave her an old-fashioned look. "He knows, certainly, who I am and that I put his dear uncle in prison. It would be best if we do not meet."

That was an understatement. "God damn my father," Maisa muttered.

Dyadya moved restlessly. "Masha mine, you should not curse your father. There are things you do not know—"

She shook her head hard. "I don't want to talk about him right now."

Maisa opened Sam's first-aid kit and found a couple of rubbing alcohol wipe packets. She tore one open and began to wash the blood from Dyadya's face.

"I do not want Jabba Beridze near you," Dyadya said in his raspy smoker's voice. He had gotten out his pack of Marlboros and was turning it over in his hands.

Maisa frowned as she worked. "Better not open those here. Sam won't like the smoke in his house."

Dyadya winced as she finally got to the small cut near his temple. "Americans are so very self-righteous about cigarettes, are they not?"

"He's not." She tossed aside the wipe and tore open another.

The cellophane on the Marlboros crinkled in Dyadya's fingers. "I like Samuel West. He is, you say, a real man, yes?"

He always pretended that his English was worse when he was trying to get on her good side. "That's not how I would say it, but some would."

The cut wasn't so bad—it'd already stopped bleeding. She searched through the first-aid kit for a large Band-Aid.

Dyadya ignored her tart reply. "He is a straight shooter, but he does not let others borrow his money or use him. He drinks, but does not fall down drunk. He would make a woman a good husband."

Maisa found a square Band-Aid and tore open the wrapping.

"But not for you," Dyadya finished his lovely little homily.

She stuck the Band-Aid on his cut and started putting the first-aid kit back together. "I'm not thinking about marrying Sam West."

She gave him a last glare and went to the door. Sam had left the two black suitcases there. She picked them up and lugged them toward the kitchen coat closet.

"Good," Dyadya called.

She ignored him, shoving the suitcases inside the closet, behind a huge bag of dog food, and shut the door.

She heard a click and then smelled the faint whiff of smoke.

"You put out that cigarette or I'll throw it out the door, Dyadya." She marched into Sam's spare room and dragged out the pseudo bomb suitcase. She shoved that in the kitchen closet as well and then looked at her uncle, hands on hips. She felt an odd urge to cry.

"I would never, my Masha," he said gently.

"Sam's a cop. We're robbers. I *know*. You don't have to keep telling me."

Dyadya tilted his head, musing. "Not exactly robbers—"

"Then what?" She felt as if ants were jittering beneath her skin, trying to dance their way out. "What are we if not robbers, huh? We're not the average suburban American family, that's for sure. What are we, Dyadya?"

He looked at her, his hands still now. "I am mafiya, my Masha, I have never hidden this from you. But you, *you* can be American. You were born here, were raised here. You have the American education and you have a job—a career. A good career. The so-called American dream, you can have it."

But not and have you in my life, she thought. That American dream didn't include her uncle and who he was.

"An American dream like Mama tried to have?" Maisa scoffed. Mama had tried that with Jonathan Burnsey when she'd first come to America. She'd tried to have both a normal American life and her brother—with all his history. And when Jonathan had realized that Irina wasn't going to desert her criminal brother—even if it hurt Jonathan's career—he'd made the decision for her. "Jonathan pretty much ruined that for her, don't you think?"

Jonathan'd left them.

Dyadya looked troubled. "You judge your father too harshly, my Masha. You should know—"

"I don't want to talk about Jonathan," she interrupted.

Her uncle fell silent.

Like mother like daughter. Maisa simply couldn't have both an average life—a normal life—and her uncle.

And she would never desert Dyadya.

Maisa smiled and reached for the first-aid kit, turning to put it back in the cabinet. "Don't be silly. I've never wanted a house in the suburbs."

Chapter Twenty-Two

Ilya burst into tears. He raised his hands to his face and pressed stubby fingers into his eyes, as if he could somehow stop the sound of the crazy guy outside by blinding himself.

Sam moved to the back window and, standing to the side, checked the parking lot as he loaded the shotgun.

"I've got two SUVs in front, shooters on both leaning against the hoods," Doc said. "What do you see?"

"Nothing." Sam bent a bit to the side, scanning the parking lot. "Only thing's out there is my pickup."

"Il-ya!" came that voice again.

"It is Beridze," Ilya whimpered. He was shuddering all over now, as if in full-fledged shock.

"Shall we show your friends I am in earnest?" Suddenly a barrage of gunfire clattered out front.

Sam flinched, but kept his eyes on the back.

Doc swore. "He's shot out the front window of Tracy's Antique Shop."

"She'll hate that," Becky muttered. "Just had that window put in last summer."

"No one's in town," Doc said. "They've all gone home to sit out the storm."

Sam glanced at him. "What're you thinking?"

"We've got guns, we've got ammo. If they storm the door, we'll take them down," Doc said.

Becky silently got up and took down a shotgun and began loading it.

"How many do you see?" Sam asked. His gut was tightening, remembering another place.

"Five, no six."

Sam was already shaking his head. "We're outgunned. They'll wait until we've used up our ammunition then come in."

Doc's jaw worked. "What're you saying?"

"We need to leave."

Doc had been in Vietnam, knew how to talk down drunks with guns and face meth heads high on stupidity. He'd been doing it for over thirty years. "I don't like it. This's my goddamned station and my goddamned town."

"Of course it's your town," Sam said. "It's mine, too. But staying here's not going to help the town. It'll only get us killed."

"You don't know that," Doc grunted.

"Yeah," Sam said quietly, holding Doc's stubborn stare. "I do."

Doc scowled for a second, then looked away. "What do you have in mind?"

"Switch with me a second."

Doc came to the back window as Sam went to look out the front. Two SUVs had been skewed across the street, shooters leaning over the hoods, while a single man stood in the center of the street. He glanced up as if he'd felt Sam's eyes on him.

Jabba Beridze was kind of ordinary looking for a notorious mobster. Slightly shorter than average height, he wore a black ski jacket with no hat, and even though the wind blew viciously against the side of his face he didn't seem affected. In fact, though there was a delicate pink tint to his cheeks, and what looked like a bruise at his temple, overall he was as pale as death. As if no blood flowed in his veins.

"Still no one back there?" Sam asked Doc, keeping his eye on the Russian mobster.

"No."

"Okay." Sam took out the keys to his pickup. "You'll take Ilya and Becky out the back, get in my truck, drive to my house. May and George are there." He tossed the keys to Doc.

Doc caught them one-handed. "Now wait just a moment. What're you going to be doing while we're running?"

"Making sure you get out alive," Sam said.

Sam turned from the window, staring first at Ilya then at Becky. Ilya was still curled in the chair. Becky was looking determined despite her pale face. They would die if Sam didn't get them and Doc out of here.

"Becky, put your coat on." Sam went to Doc's desk and pulled open the second drawer down on the right side. "Do you have a lighter?"

"Sam, what—?"

"I need a lighter," Sam said, taking out Tick's confiscated firecrackers.

Becky stared at him a beat, then she pulled open a drawer on her own desk and handed him the lighter she kept there for the scented candles she sometimes brought in.

Sam took it from her. "Okay. Doc, you're going out the back. You first, then Ilya, then Becky. Don't stop for anything until you're in the truck. Got it?"

Becky nodded grimly.

"Yeah, I got it, Sam," Doc growled. "What, exactly, are you doing in the meantime?"

"Going out the front."

"Sam, God damn it—"

"We don't have time, Doc."

Ilya began moaning.

"Come on." Becky got a hand under Ilya's arm to help him up.

Tick's confiscated firecrackers were in three big rolls. Sam quickly laid them out, two under the windows overlooking Main, and one under the back windows. He lit all three fuses, picked up the shotgun, and ran to the stairs.

He heard the first bang halfway down.

Doc was right behind him. Sam didn't have time to double-check, but he knew the older man would follow his orders.

The firecrackers were exploding all at once now, a series of loud, constant pops. Mingled in with the pops were gunshots and the crash of shattering glass.

Sam ran across the lobby and pumped the shotgun. He cracked the front door, shotgun at his shoulder and fired without bothering to aim.

Behind him, he could hear the back door slamming open.

Beridze was nowhere to be seen. He must've already taken cover. Sam pumped the shotgun and took out one of the men behind the SUV to his right.

He pumped the shotgun and swung toward the second man.

Behind him, there was the sound of gunfire and Becky screamed.

No.

Sam fired and wheeled to the back, pumping as he ran.

A shotgun blast.

He'd miscalculated. *Again. God damn it, no.*

In the back parking lot Becky's shotgun was smoking. She stood over Doc on the ground as Ilya cowered to the side.

A gunman was running toward them.

Sam shot him in the chest. "Get in my truck."

Becky swung on him, wild-eyed. "Doc's shot!"

"I've got him." Sam bent and looped Doc's arm over his shoulders. The police chief groaned. Blood was creeping down Doc's right pants leg, but he appeared to be alive, if in shock. *Thank God.* "Get Ilya."

Becky blinked and then grabbed Ilya.

Doc still had the truck keys clutched in his fist. Sam pried them loose. He tore open the Silverado's back door and piled Doc inside. Slamming the door, he swiveled, pulled open the front door, swung into the driver's seat, and shoved the keys in the ignition.

Gunfire rattled against the tail of the truck, and then Becky was pushing Ilya into the back of the Silverado. "Go!"

Sam revved the engine and set down the plow.

One of the SUVs tore around the corner, skidded, and bounced off the corner of the municipal building, taking a few concrete blocks with it.

Sam rammed the back bumper of the SUV. He bore

down on the accelerator and the plow blade scraped with a sickening shriek across the SUV, shoving it aside. The Silverado jumped as it sprang free from the SUV. The big pickup bumped over a concrete barrier, hidden beneath the snow, and for a heart-stopping moment the back wheels spun.

Then they caught, and the Silverado roared down the alley and out of town.

He needed to get Doc to safety, needed to see how bad the gunshot wound was. Needed to return to May and keep her safe.

But first he had to be sure no one was following them.

Chapter Twenty-Three

❦

"Where is he?" Maisa pushed up one of the front window blinds to look out on Sam's front yard. It'd been three hours since he'd left, and it was already getting dark—in midwinter the light began fading midafternoon. There really wasn't much to see outside.

Still. She couldn't stop herself from looking.

Beside her, Otter whimpered.

Maisa glanced down at him absently. Maybe he had to be fed—although he had eaten quite a bit of leftover breakfast.

"He will return," Dyadya said.

She looked at him. He sat in one of the mission chairs facing the window overlooking the lake. He had another cigarette between his lips, though so far he'd abstained from lighting it. Maisa couldn't tell from his voice whether he truly believed that Sam would return safely or if he was just trying to placate her. He looked so calm, so relaxed, while she hadn't been able to sit for the last hour or so.

Maisa huffed out a breath and went to the kitchen closet. "How do you know Ilya Kasyanov?"

Dyadya waved a hand. "When I was Gigo Meskhi's man, many years ago in Moscow, Ilya was a young boy, just learning to bake the books."

Maisa frowned over that one for a second before her brow cleared. "Cook the books."

"*Da*. That." She saw the back of Dyadya's head nod. "He was a vain man but very intelligent—though, perhaps, not as intelligent as he thought himself."

Maisa snorted and dragged out the big bag of dog food. There was enough in there to feed Otter for at least a year. The terrier had trotted after her to watch and he barked when he saw what she had.

She smiled at the little dog. "Just wait a minute."

Otter didn't even look at her. His eyes were fixed on the happy yellow lab on the dog food bag. He whined and pawed at the bag.

There was a dog food bowl and water dish in the corner of the kitchen, and she dragged the bag of dog food over to them. "So he followed Meskhi to the U.S.?"

Dyadya shrugged. "Yes, though by then he was one of Meskhi's main accountants."

"Then why wasn't he imprisoned when Meskhi was?"

"Because he was crafty," Dyadya replied drily. "He'd moved on to working with Beridze by the time Meskhi was at trial. A smart move, but perhaps a dangerous one. Meskhi is a murderer, but he is not crazy like his nephew."

Maisa shivered at her uncle's words. *Crazy*. The word was overused to mean someone mad or out of control, but from what she'd seen and heard, Beridze wasn't just that. He was truly crazy: a psychopath.

Otter was practically dancing in front of his dish. She blew out a breath and concentrated on feeding him.

There was a scoop already in the bag and she used it to fill Otter's dog food bowl. Although . . . She looked doubtfully at the dog noisily gulping the food. It seemed like quite a lot for such a small dog.

Otter looked up suddenly, his little body tense.

Then he exploded, barking wildly, his claws scrabbling on the floor as he raced to the front door.

Maisa grabbed for something, anything, and ended up gripping a pewter pitcher from the counter.

The front door opened and Otter launched himself at it.

Sam came in, holding Doc Meijer against his side. There was blood on Doc's leg, on Sam's side. Blood on the floor.

Maisa dropped the pitcher. It clattered against the kitchen tiles.

Sam's face was like granite: hard and still and cold.

"What's happened?" Dyadya asked sharply.

Sam nudged Otter aside. He was looking straight at her, ignoring everything else in the room.

She didn't know how she crossed the room, but she was in front of him suddenly, searching his expression, almost afraid to touch him or Doc. Sam's electric blue eyes were the only sign of life in his face.

"Doc's been shot," Becky said from behind Sam, she held two shotguns in her hands. "He's losing blood. We need to get it stopped."

"Of course." Maisa ran back to the kitchen to fetch the first-aid box. But it held mostly Band-Aids. Those wouldn't stop a bullet wound from bleeding.

"May, go upstairs and get some of my T-shirts," Sam said, his voice calm and steady in the midst of Maisa's frantic thoughts. "Second drawer down in my dresser."

She nodded, turning to run up the stairs. It wasn't until she was rummaging through his T-shirts, wondering if it made a difference if they were colored—*of course it didn't!*—that she realized she was crying.

"Stop it," she whispered fiercely to herself, wiping her face with her sleeve. The last thing Sam needed was her going into hysterics. She took a breath and dashed back down the stairs.

Sam and Becky had Doc on the futon in the spare bedroom. They'd removed Doc's boots and Sam was cutting off the right leg of his jeans.

Sam didn't look up as she entered. "Put the T-shirts there." He jerked his chin at the table next to the futon. "Becky, I've got a bottle of rubbing alcohol in my downstairs bathroom cabinet."

Becky left without a word.

Maisa stood there, staring at Doc's bloodstained leg, feeling completely useless.

"Didn't hit the artery at least," Sam muttered. Carefully he raised the leg, ignoring Doc's groan. "Looks like the bullet went through."

"That's good, right?" Maisa said.

Sam didn't answer her.

Becky came back in with the bottle of rubbing alcohol.

"Okay, Doc," Sam said, sure and steady. "We're going to disinfect the wound as well as we can here and patch it up until we can get you to a hospital."

He unscrewed the bottle cap and poured the rubbing alcohol directly in the bullet wound.

"Fuck!" Doc gasped. "Fuck. Fuck. *Fuck.*"

"Turn a bit so I can get the exit wound," Sam said, ignoring him.

Doc complied.

Sam repeated the process on the back of his leg.

Doc grit his teeth and then exhaled hard. "Son, I'm rethinking that promotion I was pushing you into."

"I bet you are," Sam said, his voice firm but his hands gentle. "Worst is over now."

He took two T-shirts, made them into pads, and bound them tight to Doc's leg before pushing a couple of pillows under the leg to raise it.

By the time he'd finished, Doc was half asleep and Maisa could see the weariness in Sam's eyes.

She looked at Becky. "Can you stay with Doc?"

"'Course," Becky said, her chin lifted.

Maisa smiled at her in gratitude. "Come on." She took Sam's arm. "You need to wash your hands."

She led him back into the outer room where Ilya had collapsed on one of the chairs by the kitchen window. Dyadya was in the other, talking quietly to the Russian.

Sam went to the kitchen sink. He turned the faucet on and thrust his hands beneath the running water.

The water turned pink in the sink.

Maisa watched him for a second and picked up the bar of soap by the sink and put it in his hands. "What happened, Sam?"

"Beridze showed up at the police station." He was rubbing the soap between his hands. "Demanded Ilya. We were outgunned so I said we ought to make a run for it, but..."

His hands were clean so Maisa turned off the water. She picked up the towel hanging by the sink and carefully dried his hands.

Sam suddenly looked up. "It was my fault."

Her heart twisted, but she kept her voice steady. "How do you figure that?"

"I didn't see anyone out back, but they must've been waiting for us to run. They shot Doc."

Maisa threw aside the towel and silently wrapped her arms around Sam's waist, giving comfort. She knew how important Doc was to Sam.

"What would've happened if you'd stayed?" she asked.

He shook his head.

She pulled back to look at him. "You already said you were outgunned. Sounds to me like you didn't have much choice."

He shook his head and pulled her back into his arms. She felt Sam bury his face in her hair and exhale. "We lost them pretty quick outside of town, but then the Silverado got stuck on a back road. Took me a couple hours to get her shoveled out." He raised his head and looked at her and she saw that his eyes were hard. "I need to go back out and find Beridze."

Tears pricked at her eyes again. *No. Oh, no.* "That sounds like a real good way to get killed."

His mouth tightened. "There's no telling what Beridze and his men are doing in town. I—"

Maisa placed her palm on Sam's cheek, feeling the chill of the outside air, the end-of-the-day rasp of stubble. "Have you eaten since breakfast?"

He frowned. "No, but—"

"I found some ground meat in your freezer and a couple of cans of black beans in your cupboard. Do you like chili?" She used the cuff of her shirt to swipe at her eyes.

"May—"

"We all have to eat," she said firmly. "You can't leave us, Sam."

"I can't just leave them in my town."

"I know." She patted his chest, blinking back tears again. "I know, but it's dark and there's only you. Can't we wait until morning? Until the other policemen show up?"

He ran his hand through his hair. "We don't know where Tick and Dylan are—the radios are down and none of the cell phones work."

"All the more reason to wait until morning," Maisa said, her voice calm and steady, as she led him into the kitchen. If he went out now, tired and hungry and with the light almost gone, he might not return. "Sam, if we lose you, we'll be all by ourselves. They need you. *I* need you."

"Yeah. Okay." He frowned as he caught sight of Otter attempting to eat the entire bag of abandoned dog food in one go. He squatted and scooped the terrier up in his arms, ruffling his ears absently. "But in the morning I've got to go out, May." He looked up, and she wanted to weep at the stillness in his eyes. "It's my town and I have to protect it."

Chapter Twenty-Four

❧

Sam sat at his kitchen island and wondered how he could eat a second bowl of chili when Doc had been shot. 'Course, this wasn't the first time he'd eaten or slept or pissed or otherwise went on living when someone he knew—someone he'd liked and respected and...cared for—had been hurt.

Had died, in some cases.

God willing, though, it would be the last.

"Do you think Otter the Dog's made himself sick?" May was watching the terrier worriedly. Otter was zonked out on his dog bed in front of the kitchen broom closet. His belly was distended.

"No." He cleared his throat. "He's got a cast-iron stomach."

May had put together supper and served it and then had found a sleeping bag and talked Becky into lying down next to the futon in the spare room. She was taking care of them all, he realized. She liked to pretend toughness, but she was so soft, so caring, underneath it all.

God, he had to keep his May safe.

He watched as George took another beer from his

fridge. The older man hadn't said much in the couple of hours since they'd made it back. Hadn't made any explanations. Hadn't offered any apologies. Something about that just didn't sit right with Sam.

"Did you know?" Sam asked.

George looked at him warily. "Know what?"

Over by the sink May stiffened.

Sam put down his spoon. He carefully placed his hands palms down on the table, bracketing his chili bowl. "Know the Russian mob was coming here to Coot Lake?"

George's eyes narrowed. "I did not know at first."

"Dyadya had no idea—"

"Hush, May," Sam said gently without looking at her. "You knew he was mafiya, though, didn't you?" He jerked his chin at Ilya, sitting in the corner, still in his red jacket, a half-eaten bowl of chili clutched to his chest. "When did you know he was coming into town?"

"Ilya and I are old...acquaintances." George deliberately twisted off the beer bottle cap, using only the three fingers on his right hand. "He called me yesterday morning, very early, and asked to see me. So, yes, I suppose I should have realized that the mafiya might be arriving in the so-gentle Coot Lake."

"And you told no one," Sam said, hard.

"Sam!" May went to stand behind her uncle. She couldn't have made her allegiance any more obvious if she'd screamed it.

Something dark gathered inside Sam. Her unwavering loyalty was part of the reason he wanted her, but in this she had to be on his side, not her uncle's.

"No," George murmured, his accent thick. "No, I did

not tell anyone that my old friend Ilya was coming—and that the mafiya might be not far behind. That is what you want to hear, yes? That the suffering of the noble police chief Doc Meijer is my fault? *Entirely* my fault"—George's voice lowered almost to a whisper—"and not his or yours."

Sam stood so fast his stool fell over.

Otter lifted his head and gave a single, startled bark.

May pushed in front of Sam, scowling, hands on hips. "This isn't Dyadya's fault—you know that. He has as much to fear from the Russian mob as you do—more, in fact. His testimony sent Beridze's uncle to prison."

Sam felt his fists clench as he looked over her head at the old man. "So he'll be after you, too."

George just watched him, his face closed.

Which was answer enough, Sam guessed. "You sat and waited and *chose* to remain silent when you knew thugs with automatic weapons were coming to my town."

"You know I am mafiya." George shrugged. "Did you perhaps expect otherwise?"

May looked exasperated. "Dyadya!"

Sam's lip curled. "You endangered this town—endangered *May*—and didn't give a fuck, did you?"

"Sam!" May puffed up like a bantam hen. "You can't talk to him like that."

"Go upstairs, May."

"No."

"I *said*—"

"And I said *no*." She reached up and grabbed his chin.

He looked down at her, incredulous.

"I'm not going to be pushed to the side like a good little girl," she said low and fierce, "while you big men settle your asinine argument. This is the twenty-first century, not the Middle Ages."

Sam's nostrils flared. "I let you get away with a lot, sweetheart, but that doesn't mean I don't have a line."

She blinked, but didn't back down. Instead she crowded up against him, well within his personal space. "You knew exactly what I was like when you decided to keep chasing me, Sam West. I'm not some sweet young thing who'll tell you your cock is the biggest I've ever seen. I'm a cranky bitch with a career, an education, and opinions. Take it or leave it, but don't start acting like you had no idea who I am. *What* I am." She pointed behind her, straight-armed at her uncle without looking away from Sam. "Dyadya is everything to me. If you force me to make a choice I'm going to pick him. Every. Single. Time." She inhaled and her voice suddenly dropped as if all the steam had gone out of her. "So don't force me, Sam."

He stared at her a moment longer and suddenly realized that he'd already made a choice of his own—whether she liked it or not. Old George and Ilya were still in the kitchen watching, but he ignored them, because this was between him and May, and it was important. "Go on to bed, May. I'll be up in a minute."

"Dyadya—"

"I'm not going to hurt your uncle." *Tonight.*

She looked at him suspiciously as if she'd heard his unspoken amendment, but in the end she nodded and turned to the stairs without protest. Despite what she'd just yelled at him.

Not that he was stupid enough to point that out.

George wasn't a fool, either. He waited until May was

out of earshot before he raised an eyebrow at Sam. "So, that is settled, I think."

Sam looked at him, flat. "Don't bet on it, old man." He jerked his chin at the mission chairs by the windows. "You and Ilya can bunk in the chairs—they fold down nearly flat. Spare blankets in the closet by the back door. Sorry I don't have anything better," he added without really meaning it.

George nodded cautiously anyway. "I thank you. And you, you'll be, uh, *bunking* with my niece upstairs?"

Sam looked the man in the eye. "Got a problem with that?"

George actually chuckled. "Oh, I am not the one you should worry over."

Sam grunted and turned toward the stairs and his loft, because he figured Old George had it right: He might have May in his bedroom, but that didn't mean he had her in his bed.

Yet.

Chapter Twenty-Five

❧

Maisa stopped at the top of the stairs. God, what was she doing? She stared blankly at the simple platform king bed. Beside it was an old wooden footstool serving as a bedside table with a small lamp on top. A massive antique chest of drawers stood against one wall next to a straight-backed chair, and that was it for the furniture. There wasn't a bedspread on the bed, just a Hudson's Bay blanket on top of red flannel sheets. She laid her hand on the cream blanket, stroking over the scratchy red, green, and yellow stripes. It looked warm and inviting.

Maisa shivered and stepped away.

She should go back downstairs, maybe see if there was room for her on the futon with Becky. Anything she might do up here would be very, very foolish. And yet . . .

And yet there'd been something in his face tonight that she was unable to walk away from. Doc had been *shot*. That was just—

His steps sounded on the uncovered wooden stairs leading to the loft, his pace unhesitating. She snorted to herself at the thought. Had Sam ever hesitated at anything in his life?

She took a breath and turned.

He stood just at the top of the stairs watching her. The only light was a soft glow from downstairs. She'd forgotten to flick on the light up here and his face was partly in shadow.

"He didn't mean it," she blurted. She wasn't sure if those below could hear them up here, but she kept her voice low. "He likes Doc."

He didn't say anything, just watched her, and she felt immediately angry with herself. This was why she'd vowed never to defend Dyadya: other people didn't understand his motives, didn't believe he was anything beyond the tattoos on his hands.

"Forget it." She huffed an impatient breath and moved to stride past him. "I should go sleep downstairs."

"May." He caught her arm. His grip wasn't hard—she could've pulled away had she tried—but she stopped dead.

She looked up at him in the dimly lit room. He should've looked sad and lonely and hurt because of what had happened to Doc. She should've felt sorry for his vulnerability. Should've felt sorry for *him*.

Except he looked anything but vulnerable.

The breath caught in her chest. If anyone was vulnerable it was she. "Let me go."

"Never," he whispered, and pulled her against him.

His mouth was hot and tasted of hops. He combed his fingers into her hair, holding her, bending her back so she felt off balance. Relying on him to keep her upright. He thrust his tongue into her mouth, and she heard herself moan. Her hands fisted the soft chamois of his shirt, as he angled his head and pried her lips wider. He was a winter storm, overwhelming and relentless, and she was only a woman. Only a mortal. There was no way she could be expected to withstand someone like him. She could only hang on and hope to keep her sanity in the face of such an assault.

She whimpered at the thought, and then the backs of her knees hit the bed and she realized that he'd been bearing her toward the bed all this time.

She fell, out of control, and he came down, too. He landed on her, his hands braced on either side of her shoulders, and immediately brought his mouth to hers again.

He bit her. He caught her lower lip between his teeth, gentle, but with a definite threat, and tugged.

That shouldn't have turned her on. Only a woman with very strange tastes in bed would be turned on by that. But an electric shock shot through her, hitting that place between her legs, so maybe she was that woman.

She arched up and tore at his soft shirt as if she'd lost the ability to figure out buttons.

He chuckled, deep in the back of his throat, and that would've normally made her mad, but right now it just made her want to get all his clothes off. It'd been so very *long* since she'd felt his skin against hers.

She gave up on his shirt and went straight for the front of his jeans instead, wriggling her fingers between their bodies, shoving, twisting, until her hand held him. Until she found the long, hard length of his penis through his clothes and squeezed him.

He stopped chuckling.

Oh. Oh, this was very nice. How long since she'd held all his strength and want quite literally in the palm of her hand? She was an idiot for refusing this. For staying away from Sam.

She ran her fingertips over worn denim, exploring delicately, blindly, panting against his teeth, until she reached the head and squeezed.

He groaned into her mouth.

She wanted *more*. Wanted . . . wanted . . . *everything*.

Tomorrow, half an hour from now, she might come to her senses. Might talk herself out of this, and she wanted—*needed*—to feel all of him before that time. Needed to have something of him to keep when she went back to her lonely, *solitary* existence.

She pushed his shoulders, and at first he wouldn't move. That only made her frantic, and she heaved against him, shoving at his great big, heavy, *male* bulk until he must've realized she wasn't going to stop.

He gave way and rolled off her and onto his back on the bed. "May, sweetheart, don't—"

But whatever stupid protest he was going to make died in his throat when she climbed on top of him.

She sat on his legs, leaning over him, and went for his fly. And wonders of wonders, her fingers, which had been unable to figure out shirt buttons, turned out to be pretty swift with a zipper. She pulled it down, popped the tab, and paused to take a deep breath of greedy anticipation.

She carefully—*tenderly*—laid wide his fly. He wore gray knit boxer briefs. His cock was clearly outlined beneath, pointing up and to the side. She touched her tongue to her upper lip and pulled down the elastic waistband. Slowly, because she wanted to savor this, the pulse beating strong at her neck and in her ears, her thighs clenching, and because she'd named herself a bitch and in that, at least, she'd never lied: She *liked* to tease.

She heard him mutter something that sounded impatient.

The head of his penis poked out of the waistband of his underwear and it really was a lovely sight. Fat and cut, reddened with the blood that made it hard, the slit just slightly damp. She crooned at the beautiful thing, running her fingertip over the top, petting like it was her favorite toy.

Oh, he was hot—so hot. And she could smell his musk, this close to all that was most vital about him.

She couldn't help leaning down to flatten her tongue against the warm, bitter tip.

"Jesus, May," he rasped, and she glanced up to see that he had a hand in his hair as if to keep himself from grabbing her. At her look, though, he reached down with his other hand and softly brushed his fingers through her hair.

She met his eyes and took the head of his cock in her mouth.

"God," he breathed, his hips bumping up just slightly. As if he couldn't help himself. As if he teetered at the very edge of his control.

She liked that thought. She closed her eyes and tasted his skin, swiping her tongue back and forth over the top of his penis, not trying to give a proper blowjob. This really wasn't for him.

It was for her.

She suckled softly, inquisitively, tasting more salt, smiling in secret when his hips jerked again. She ran her hand under her chin and into his briefs. It was close quarters there, but she could feel his balls, drawn up needy and hot, and she rolled them tenderly in her fingers, such delicate things on a man. The very center of him held in her palm.

She pulled his shorts down farther until she exposed all of him, cock and balls, in the V of his jeans. Oh, he was beautiful: his penis heavy and veined, nestled on the blue of his chamois shirt. There was something obscene about his crude nudity there—only there—while he still wore shirt, jeans, and socks. She'd debauched him, her clean-cut cowboy. She smiled to herself, secretly, as she mouthed his length, tonguing the large vein that snaked down the underside of his cock. His penis leapt beneath her mouth, alive and hot, and she scraped her teeth gently—so gently—against him before burying her nose in the juncture of balls and cock and inhaling.

He had both hands in her hair now, moving restlessly, lightly, as if he only just kept himself from taking over. She liked this feeling—that he held himself back with the thinnest of threads, that any moment his willpower might break.

That she might *make* it break.

She lifted her head, tugging at his jeans. She wanted him naked. "Off."

"Yes'm," he drawled, his voice like gravel. He tilted his hips, helping her to shuck his jeans and sat up to pull his shirt over his head. Apparently he couldn't wait for buttons, either.

She scrambled to stand at the foot of the bed, rapidly tearing off her own jeans, shirt, bra, and panties. She didn't take her eyes off him the entire time, and when he lay back, nude and waiting, she stood for a moment, just looking. Sam West was long and lean with shoulders that made her want to touch: wide and muscled. He didn't look like an overly ripped gym rat. He looked like a man who used his muscles to work. A man who was real. There was hair on his chest, sparse and curling, circling his nipples and navel, trailing down his belly to end in a tangle highlighting that gorgeous, ruddy cock.

He watched her watching him, and the corner of his mouth lifted, a wry twist. "So I'm not the biggest you've seen."

"I didn't say that," she whispered, climbing onto the bed to kneel by his side. "I just said I wouldn't *tell* you if you were."

"No point in inflating my ego." He nodded as if that made sense and trailed his fingers over her hip. "I guess I'm not that worried about your ego. You're the most beautiful woman I've ever seen."

Her lips parted at the blunt words. "You don't have to tell me that. I know I'm just ordinary."

He cocked his head against the cream blanket. "No, you're not. Not to me. You're the only one for me, May. Don't you know that by now?"

Any other man and she would've eviscerated him for lying. For thinking her so naïve she'd fall for false flattery. Except this was *Sam* and his flattery . . . wasn't flattery. He was telling the truth as he saw it.

"You're not supposed to say that," she whispered.

"Why not?" He trailed his fingers down her bare side. "Why shouldn't I tell you how much you mean to me? You think trying to hide it makes it any less so?"

"No." She shook her head, almost frightened by his bluntness. "But I don't understand why. Why me?"

"Because." Something close to anger crossed his face. "Anytime you walk in the room I can't take my eyes off you. Anytime you walk out I have to physically stop myself from following you. I like your bitchiness. I like that you get right in my face. And sweetheart, I adore the way you stand by your criminal of an uncle. You're everything I've ever wanted, May."

"I don't know what to do with that," she whispered, the words pulled from her very soul. "I don't know what to do with *you*."

"Don't you?" he asked and his thumb brushed her nipple. "Maybe you should just kinda stop thinking about it. Just do what feels right."

"That's the problem. I don't think I know right from wrong. I only know who I care for."

"Okay." His hand cupped her breast. "Then care for me, May."

"I can't. I have to—" She gasped, arching under his hand "—have to..."

"You don't *have* to do anything, sweetheart," he said so tenderly she caught her breath. "You can care for anyone you damn well please."

"That's too simple." She bit her lip to hold back a whimper.

"Is it?" He shrugged. "I guess I don't think so. Just let go."

She shuddered. At his hand, at his words, she didn't know anymore.

He watched her as he weighed her breast in the palm of his hand, dragging his thumb back and forth across her nipple until it hardened.

She glared at him. "Do you have a condom?" If he didn't she just might kill him.

Without looking away from her, he reached under the mattress and took out a strip of condoms.

"Suave," she mocked.

He tilted his chin at her, chiding. "Put one on me, May."

The sound of the packet tearing between her fingers seemed very loud in the loft and for a moment she wondered if anyone below could hear.

And then she decided she just didn't care.

She sat up on her knees and unrolled the condom onto his cock. Her fingers trembled, but he made no comment at her weakness. She held him upright and swung her leg over him so that she straddled his hips.

He moved finally, then, placing his big hands on her hips. "May, I—"

But she gave him no chance to make any confessions. That wasn't what this was about tonight. She lowered herself, surprised at how slippery she already was, and rubbed him through her folds. Up to her clit, down to her entrance, and back up again, the sound of their flesh sliding together wet and obscene in the darkness.

He closed his eyes. His fingers gripped her hips, and she wondered if he was that close already.

She smiled at the thought.

Then she notched him at her entrance and bore down.

There hadn't been anyone else since last August—though she'd die a thousand deaths before telling him that—and the feel of him stretching her made her inhale. She shifted, lifting up a bit, before lowering herself again, working him in slowly.

She wasn't quite seated fully when she placed her palms on his chest and leaned forward, her breasts dangling in his face. He turned his head and mouthed one, and she had to arch her head back and bite her lip. *So good.* So good to have him inside, to feel his hands on her, his mouth making love to her breasts. This feeling with him was something she could get lost in, forget all that she'd fought for before.

If she let herself.

She inhaled and lifted up again, careful not to let him slip entirely out. He seemed content to let her take the lead—or at least he was good enough to hold himself back. She twisted her hips a bit as she screwed down on him. This time she took him all the way inside, until her pubic bone met his. Until her clit rubbed sweetly against him.

Oh, that felt nice.

She flattened herself against him, sliding back and forth, grinding a bit.

He let go of her breast and switched to the other, sucking her nipple strongly into his mouth.

She moaned breathlessly.

But then he was sneaky. He slid his palm inward toward her center and slipped his thumb between their bodies. She lifted up just a little, and then he was pressing just there, against her clitoris, and the spark of pleasure, the sudden wave of pure, exquisite feeling, was so strong that she bent and grasped his head between her hands.

She kissed him as if he were oxygen. As if she sucked life from his lips. And she moved. Not well, not gracefully, because she half lay on him now, but she wanted the sensation, wanted his lips, too. Wanted everything that he was.

Something broke then, the thread that had held him back, perhaps. He surged up against her, his hips moving fast and hard, thrusting into her.

She sobbed into his mouth, giving up the control of their lovemaking even though she remained on top. She held on and kissed him and braced herself so that he could move strongly between her thighs.

Sam. Sam. Sam. He was the whole and the entirety of her person right here, right now, and she never wanted this to end.

But it must; they couldn't struggle so sweetly together forever like this. He was slippery beneath her now, sweat filming his chest as he labored under her. His thumb stroked wetly against her, and she threw back her head, gasping, grinding her hips against him frantically. Just there...just *there*.

She saw lights, blue and yellow and white, behind her eyelids as she came. Her body shook with hungry pleasure and then shook again on another wave. Endless, endless, pleasure.

She opened her eyes finally, with great effort, and saw him, his teeth bared, his eyes wide, the blue almost glowing as he hissed out a long, silent breath.

She watched Sam West come inside her and was afraid.

Afraid of how easy it would be to love him.

Chapter Twenty-Six

DAY THREE

When Sam had woken that hot August morning six months ago, May had already crept out of the motel room. Sam might not have been the smartest guy in the world—certainly not college educated—but he liked to think he knew how to learn from past mistakes.

So when he woke in the dim winter dawn to May edging from his bed, he didn't bother debating the matter. He simply grabbed her and rolled.

She squeaked kind of adorably, like a mouse startled by a swooping hawk.

Except mice didn't usually give a death glare.

"Get off me," she hissed, good and mad—or at least trying to look mad. He noticed she kept her voice down.

"Nope." His brain was still a bit foggy from sleep, but his dick was already with the program, hard and pressing into the warm softness of her thigh. Her eyes might be sparking at him, but her body was relaxed and unguarded under his. The covers were still heaped over them, making a moist, warm cave, shielding them from the chill of the room.

He nudged the side of her face with his nose. He could smell himself on her and it made something within him stretch in satisfaction.

"May," he said, in greeting or simple acknowledgment: May, here with him. May.

He opened his mouth over her earlobe, tasting a hint of salt.

She brushed her hand into his short hair. "Look..."

"Mmm." He tongued down the side of her neck, making her shiver. Making his hips shove into hers.

"We can't—"

"Hush," he whispered, doing a push-up over her. He wanted to see her breasts. It'd been dark last night and he hadn't taken the time to look.

Now, though...now he had all the time in the world.

There they were, round and perky, her nipples shockingly dark against her fair skin. Her tits looked kind of happy to see him.

Unlike the rest of her. "Sam," she complained, wriggling beneath him.

He winced as a sharp knee nearly took out his morning joy.

"They'll hear you, you know," he murmured, lowering his mouth to one brown nipple. He'd given up way too soon last time. "You want that? Them listening?"

She stilled at his words—or maybe it was because he was licking her nipple.

"I...I don't think..." Her husky voice trailed away as he sucked her into his mouth and he hid a grin.

Good. Her thinking had never led to anything positive for the two of them. Better to not let her think at all.

He tongued his way across the skin of her chest, the

delicate bones beneath, to her other breast. He licked all the way around that nipple before opening his mouth over it.

She whimpered softly—sweet, sweet music to his ears. "We...ah...we shouldn't. Sam..."

She might be voicing doubts, but her legs opened, welcoming him in. He let his weight settle against her, his cock sliding on her moist skin. He could feel the rough little curls over her pussy, the heat and slipperiness below. Suddenly he had a driving need.

He raised his head, looking into her wide, dark eyes as he nudged himself into her folds, sliding. "May."

She was wet. Her eyelids drooped to half-mast. Her cheeks were pink, a crease from the sheets still imprinted on one, and her hair was flattened against the side of her head from sleeping.

She was the most beautiful thing he'd ever seen.

He kissed her because he had no other way to tell her how big his heart was right now—swollen to bursting with need for her. She was so small, so vicious, so vulnerable. All that packed into one feminine body, one lightning-quick mind. How could he ever keep up? How could he ever let her go again?

He pushed his tongue into her mouth too soon, not letting her get used to what they were about to do.

He angled his head, taking her mouth, staking a claim on her.

He opened his eyes and glanced at the side of the bed. He had more condoms under the mattress, if he could just reach them...He felt with his left hand, fumbling with the blanket hanging over the edge of the bed. The crease was just there...

She murmured something and he growled back, nipping at her bottom lip. His cock pulsed with blood, with heat and need, and he wanted to put it in her. Where was the damned condom?

His fingers found the square packet just as she arched under him, rubbing her pussy against him.

Jesus. He nearly went cross-eyed.

He broke away from her lips, gasping. "Hold on."

"Hurry." Her single, moaned word made his hips jerk against her. He had to get that condom on.

He knelt up, tearing the square open with his teeth, hands vibrating as he concentrated everything he had on rolling the thin latex down his cock.

When he glanced up he couldn't help but catch his breath. She lay on his bed, spread and open like a thirteen-year-old's wet dream.

Like everything he'd ever hoped for in this life.

Her eyes glinted in the dawn's light as he took his cock in hand and lowered himself.

"May," he whispered, and he didn't know if she could tell that he was bleeding from the soul as he found her opening. As the head of his dick nudged inside.

Hot. Soft and tight and hot.

God damn. So fucking good.

He closed his eyes for a moment, praying, gritting his teeth, teetering on the edge of bursting.

She wrapped her slim legs around his hips and pulled, and he grunted as he slid all the way into her.

Her hands were skittering over his shoulders, her mouth open, panting. "Move."

He withdrew slowly, carefully.

She arched beneath him, her head tilted back on

her graceful neck. Her throat was damp. "Move, move, *move.*"

And he did. Shoving hard into her, riding her roughly, making the bed rattle against the wall. Blissed out on fucking May.

She moaned, loud and uninhibited, and the sound sent a shock of lust through his spine, electrifying every nerve. He propped himself up on his elbows and pounded into her, watching her face, sharing her breaths. Her breasts jiggled against his chest with each thrust, and even in this animal state with nothing on his mind but the feel of her around him and how ever-loving *good* it was, even now he was aware of the thin wisps of regret and longing and sorrow, hanging like cobwebs in the corners of his brain. He wanted this forever. Now and tomorrow and all the days afterward, him and May together, amen.

If she'd only let it be so.

He rode her until his chest was heaving and his heart was racing and the breath sawed in and out of his throat and he might have a heart attack at any moment. Until the pleasure raced up and down his spine, looking for outlet. Until she gasped his name, soft lips trembling. Until he couldn't stand it anymore and bent to lick the sweat from her beautiful throat. Until he felt her orgasm hit, hard and overwhelming, squeezing tight around him, holding him like she'd never let him go.

Until his sight whited out with his own release.

He slumped against her, twitching helplessly from the aftershocks, his brains blown out. He knew he was heavy, probably crushing her, but he just couldn't move. He had to wait for his brain to reboot.

"Sam." Becky's voice came from below, sounding high and panicked. "Sam!"

He jolted up, throwing the covers over May even as he reached for the Beretta under the bed.

"What?" he yelled back, fumbling off the condom and taking a few painful short hairs with it. "Becky?"

Where the fuck were his jeans?

George answered him. "There are people outside this house. With dogs."

Chapter Twenty-Seven

❧

"I'm allergic to dogs," Walkingtall said for the fifth time—or maybe the hundredth—as Cookie led the team into Sam's road. The sled bumped over a mound of packed snow and Karl didn't even try to hide his grin when Walkingtall grabbed wildly for the rails to either side of him. He was sitting in the basket in front of Karl. His sled was kind of small for a passenger, which meant Walkingtall was hunched over his bent knees like a confused great blue heron. The other man snuffled wetly before sneezing which, what with the "wetly," was pretty gross.

Karl rolled his eyes because, really, the guys's allergies were getting old. Behind them, Stu was whooping in the cold morning air. 'Course, he was probably feeling cheery because *his* passenger was Molly, which was simply unfair. It wasn't Karl's fault that Walkingtall had insulted Stu and his team early into the proceedings by mentioning that Stu's lead dog, Axel, looked kind of like a rabid wolf—which he did, in point of fact, but most were smart enough not to *say* that to Stu's *face*. Not, apparently, Walkingtall. Karl had suggested just leaving the guy at the Coot Lake Inn with Norm—because why did they need him, anyway?—but Molly had given him *that* look, and the next thing he knew he had an unwelcome passenger.

Karl began yelling "Whoa" as the team neared Sam's drive—sometimes they got a little enthusiastic and didn't want to stop for, like, a half mile or more. But today Cookie was on her best behavior. She was a big silver-and-black malamute with blue eyes—prettiest thing you'd ever seen as long as you didn't get too close. The team even made it into Sam's drive without overturning the sled—which, on the whole, wasn't something Karl had been too worried about anyway.

He set the brake, and Cookie immediately turned to snap at Bug right behind her. Bug, who'd just been minding his own business lifting his leg at Sam's front tire, looked startled.

Karl sighed and scrambled to pull Bug away before he did something stupid like snap back at Cookie. The dogs hadn't had a decent run in days, and Cookie kind of had permanent PMS. Bug might lose a nut—or more important, an ear.

"Those dogs aren't safe," Walkingtall muttered in a stuffed-up voice as he unbent his long legs.

" 'Course not," Karl scoffed. "Sled dogs never are."

Walkingtall looked confused at that, and Karl had a little moment of joy, and then Stu pulled up kind of showy, and Molly was there looking all worried and grim.

The front door to Sam's cabin opened and Sam stepped out, wearing only jeans and boots and holding his gun down by his side. Karl was pretty impressed: going bare-chested in the wind was hard-core. Sam must be freezing, but his expression was stern and he wasn't shivering. His nipples were little pointy points of *ow*, though, which, of course, Karl only noticed in a *scientific* sort of way. As bros do. Karl snuck a look sideways to see if Molly was staring at Sam's nipples.

But she had her gaze well above his clavicles as she climbed out of Stu's sled. "Sam, the motel and police station have been shot up and Doc's missing."

And like that, things got serious.

Karl watched Sam because he knew this had to hit his friend hard—Sam and Doc argued a lot, but anyone could tell they were tight.

Sam's face hardly moved, though. Just a faint tightening of his jaw as he squinted into the morning sun. Kind of like Clint Eastwood facing down a passel of really dirty outlaws.

"We've got him here, Molly," Sam said. "He's been shot, but he's okay." His voice was deep and gravelly, which Clint had never been able to manage, despite being possibly the greatest actor to ever live.

Next to Bruce Willis, of course.

There was a movement behind Sam, and Maisa Burnsey peeked over his shoulder and—*whoa!* Maisa wasn't wearing much besides a chamois shirt that had to belong to *Sam*.

Karl couldn't help but grin. He shot a look at Molly to share in the discovery of sexy shenanigans in Coot Lake. Molly kind of frowned back at him.

Oh, yeah, not the time.

Karl coughed and hastily rearranged his face as Maisa said, "Why don't you all come inside?"

Otter nudged his way past her knees and came out barking, real buff and macho, but then saw his yard full of bigger, tougher sled dogs. The terrier made an immediate U-turn and hustled his furry ass back inside.

Just then the last of their party pulled up. Doug had made the musher meet after all, despite the weather, which for some reason had kept nearly everyone else away. He listed a bit to the right, still recovering from his little broken-legs problem. Unlike his cousin Stu, Doug was a stump of a guy, nearly as wide as he was tall, but not because of fat necessarily, just sort of *bulk*. He was a good musher, though, one of the best. His dogs were almost uncannily well behaved. In Karl's experience sled dogs tended to lean less in the direction of fluffy-and-sloppy kisses and more toward the rabid might-kill-and-eat-you-in-your-sleep.

He glanced fondly at Cookie, who was lunging at her lead, trying to get to Doug's dogs.

Haley Anne Lingstrom sat in Doug's sled, wearing a fake fur jacket that came only to her waist and must've left her butt freezing in the cold. It looked good on her, though. She was already struggling up as the sled slowed. She hopped off as soon as Doug set the brake, running to Sam in furry knee-high boots.

"Sam, those crazies have Dylan!" Haley Anne was not so much worried as mad as a hive of hornets hit by a base-ball bat—something Karl had learned by experience not to do.

Everyone turned and stared at Sam.

He nodded. "You'd better come inside and tell me what's happened."

And they did, trooping in like refugees hoping to find someone to take them back home.

George Johnson was standing on the other side of Sam's kitchen island, his face careful and blank, and his hands hidden. Peering around the door from what looked like the bathroom was the tubby Russian from yesterday—that Kasyanov guy. Karl kind of started at the sight of him and narrowed his eyes in case the Russian whipped out an automatic weapon and began shooting. Kasyanov didn't really look the type, but who did?

Then Becky came out of Sam's spare bedroom. She looked real tired, lines on her face that hadn't been there before. "Doc's sleeping still, but his color is good."

"Oh, Becky!" Haley Anne crumpled into the older woman's arms. "I'm so sorry about Doc."

"I know, hon." Becky looked at her, shrewd. "What's going on?"

"They've got Dylan."

Becky patted her back, making female comforting sounds. Molly went over and without saying a word, wrapped her short little arms as far as they would go around both women. Maisa hovered a bit, not touching anyone, but looking real concerned.

Karl gave Sam the side-eye. Should he go over and hug him in a manly, we're-all-bros sort of way? Or would Stu take an honest, heartfelt gesture like that and run with it, ragging Karl relentlessly to his grave?

Fortunately, he was saved from the social dilemma by Sam's interruption. "What happened, Haley Anne?"

The girl pulled back, wiping her eyes. "Yesterday afternoon Dylan came to pick me up from work 'cause the snow was so deep, y'know?"

Everyone nodded because of course they *did* know.

"And the roads were pretty bad so we weren't going too fast, and then we saw an SUV by the side of the road like it was stuck and naturally Dylan stopped. It's his job, after all." Haley Anne glared then, planting her fists on her skinny hips. "I should've known something was up after what Jim Gustafson said at the café and you questioning him, Sam, but I swear to God I hadn't a clue in the world. I was too worried about if we were going to make it through the snow to my mom's house and if he should just stay there with us if we did."

"You couldn't have known," Becky comforted.

Haley Anne nodded shakily. "Anyways, they had guns on Dylan as soon as he got out of the squad car. Big guns, like something soldiers would have, and they made him kneel down in the snow. I thought"—Haley Anne gasped, tears welling in her eyes—"I thought they'd shoot him dead right there in front of me."

"Oh, hon," Becky murmured, patting her shoulder.

Haley Anne gripped the other woman's hand and shook her head. "But they didn't. They made me get out of the car and had us climb into their SUV. It was black, just like Jim said, Sam." She glanced at Sam. "Big and square and expensive, like a BMW or something."

"That's real good you remembered a detail like that, Haley Anne," Sam said, soothing like. "What happened then?"

"They drove us back into town to the police station. It was all shot up and there was blood on the ground in the parking lot. Is that where...?"

Becky nodded grimly.

For a moment no one spoke.

Karl shot a glance at Sam, but his expression didn't reveal anything. His face had shut completely down. Made you wonder if you ever really knew a person, deep down like, until Armageddon showed up.

Haley Anne inhaled noisily, breaking the silence. "They took us upstairs and there were more guys there. They put us in that cell, and I gotta tell you Sam, there is *no* privacy for the toilet, none at all. I had to get Dylan to stand in front of me, facing away, just to pee."

Karl had to agree on this last complaint. Not that he'd been a visitor to the Coot Lake Police Station holding cell all *that* often, but when he had, he'd felt a certain lack of respect for the more intimate bodily functions a prisoner might have to perform.

Sam didn't seem too worried about prisoners' rights at the moment, though. "Duly noted," he said evenly. "How'd you get here, Haley Anne?"

"Okay." She scrubbed her hands on her thighs. "Well, there's this guy in charge. Not tall or, like, big or anything, but he's real scary." Her brows knit like she was confused. "I can't even tell you why. He's pasty white and has tiny eyes and he just *looks* mean. He was smoking these little black cigarettes the entire time, just watching us, and it made me nervous. Dylan, too. Dylan kept me close all night long. But in the morning, real early, the boss had one of the other guys point a gun at Dylan. They said they'd shoot him if I didn't come out of the holding cell. Dylan didn't want me to, but what was I going to do? They would've shot him. I could see they meant it, too." She looked appealingly at Becky.

Becky shook her head. "You did the right thing."

Haley Anne nodded, still trying to convince herself. "So I came out and the nasty one in charge, he said that I was to find you, Sam and give you a message. They shoved me out on Main. I knew my little Honda wouldn't make it in this snow so I started walking. When I got by the motel, that's when Stu saw me. I told him what was going on and we all decided to come here."

"What did Beridze say to tell me?" Sam asked quietly.

"He said that he'd kill Dylan—" Haley Anne gulped "—if you didn't bring him what he wanted."

"Shit," Karl said. "What did he want?" They hadn't actually got that far before deciding to find Sam.

Haley Anne shrugged. "He said you'd know, Sam."

So everyone looked at Sam. Well, everyone except Kasyanov, who tried to sneak out of the bathroom and to the front door. Karl snagged him easily by the back of his red jacket—which was beginning to look kind of ratty—and Otter helped by growling at the Russian.

"Hey!" said Kasyanov. "I go outside to have a smoke, yes?"

"No," Sam said and he didn't sound angry or curious or even worried. He didn't sound like anything at all. Karl had known Sam West for three years now, and the policeman was laid-back and cool, and kind of drily funny. A regular guy. A guy good for fishing early on a Sunday morning or brewskis down at Ed's late on a Friday night. Karl would never have guessed in a thousand years that his friend could sound so completely and utterly *blank*.

"No, you're not going anywhere," Sam continued in that same *not* tone, making Karl's spine crawl like he had a thousand ticks on his back. "You're going to sit down and tell me what Beridze wants with you. What made him chase you to my town."

Kasyanov's eyes widened. His face had turned greenish around the edges and he opened his mouth. And then shut it.

"Diamonds," George rumbled from the kitchen, making Karl start because he'd almost forgotten George was there. "Beridze has come to take back the diamonds Ilya stole from him."

At the word *diamonds*, Karl's grip on Kasyanov's collar loosened in surprise. The Russian wriggled like a just-caught fish, nearly escaping. Otter jumped up and barked.

Karl absently yanked him back again and Kasyanov sagged, defeated in his hand. "Wait, *what* diamonds? There're diamonds? In *Coot Lake*?"

He glanced around the room to see if anyone else had known about the diamonds, but everyone looked pretty surprised, mostly.

Well, except for Old George, who was staring significantly at Kasyanov. "Yes. Pink diamonds, cut into the shape of hearts. Perfectly matched, beautiful and rare, and worth…" George held up his hands as if trying to cup the words to describe such wealth. He shook his head helplessly. "Worth more than any of us will ever see in this lifetime."

For a moment the room was silent as if in awe.

Karl shook the little Russian, just to see if any diamonds would rattle out. "You got diamonds, man?"

"You!" Kasyanov rounded on him. "You…you thief!"

"Hey." Karl was really hurt. Sure he and Kasyanov hadn't had time to form a true bro relationship yet, but that was no reason to go around calling people *thieves*.

"Yesterday. In the lobby of that shit motel—"

"Now wait a—" Karl started.

But Kasyanov was red-faced and at full steam now. "You stole my suitcase and put your own in its place!"

"What?" Karl reared back. "What? No . . . what are you talking about?"

"I take my suitcase to my room and when I open it, fa!" Kasyanov made some kind of foreign-y noise with his lips and tongue that resulted in spit flying through the air.

Karl flinched.

"Fa!" Kasyanov spit again. "My diamonds, they are not there. Instead there are shitting—"

George sighed loudly and interrupted the confusing rant. "Ilya, you fool, Karl does not have your diamonds."

"Thank you!" Karl exclaimed, glad someone had some sense.

"When you arrived at the motel, you had already lost the diamonds," George said.

He turned to the kitchen closet behind him. Otter, who had been quietly growling under his breath at Kasyanov all this time, lost interest in the Russian and trotted over to look in the closet. George bent and took three identical black suitcases out of the closet. They all looked like *Karl's* suitcase.

He began to have a bad feeling.

George looked at Kasyanov. "My niece, Maisa, had the diamonds when she came to my house yesterday."

Kasyanov jerked his head in the direction of Maisa Burnsey. "This is your niece?"

George nodded and lifted one of the suitcases onto the island in Sam's kitchen.

"But . . ." Kasyanov looked like the air had been let out of him. "But I did not know you had a niece."

"That is because I wanted it so," George said and flung open the suitcase.

A red bra flopped halfway out.

Everyone stared.

The bra was filmy and had tiny sparkles all along the upper edge. Karl was pretty sure he'd seen one just like it in the last Victoria's Secret catalogue—which he got for the articles, of course.

"Dyadya!" Maisa was turning an interesting shade of pink. She rushed forward and pushed the suitcase lid closed. "That's *my* suitcase."

Karl arched his brows at that, because he'd never seen Maisa in anything but black. He eyed her chest, trying to figure out if she was wearing a sexy red bra right now.

Molly slapped him across the back of the head.

"Ow!" Karl looked at her with his patented puppy eyes. "Why did you—?"

"You know why." She turned back to the suitcases.

Walkingtall had marched over, all important, to get involved. He bent over one of the two remaining suitcases on the floor and then jumped back like it had turned into a rattlesnake. "It says there's a bomb inside!"

Kasyanov yelped and Karl recoiled a step.

"It's all right," Maisa said loudly. "Really. My uncle put that sign there to keep anyone from opening the suitcase. There's no bomb. *Right*, Dyadya?"

"Of course, of course," the old man rumbled, as if a *bomb* was nothing to get worried over. "Is a joke merely."

Karl caught the hard look Sam shot at the old man— and his niece. *Uh-oh.* Trouble in paradise.

But Sam said nothing as George hefted the last suitcase up to the counter. Everyone sort of leaned forward as he unzipped the thing and opened the top.

Styrofoam burst out and scattered.

Otter yipped and jumped up, snapping at the floating bits.

Karl's heart did a nosedive. "Uh..."

"What is this?" George muttered, lifting up a clear plastic ziplock bag with a gorgeous Clovis point made from dark caramel-colored Knife River flint. One of his best, if Karl did say so himself.

Walkingtall stiffened like a pointer with a pheasant in front of his nose. "Native American artifacts! Stolen from the Red Earth Ojibwa Indian Reservation."

"What?" Karl squawked in alarm. "No, wait, that isn't..."

Everyone looked at him. Molly's pretty brown eyes widened and she shook her head, looking sad. "Oh, Karl."

"Look, I can explain," Karl said like every single guilty asshole he'd ever seen in the movies.

"It isn't important," Sam said. "What's important is the diamonds. Where are they if they aren't in these suitcases?"

"I tell you, he has stolen them!" Kasyanov pointed at Karl, straight-armed, like one of those pod people in that movie that had scared the shit out of Karl when he was nine. "At the motel yesterday—"

"No, that cannot be," George rumbled. "For I had the diamonds this morning when I went to meet you at the café." He looked thoughtful. "Karl was also there with *his* suitcase, identical to these."

"The suitcases must've been mixed up at the café." Sam glanced at Karl. "So you *do* have the diamonds. Where's your suitcase, Karl?"

And Karl's heart, already in his toes, made a valiant attempt to burrow through the floor. He remembered picking up the suitcase after Kasyanov had knocked it over, remembered setting it under his feet. Then he'd started arguing with Walkingtall and there'd been the business with the ride to the motel, all of which meant...

He gulped. "I left it in the café."

Chapter Twenty-Eight

❦

Jabba Beridze blew out a stream of cigarillo smoke and stared out the shitty small town police station window at the café across the street. It was cold. There was heat, but many of the windows had been broken by his men when they stormed the police station. Bits of cloth had been stuffed into the gaps, but still the wind whistled in, bringing the cold. He'd spent the night in an office chair, sleeping very little. The food was not good. Only that which his men could find in the kitchens of the restaurant across the street. Canned peaches, stale bread, and sliced meat and cheese. Jabba had endured cold, little sleep, and poor food before. It bothered him little.

What he did not like was the boredom.

Behind him, one of his men was pacing. Another was taking apart a gun, laying each piece down with a muffled *thunk* on a piece of cloth laid out on a desk. Probably it was Sasha. He liked his guns.

Jabba rose and strolled to the little cell where the young policeman sat on the cot. His head had been bowed in thought, but he looked up as Jabba drew near.

The policeman had hair the color of piss—so yellow

it looked dyed, like a woman would do. His face was unlined, his hands broad but boyish, as if his body might decide to grow yet still. He had probably never gone a day without food.

This boy stood and looked at Jabba. He tried to do so without fear, but that, alas, was something few could do.

"I'm a cop, you know," the boy said, his voice breaking. "You can't kill me and get away. Every law enforcement agency in America will be after you."

Jabba cocked his head. He was bored, after all. "And what do you think I should do instead?"

Behind him, Sasha no longer played with his gun and Nicky's pacing had stopped.

The boy tilted his chin, square and solid, facing him like John Wayne.

But then John Wayne had never fought in a real war.

"You should let me go before this gets any worse," foolish John Wayne said.

"Ah, but then my men have already shot your police chief," Jabba replied. He dropped the cigarillo to the floor and ground it out with his heel. "So I think already every American policeman will be after me, as you say. Do you not think so?"

"Yes, but..." The boy opened his mouth and then closed it. He looked puzzled. Perhaps the villains in his movies did not make such blunt statements.

Jabba took out a silver case from an inside pocket of his coat and selected a new cigarillo. He lit it while he waited for the boy to try another tack to save his own life.

When he blew out the smoke and the policeman still had not spoken, Jabba said, "I think I will do as you say."

The boy blinked, confused.

"Yes," Jabba inhaled hot smoke as he mused. "Yes, I think I will set you free, but in my own way, you understand."

The boy's voice was hoarse when he asked, "What way is that?"

Jabba smiled sweetly. "One piece at a time."

Chapter Twenty-Nine

"Have another piece of the breakfast bake," Becky said gruffly, her spatula hovering over the huge dish of eggs, bread, ham, and cheese.

Maisa smiled awkwardly and shook her head. Her mother was the same way: when Irina was sad or upset, she cooked and fed. Becky had spent the last hour putting together the breakfast casserole along with a mountain of pancakes, coffee, juice from Sam's freezer, and fruit she'd found in cans in his cupboards. She'd stayed mostly silent as she did it, letting everyone else talk and worry and argue around her.

Maisa had offered to help just once and had been directed to set the table and eat. Realizing that it was better to let Becky work through her anxiety at the stove, Maisa left her to it. But now, having finished eating, she felt kind of useless. She didn't want to take away what comfort Becky found in serving others, but she didn't quite know what to do herself. Everyone else seemed to know their roles, to know their place in this gathering.

She was the only one at loose ends.

She cradled her mug of coffee and watched as Sam

studied the Coot Lake Chamber of Commerce map of the town, spread over the remains of breakfast on his kitchen island. His short, dark blond hair was ruffled. He'd taken a quick shower but forgotten to comb it, and she had an urge to get up and stroke it into place, feel the damp strands beneath her fingers, the warmth of his scalp underneath.

She took a sip of her cooling coffee instead.

Sam wore a faded denim shirt, a shade lighter than his eyes, the sleeves rolled up above a red thermal shirt. Both arms were braced on the island as he peered down. He looked grim, deep lines bracketing his mouth. Everyone else was crowded around him, and they might be arguing points of his plan, but they weren't coming up with any of their own.

He was the clear leader.

"Okay, Haley Anne has the keys to the Laughing Loon Café, and there's a back entrance here." Sam tapped a tiny loon on the map inside a brown square. "And there's a fire escape on the back of Tracy's Antiques, but it's pretty rusted. Molly's going to need a boost. Think you can get her up there, Karl?"

Karl leaned forward, peering at the map. "Yep. Remember last year when you wanted to climb that oak to check the raccoon nest, Molly?"

He turned, grinning to Molly, but visibly wilted when he saw her stony stare. Maisa wasn't entirely sure what the problem was with the arrowheads that had been in Karl's suitcase, but it had made Molly stop speaking to Karl. Maisa didn't know the other woman that well, but Molly kept shooting irritated little glares at Karl and, when he wasn't looking, oddly hurt glances. The tall, handsome Native American lawyer who'd come in with Molly and

Karl was obviously on her side. He whispered something to her once in a while, but his words didn't seem to make Molly any happier.

Otherwise the lawyer looked kind of lost, which wasn't surprising. It must be strange to be an outsider in all this.

Then again, she was an outsider, too.

Maisa stared down at her coffee mug as the realization hit home. Molly, Haley Anne, Stu and Doug, Karl, the lawyer, and Dyadya were all crowded around Sam. Becky kept her head cocked, listening in on the discussion, and even Ilya said something once in a while. The only one not participating was Maisa.

Well, that made sense. She wasn't from Coot Lake. She had her own little apartment in Minneapolis. When all this was over, she'd get in her Beetle and drive back to the Twin Cities, continue sewing retro dresses and eating Lean Cuisine. She didn't belong here. She wasn't even sure she *liked* small towns. Everyone knowing her and her business would just get on her nerves. And beyond that, beyond living elsewhere and not being from Coot Lake, beyond all that there was still one fundamental difference:

She was mafiya. They weren't.

Dyadya glanced up, his sad, hound-dog face looking quizzical as if he'd heard her thoughts, and he nodded at her.

"He said he'd kill Dylan," Haley Anne burst out. "What if he just shoots him before we get there? What then?"

"He won't," Sam said, calm and sure. "I'm going to get him out alive, Haley Anne. Trust me."

"I'm just . . ." Haley Anne choked and suddenly lunged at Sam, wrapping her arms around his neck.

"Hey, hey," Sam murmured. "It'll be okay."

"Yeah," Haley Anne said shakily. "Yeah, okay, Sam."

And Maisa marveled. They'd all turned to Sam, let him make the decisions, trusted him to do the right thing and get Dylan back. Basically defend the town against armed mafiya thugs. They either didn't know or were ignoring how much the odds were stacked against them.

But Sam must know. He was a small-town cop, but he'd served in Afghanistan and was smart besides. What would it do to him if they failed? How would he feel if Dylan died after he'd assured Haley Anne that he could save them?

Maisa looked away, suddenly angry. These people had no right to put such a burden of responsibility on Sam's shoulders. He was only one man.

"Everybody know what they're doing?" Sam asked, looking each person in the eye one by one. He looked at Maisa last, his electric blue eyes intent. He held her gaze as he rolled up the map. "Okay, get your stuff together. We'll leave in fifteen minutes." He waited until everyone got up and scattered before walking over to stand next to Maisa. "You got a minute?"

"Sure." Her voice came out a squeak and she frowned to cover it. So they'd spent a night together. So they'd made love—*twice*. So he'd made her come so hard she thought her eyeballs might explode. No biggy, right?

But she found herself docilely following him up the stairs to his loft bedroom, trotting after him like Otter. Maybe sex hormones had fogged her brain.

At the top of the stairs he stopped and suddenly turned, pulling her into his arms without a word. His mouth covered hers, the taste of coffee bright on both their tongues.

He thrust his thigh between her legs and she forgot every-thing but the hardness of his chest, the steady heartbeat beneath, and the press of his leg against her.

He pulled away and she actually followed him with her mouth before she caught herself and blinked up at him.

"How are you?" he asked.

"Fine. Okay." She tried to sound adult, composed, but it was a little hard when she was still riding his thigh.

"Did you know?" he asked, and she realized she needed to get it together pronto.

She stepped back—or tried to.

He held her upper arms firmly. "May, answer me."

She shook her head. "Know what?"

"About the diamonds."

She inhaled, bracing herself. "Yes. I opened what I thought was my suitcase the night I arrived at Dyadya's house. I saw the diamonds then."

"And you didn't tell me."

"I...no." She could explain about Dyadya and the mafiya and the suitcase he'd left her with the warning *BOMB* on it, but in the end, it wouldn't matter anyway.

She hadn't told him.

He stared down at her, his face hard and closed and she realized she didn't like that look aimed at her. In fact, she hated it.

But there wasn't much she could do. She was who she was and he was who he was. He'd known. He'd *known* before they'd got into bed last night that she wasn't to be trusted.

Still. Something withered inside her.

"Okay." He let her go and she wobbled a moment, off balance without his support, her arms suddenly cold. He looked at her speculatively a moment and then nodded as if coming to a decision. "I have a job I want you to do. Will you?"

"What?" Did he really trust her enough to help? "I..."

"May," he said, "I don't have a lot of time. Will you do it?"

He wanted her to commit without any idea what she was committing to? He had to be crazy. There was no way she'd do that, and besides, she'd just proven herself untrustworthy.

"Yes." She blinked, surprised, but then she opened her mouth and said it again. "Yes."

"Good." He kissed her, hard and fast. "I've got some spare long underwear." He turned to rummage in his dresser drawer. "You can cut the legs to fit. It won't be perfect, but it's better than nothing. You know how to ski, right?"

"Um...I haven't been on the slopes in years." She watched as he took out a pair of wool socks.

He shot a glance at her. "Cross-country."

"Oh." She felt her ears heat at her stupidity. "Yes, of course."

"Good," Sam said absently. "I'm pretty sure I've got some women's ski boots in the downstairs closet."

Maisa picked up the wool socks and the pair of men's long underwear and stripped to put them on, wondering rather viciously whose ski boots were in Sam's closet.

He put on long underwear, two pairs of socks, and a sweater over his denim shirt.

"You ready?" He turned around and looked at her and this was it. They were going out to face murderous mafiya thugs and she didn't know what to say. How to act.

He wasn't her boyfriend, maybe wasn't even a lover—
at least in the long-term—but he was *something* to her.
Something important, no matter how much she struggled
against it.

She stared at him. "You don't snore."

A corner of his mouth quirked. "You know that now?"
His voice was unbearably gentle.

"Yes."

He crossed to her and took her face in his hands,
smoothing her short bangs back from her face. "May."

That was all he said, but somehow it was enough.

He leaned down and kissed her again, but this time it
was soft, almost chaste, his lips tender against hers.

It made her want to cry.

"You all coming?" Stu's shout came from below.

"Yup." Sam took Maisa's hand and led her down the
stairs.

On the main floor everyone was gathered by the front
door. Molly and Karl were already in parkas, Molly with
a rifle held under her arm. Stu was bouncing nervously on
his big feet. Doug must already be outside.

Sam went to his closet and began taking out skis and
boots. "Here." Sam slapped a huge fur-trimmed hat with
flaps on her head. "Warmer than your beret."

She peered up out of the huge, silly hat. "Thanks."

"No problem." He turned with a small revolver in his
hands. "Almost forgot."

Maisa's instinctive reaction was to back away when he
held it out to her. She'd never touched a gun before in her
life. But she made herself stand still.

Sam turned the little handgun over. It had a black grip
and a shiny metal barrel. "It's a .22. Not too heavy for

you, I hope. Keep it in your pocket and if you need to, point and shoot."

"And do not stop," Dyadya rumbled.

Maisa glanced at her uncle and then back to Sam.

Sam looked irritated, but he nodded. "He's right. Once you start shooting at a man, empty the chamber. Shoot to kill."

"Okay." She took the handgun and shoved it in the pocket of her coat, zipping it closed. The coat sagged on that side.

"Lock the doors and stay away from the windows once we leave," Sam told Dyadya.

"You're just going to abandon us here?" Gerard Walkingtall hadn't said much since he'd entered the cabin, but now he looked perturbed.

Sam looked him hard in the eye. "Too many people will just get in the way."

Gerard jerked his chin at Maisa. "But you're taking her."

"Yeah, I am," Sam said, slow and deliberate. "She's one of us. I trust her. You got a problem with that?"

"I . . . no." Gerard scowled and turned away.

Sam nodded. "Anyone else?"

"We'll be fine, Sam." Becky spoke for everyone staying behind.

Sam looked at her. "How's Doc?"

"He's okay for now." Becky drew a deep breath. "You just be safe—all of you."

Stu blushed and stumbled out the door.

"Thanks, Becky." Sam nodded at Karl and took Maisa's arm. "Let's do it."

And then they were out in the cold.

Chapter Thirty

The cold hit Sam like a smack across the face. He braced himself in the basket of Stu's sled as the dogs galloped down the highway. There wasn't a vehicle in sight. Nothing moved in the still winter landscape except the dogs.

Afghanistan was nothing like this. It'd been hot and dry—dry as a bone, a desert of sand-colored rock, mountains, and tufts of grass. He'd never figured out how the goats the locals herded had found enough to eat. It hadn't been a place humans should've chosen to live, and despite the difference between that barren land and the cold of Minnesota, he couldn't stop thinking of Afghanistan.

It was where he'd last gambled on the lives of others—gambled and lost.

He wasn't going to lose any more men if he could help it.

The dogs loped past the Coot Lake Inn as County Road 23 turned into Main, slowing as they got close to the center of town. They passed the old library—boarded up now, the books moved to a smaller, newer building—and Sam leaned out of the sled and tossed his skis and poles to the side of the building. They sank partially into the snow and then they were past. Stu let down the break and Sam gathered himself to jump off.

He glanced back at Stu. "Good luck. Stay safe."

Stu nodded. "You, too, man."

And then Sam was leaping and running as Stu gained speed again to dash by the police station.

Sam flattened himself against the doorway of Tracy's Antiques and drew his Beretta. He was across the street and a little ways down from the police station, and as he glanced that way he saw spots of blood in the snow where he'd shot the two Russian mafiya thugs.

The bloodied snow was right in front of the police station, in plain view of the windows. This wasn't going to be easy. 'Course, there were windows in back of the station as well. No matter which way he went in it would be hard.

A whoop came from up the road, and then Doug barreled into sight, alone on his sled. He'd already dropped May off. Sam was grateful that she, at least, was out of the line of fire.

He crouched, readying himself.

Just as Karl came around the bank from the opposite direction.

A barrel pointed out the window of the police station and the snow burst in a staggered line just behind Doug's lead dog. Belatedly, gunfire echoed off the Main Street buildings. Doug's team was good, though. The dogs didn't swerve or hesitate, just kept going as Doug made the end of the street and turned to come back.

There was a loud *crack!* and the window where the gun barrel had been exploded.

Sam grinned grimly. Molly Jasper was the best shot in

the county, and while she sat on the rooftop, there was no one to touch her.

A shout came from the back of the police station and the sound of gunfire, so Stu must be doing his part creating a diversion in the parking lot.

Sam ran toward the police station as Molly shot out another window. They were taking a risk, not only in him and the mushers being out in the open, but that Dylan wouldn't get hit in the crossfire. He was hoping the policeman was smart enough to hit the floor the moment he heard shots.

Sam reached the municipal building's front and flattened himself against the façade, making himself as small a target as possible as he scrambled for the front door. Beridze's men had obviously broken it open when they stormed the building yesterday. Sam had expected them to barricade it, but apparently the mafiya were too confident for such measures.

He smiled grimly. Their mistake.

He pushed open the door and went in, Beretta up and ready, but no one was in the lower office. Sweat was gathering at the base of his spine despite the cold. Too bad Coot Lake didn't have the funds for body armor—it would've been nice right about now. Outside he could hear Karl whooping as Molly blew out another window.

Now or never.

He turned quickly into the enclosed staircase, meeting a thug coming down. The man's eyes widened as he shouted something in Russian.

Sam shot him once in the chest and again in the head as he passed him on the stairs. He ducked as he burst into the upper police station, keeping himself low. And a good thing, too—the first volley of gunfire went over his head. Sam rolled to the side, behind Tick's desk, and shot a charging mafiya. Only two men remained—where the hell was everyone else? One raised his weapon. *Shit.*

The air filled with the thunderous rattle of automatic gunfire as the desk burst into splinters.

Sam lay low, breathing, waiting for his moment, as shards of wood pelted his arms and the back of his head. Auto was scary as hell, but it ate bullets.

A pause.

Sam popped out and took out one of the shooters.

The other was frantically fiddling with his gun. He looked up, wide-eyed, and threw the weapon at Sam, turning to dive for the dead man's gun.

Sam shot him as well.

In the sudden silence, Dylan swore.

Sam got up and checked the men he'd shot—all dead or close to it. Then he took the cell keys down from the wall.

Dylan had taken cover under the cell bunk, but now he got up. "That last guy—his gun jammed."

"Yeah," Sam said. "How you doing?"

"I'm...I'm good," Dylan replied. His face was white, but he picked up one of the fallen semiautomatics. "Did Haley Anne get to you?"

"Yup, she's fine."

"Oh, thank God."

"Okay," Sam said as he reloaded the Beretta. "We'll go out the front and we're moving as fast as we're able. Got it?"

"Gotcha," Dylan said.

"Going down first," Sam said, turning to the side and descending the steps. "Clear!"

The lower reception room was dark and cold. Had he

underestimated Beridze's men—or were they waiting somewhere?

Dylan made the bottom of the stairs just as the door to the back started to open.

"Out the front!" Sam shouted as he shot through the back door.

A bang and the reception counter exploded.

Sam returned fire and glanced over his shoulder. Dylan right behind him. Damn it! Were they walking into a trap?

He backed toward the front exit, still firing, just as Dylan opened the door.

Nothing.

"Out!"

They tumbled through into the white snow-covered street.

Then Stu was there beside them, the dogs all yapping. "Get in!"

Dylan threw himself into the basket and looked up at him. The younger man's brows knit. This close Sam could see that he had a nasty bruise on his forehead and a dried spot of blood on his upper lip. "What about you?"

"I've got a way out." Sweat poured off Sam's forehead. "Go!"

He didn't wait to see Stu drive off before breaking into a run in the opposite direction, moving awkwardly through thick snow in his stiff ski boots. A gunshot. The snow kicked up next to his boots and he felt something sting his thigh and then he was at the old library. He flung himself around the corner, panting, and found where he'd thrown the skis earlier. Sam stooped to set the skis flat. He toed them on, pocketed his Beretta, picked up the poles, and started skiing.

The snow was unbroken, crusted by wind in places and too fluffy in others, but he'd been skiing since he was a kid. His body fell into the long, loping rhythm, not pushing too hard because he didn't want to sweat anymore than he already had. Sweat could be dangerous in cold like this.

And then behind him he heard the one thing he hadn't planned for: a truck engine.

Chapter Thirty-One

⟨⟨⟨⟩⟩⟩

A truck engine revved somewhere, and all Maisa could think inside the Laughing Loon Café was that Beridze must really be insane. Everyone knew you couldn't drive on snow like this. It was simple common sense.

But there was something about a man disregarding the laws of nature—of common sense—that sent a shiver of dread down her spine. That SUV—if that was what it was—shouldn't be able to move in knee-deep snow, and yet it seemed to be getting nearer.

Dear God, Sam couldn't outrun a truck, no matter how slow the snow made it.

For a moment, she wavered. She'd watched him get Dylan into the sled, seen Sam run off afterward, and breathed a sigh of relief. He was no longer in the line of fire. But if the mafiya could get that truck moving, that wasn't necessarily true, was it? He might be killed as she stood here, dithering.

No.

She actually reached out to catch one of the booths. No. She couldn't think about that right now. Sam was trusting her—above Karl and Stu and Doug and even

Molly, trusting her to get the diamonds. And she wasn't going to let him down, damn it. All she had to do was pocket them and leave.

He was the one trying to out-ski a truck.

She inhaled and blew out a breath forcefully and then continued methodically looking under the booths. A minute more and she found the suitcase, shoved way to the back under a booth. She hauled it out and unzipped it. There, twinkling among the awful men's briefs was the ziplock bag with the pink gems.

Maisa pocketed the bag and stood, listening.

A shadow crossed in front of the big front window. A man, silhouetted against the outside sunlight, a gun in his hands.

Maisa froze. She was in the middle back of the Laughing Loon and, yes, the lights were off, but all the gunman had to do was turn his head and maybe squint.

She was standing right out in the open.

Carefully, moving slowly, inch by inch, she eased her right hand into her parka pocket, closing her fingers over the cold grip of the little revolver Sam had given her. She could do this. If he turned, if he lifted the gun, she'd have to be quick and act without hesitating. She had a revolver.

He had an automatic weapon.

And then he simply walked past.

She swallowed, nearly choking on the dryness of her throat. Oh, God, that had been close. Too close.

Maisa turned and walked quickly to the back of the café. Her ski boots tapped against the black-and-white linoleum floor—they weren't made for stealth—and she winced at the sound. If anyone entered the kitchens in back, they'd know at once that she was in here.

She almost couldn't open the door to the kitchen. She'd seen too many horror movies in which the monster lurked behind the closed door. But that was silly. She was a grown woman and she had to get out of here.

So she shoved through quickly, scanning the room, her hand still on the revolver in her pocket.

Empty.

A burst of gunfire out front nearly made her shriek.

She gulped again and scurried across the kitchen. Outside it was so cold the warm air in her nostrils caught. Her skis were just outside the back door. Dark clouds had begun to gather in the sky, and she glanced at them anxiously as she put her skis flat on the ground. The very last thing they needed was more snow.

She was about to step into the skis when she heard it: the crunch of boots in snow. Had Sam come back for her? Or maybe Molly was on the ground?

Or of course it might be someone entirely different.

Maisa felt herself panting as she picked up her skis and looked around. There was a Dumpster beside the back door, but anywhere she went she'd be trailed by telltale footprints in the fresh snow.

The crunch of snow was coming closer.

Maisa thrust the skis behind the Dumpster and slipped back into the Laughing Loon.

Chapter Thirty-Two

Karl peddled with one foot off the runner as he walked the dogs around the back of Tracy's Antiques—not an easy maneuver because what with the shouting, the gunfire, and the revving of that truck, they really wanted to race. Phase One of The Plan had already been implemented: Sam had rescued Dylan, and Maisa had presumably grabbed the diamonds—Maisa's getaway skis by the back of the Laughing Loon were missing, so she was gone, anyway. Now it was time for Phase Two: Super-Cool Sledding Action Plus Bonus Badass Molly Shooting.

For some reason Sam had shot down Karl's suggestions for plan titles.

"Whoa. Whoa!" he hissed at Cookie, who was straining against her harness and pretending she'd gone suddenly deaf. He had the drag pad down—a sort of auxiliary brake—but it was hardly slowing Cookie in her present mood.

"Molly?" If he missed her, it'd spoil Phase Two: SCSAPBBM, *and* she'd be stuck on the roof of Tracy's Antique's, and then who knew what would happen to her? "*Molly.*"

"Why are you whispering?" she asked in a normal voice from behind him, nearly giving him a heart attack.

Karl stomped on the drag pad, bringing the sled to a halt. "Because of *bad guys*?"

She rolled her eyes and climbed in the basket, holding her rifle across her knees. "Like they wouldn't hear the team coming from a mile away."

Karl kicked off and let Cookie have her head as they skimmed. "Well, okay, sure, but that doesn't mean we need to be—"

He broke off with a shriek that wasn't at all unmanly as they rounded the corner to cross Main and came face-to-dog-muzzle with an armed mafiya.

The thug looked nearly as startled as Karl felt.

"Haw!" Karl yelled, trying to get the dogs to turn to the left so they could get the hell out of there. "God damn it, *haw*!"

But Cookie took one look at the hulking thug, laid her ears flat, and lunged.

There was a rattle of automatic gunfire, growling, a scream from the thug—*really* girlish—and a thump as the dogs kind of ran over him. The sled ricocheted off the sprawled man and then they were past.

Karl whooped and pumped his fist in the air as they shot across the street. Molly hadn't made a sound but she was gripping the sides of the basket hard. Cookie was ready to race off into the country and maybe not stop until she got to Canada, but Karl somehow got her under control—well, *partly* under control—and they turned by Mack's Speedy, bumped along the snow next to the gas station, and then turned again onto Fourth, which ran behind the buildings on the south side of Main.

The wind blew in Karl's face, the dogs panted and galloped, and somewhere up ahead shots were still being fired. Electricity zinged in Karl's veins. This was by far the coolest thing he'd ever done, even including that time he'd made bat wings out of tinfoil and coat hangers and tried to fly off the top of the Red Earth Elementary School, a one-story structure that, as it'd turned out, was just as well. One of the lilacs planted along the foundation of the school still looked kind of stunted after all these years, and Molly always glanced at him a bit suspiciously when she saw it.

Karl smiled with affection at the back of Molly's head. "Think Doug got to the fuel tank in the municipal parking lot?"

Molly shrugged, not bothering to turn around. "I saw him go back there. Guess we'll find out soon enough."

The back of the municipal building came into view—along with the shed at the end of the parking lot that housed the back-up generator. The door to the shed was open. Thank God—Doug must've done his job. Time to implement the second half of Phase Two: Badass Molly Shooting.

"Whoa!" Karl called, stomping on the drag pad. "WHOA, God damn it, Cookie!"

For once the dog listened, which was kind of odd, but Karl was just happy he wouldn't have to do another lap around the town to come back.

Molly heaved herself up and stepped out of the sled.

"What are you doing?" Karl asked nervously. The last thing he wanted was the sled taking off without Molly.

"I can't hold the rifle steady in the sled," she said quietly.

He watched as she braced herself, standing tall—well,

tall for five foot two—and bent over the rifle sights, aiming at the fuel tank in the municipal parking lot shed. In theory Doug had already been by and taken off the tank cap. With any luck there'd be a build up of fumes in the little building.

Well. If all had gone according to plan.

Molly inhaled quietly, steely calm even though there was still a truck revving somewhere and gunshots now and again. His chest swelled with pride. Molly was the best damn shot in the county.

Crack.

He flinched without meaning to, both hands flying up to shield his face.

Nothing happened.

Molly took a breath and slowly exhaled.

Crack.

Nothing.

The truck engine was coming closer, and for a split second Karl felt admiration for *anyone* who could drive in this snow. Then a jittery feeling began jumping through his veins.

He glanced behind them. A truck grill rounded the corner down by Mack's Speedy. *Fuck.*

"Molly—"

Crack.

He turned back to her, well into full-fledged, lets-get-the-fuck-outa-here panic. "*Molly!*"

BLAM!

The shed went up in a humongous volcano of orange and black fire, like something straight out of any movie Arnold Schwarzenegger had ever made in his life, and it was so incredibly awesome that Karl would've cried.

If it weren't for the fact that they were about to die.

"Getingetingetin!" he babbled at Molly, not losing his cool at all, and Molly tumbled into the sled and he let the brake go, jumped off the drag pad and screamed, "HIKE!"

Cookie took off like a bullet out of a gun, nearly giving him whiplash, and the sled bumped and swung wildly onto the street.

Karl clung to the bar and risked a glance behind him.

The SUV was roaring up their ass. As he watched, a gunman hung out the window and took aim at them.

Karl turned back around, yelling at the dogs. He wasn't even forming words anymore, it was more like inarticulate screaming.

The automatic rattled behind them and for a horrible moment Karl was sure he'd been hit. But then he realized there was no blood and he was probably just having a terror-induced heart attack.

They made the end of the street and he got the dogs to head back toward Main, which was a mini-miracle in and of itself.

The SUV growled behind them.

"Shit!" Why the hell hadn't the truck gotten stuck by now? It shouldn't be able to even move in the snow. Thank God the snow was at least slowing it—the dogs were fast, but not fast enough to outrun a truck at speed.

"Head to the rez!" Molly hollered, proving that she was as smart as she was pretty.

"Yeah," Karl panted. They'd lose these assholes there, or preferably on the *way* there.

They hit the highway going like a zillion miles an hour, just flying over the snow, and for a moment Karl thought they'd lost the SUV. But then the thing roared behind them, much bigger and scarier than any *Christine*.

"Fuckfuck*fuck*," Karl chanted into the wind and then a miracle happened.

Behind them, there was a muffled *whump!* and then the awesome, wonderful, erection-inducing sound of an engine whining as the SUV's tires spun uselessly.

"Whoa!" Karl yelled, and Cookie slowed at once.

He turned to look.

There sat the SUV, spun around and half buried in a snow bank, its tires whirring as they made ice in the snow.

"Ha!" Karl yelled, making a superrude gesture he'd learned in the army. "Ha, motherfuckers, *ha*!"

"Uh, Karl," Molly said.

"Oh, sorry," Karl said at once, because it was just wrong for him to be swearing and rude-gesturing in front of Molly, even though she still hadn't even smiled at him yet today and wouldn't even let him explain about the arrowheads.

"Hey, Molly," Karl said, "about those arrowheads—"

"*Karl!*"

And Karl's chin jerked in the direction of Molly's horrified stare in time to see the SUV reverse out of the snow bank and *continue* reversing toward them, gaining speed as it loomed. Which, really, he should've seen coming.

The monster never died in the movies.

"Hike, Cookie! Hike for your life!"

Cookie leaped forward. The sled lurched and swung before catching and then they were racing down the highway, the SUV gaining behind.

Shit! They were going to die, and Molly would think for eternity that Karl was a thief.

"I didn't steal them!" he shouted into the wind.

"Take the exit," Molly screamed back.

"What?"

"Take the fucking exit, Karl!"

So he did, shouting orders at the dogs, racing down the exit ramp to the road that ran by Lake Moosewood.

Molly was clinging with both hands to the rails, but she twisted to look at him. "The ice."

And he had one of those moments that seemed straight out of the romance books he used to sneak out of his mother's room when he'd been twelve and any mention of a nipple would give him an erection: perfect and complete understanding such as could only be achieved by twin souls bound as one.

Which was just bitchin'.

"Cookie, gee!" And his lead dog, bless her crazy heart, turned to the right, bumped off the street, over a field of snow, and onto Lake Moosehead.

The wind had blown away a lot of the snow here, making the sledding fast and slick, but it was easier on the SUV, too. Karl could hear the truck racing closer, still in reverse. His back felt like one fat target.

"Can you shoot at 'em?" he yelled at Molly.

She snorted. "I can shoot at them, but I won't hit anything. Not while we're moving anyway."

"Shit." Karl searched the far shore. There was the big ugly oak that twisted to the side, there was that tacky three-story A-frame which, okay, he was kind of jealous of, but *not the time* ... and *there* was the little dip in the shoreline, totally unnoticeable unless you knew the area like your own hairy balls.

Which he did.

Karl made for that dip in the shore—the spot where Gopher Creek emptied into the lake.

Behind them something popped and the snow beside the dogs exploded.

"Crap! Those assholes are shooting at my dogs!"

Molly was usually pretty quick to speak her mind, but she didn't reply, and that fact made him even madder than the shooting-at-the-dogs thing. She was scared—he could tell by the hunch of her shoulders—and that just wasn't right.

Nobody should shut his Molly down.

They were almost to the shore now, almost to that dip, and the SUV seemed to know it. The big truck roared in their wake, suddenly gaining speed, about to crawl up Karl's ass.

Nearly there. Nearly there. Sweet baby Jesus would they ever get there?

And then they were *there*.

The dogs and sled turned, riding along the shoreline, fifty feet out. The ice looked just the same here as anywhere else on the lake, but it really wasn't. The water from Gopher Creek ran beneath, making the ice here thinner.

Dangerously thinner, especially if you were driving a three-ton SUV instead of, say, a sled and a half-dozen dogs.

The truck was right behind them, and for a bowel-loosening moment Karl thought he'd fucked it up. That they'd run down Molly and the dogs and it'd all be his fault.

Then he heard the sweetest sound in the world: a tremendous *CRACK!*

"Whoa!" He looked over his shoulder as the dogs

slowed. The SUV looked like it was bowing to him, the front end tilted down at a forty-five-degree angle.

Someone shouted.

And then the ice just gave way.

The big truck disappeared in a geyser of dark water and ice chunks, splashing out over the top of the frozen lake.

"Oh, my God," Molly whispered.

"That was..." Karl looked at her, wide-eyed "...the coolest thing *ever*."

Her eyes crinkled so beautifully, and her soft, soft pink mouth spread in a smile, and for a moment everything was perfect in Karl's world.

Then Cookie whimpered.

Cookie *never* whimpered.

He glanced up. She turned, trying to lick at her butt, and suddenly sat down as if she'd lost her balance. The snow was pink under her feet.

"Karl," Molly said in a soft, sad voice. "Karl, she's been shot."

Chapter Thirty-Three

"He's been shot."

Stu's words were matter of fact, but Sam could see the worry in his eyes for his cousin. They were gathered by the meeting place that Sam had decided on: an old, abandoned barn just outside town. It was far enough away to've lost any followers, close enough that it wasn't too hard to ski to.

Or at least Sam had thought that this morning.

Doug was sitting on his sled, white-faced, his mouth set in a grimace. His left arm was red from the shoulder down, wet with blood. It wasn't a bad injury—the bullet had gone through and the bone wasn't broken—but in the cold and with the blood loss, Doug might go into shock.

Sam turned to glance again over the snowy fields. The wind had picked up, blowing icy little snow crystals into his face.

May was nowhere in sight.

"She'll make it," Stu said.

"Should've waited for her," Sam muttered. "Made sure she was out of town."

"That wasn't the plan." Stu turned to look at his cousin. "Runner's broke on Doug's sled and besides, shape he's in he can't mush. I can let the dogs loose and put him in my basket with Dylan. It'll be tight, but we should be able to make it."

Sam nodded. "You'd best go ahead and take Doug and Dylan to my cabin."

Stu frowned, glancing back at him. "You and Maisa were supposed to ride the rest of the way back."

"You and Dylan need to get Doug out of this cold as soon as you can." Sam shook his head. "You don't have time to wait."

"Okay." Stu sounded relieved. He'd been sneaking anxious glances at his cousin. "You sure you both can ski all the way back to your cabin? Looks like we're going to get more snow."

Sam shrugged. "We'll stop if we have to."

He was more worried that May still hadn't made the meeting place.

Sam and Dylan unhitched Doug's team and helped him into the basket of Stu's sled. By the time they were done, Doug was moaning quietly under his breath.

"Get going," he said to Stu.

Stu nodded and yelled, "Hike!" to his dogs.

The dogs took off running.

Sam toed his skis back on and began heading back into town. Dark gray clouds were crowding the horizon, threatening more snow.

He needed to find May before the storm hit.

Ten minutes later, he slowed as he saw the old library up ahead.

A crackle of gunfire came from somewhere close,

making adrenaline leap into his veins. Everyone should be out of town by now. There was no reason for shooting.

He bent and unlatched his skis, stowing them by the library, then began moving into town.

Black smoke still trailed from behind the police station. Sam had heard the explosion as he'd skied out of town and a corner of his mouth twitched grimly now. Beridze and his men would be getting very cold very soon with the backup generator out of commission.

Up ahead by Mack's Speedy, another *pop* sounded. Not an automatic weapon. Was it May? His blood ran cold at the thought of May having to defend herself.

Sam drew his gun and started lunging through the snow, trying to get closer as fast as he could.

Someone came around the corner of the gas station.

Sam brought up his gun, but it was May and he hastily lowered it.

She looked at him, wide-eyed, and silently pointed behind her.

He nodded and waved her farther away.

She hunkered down by the far end of Mack's Speedy. There wasn't much cover there—only a concrete trash can—but it was better than nothing.

Sam began making his way along the side of the service station. He could hear panting close by. A muttered word, maybe in Russian.

Sam brought his gun up, ready, and paused at the back corner of the station. The wind was whistling, blowing the snow up into his face.

He couldn't hear anything.

If the mafiya thug went the other way around the gas station he'd run into May.

Sam took a breath and rounded the corner.

The guy was right in front of him, but thankfully facing the other way.

He started turning as Sam pulled the trigger.

The first shot went wide, into the space the mafiya's shoulder had been a second before, but the second shot nailed him squarely in the chest.

And then the thug's rush hit Sam, making his gun swing up. Shots three and four went into the air as Sam was flung backward into the snow. The man's breath was sour—from fear, from adrenaline, from exertion. It was a familiar smell, a smell that spun Sam back to Afghanistan and other sour-breathed men who didn't speak English.

Death's exhalation was international.

The mafiya thug shoved his forearm into Sam's throat and Sam choked. Sam fought to bring his gun back around. The guy knocked back his hands once, twice, scrabbling for the gun, trying to make Sam drop it. But he was fighting with only one hand. If he raised the arm holding Sam down, Sam would wriggle free.

He couldn't breathe. He was being slowly choked. It was animal instinct to fight the arm strangling him, but Sam brought his gun around one more time, hard and fast, pulling the trigger as he swung.

The shot deafened him.

The mafiya's face disappeared in a haze of blood.

Sam pushed the dead meat off him and stood. His ears were ringing, and he tasted blood in his mouth.

The other man's blood.

Wiping his face with the back of his sleeve, he glanced around. No one else was coming at him from the back of Mack's Speedy.

He turned.

May stood there in a shooter's stance, her face milk-white. Her lips moved and he could see that she said, *Sam*, but either the wind took the word away or his ears still weren't working.

He strode toward her and took her arm, gently lowering the gun she held. "Let's get out of here."

Chapter Thirty-Four

Sam's face was speckled with blood.

The dead man's blood.

It was all that May could think about, running in circles in her mind: he was blood splattered. And he'd gotten that way saving her.

She'd known he'd been a soldier, known he was a policeman, but watching him grappling with the thug had made her see him as if for the first time. She'd heard the gunshots, knew Sam was in danger, and had gone to help without thinking.

Except he hadn't needed her help.

Even held down by a thug who'd looked twice as bulky as Sam, he'd moved with quick, deadly precision. He hadn't panicked. He'd simply shot the other man.

In the face.

"Where are your skis?" he asked, glancing up and down the street. The snow had started, whipped nearly horizontal by the wind.

May shuddered. She'd never seen such snowfall, storm after storm, one right after another. It was almost unnatural, as if the weather were a malevolent force intent on obliterating them.

"Back by the café," she shouted into the wind. "He came after me before I had the chance to put them on."

"Did you get the diamonds?"

She patted her pocket. "Yes."

"Good." He glanced back at the café. "We could get your skis, but they might be waiting there. I don't want to take the chance."

She gasped as the wind blew straight into her face. "So what do we do? We can't walk back to your cabin in this."

"I know another place."

He had to let go of her hand so that they both could make their way through the snow. It was knee-deep on him, nearly hip-deep for her in places, and it was slow, awkward, sweaty work.

She kept her eyes on him as they made their way. His face was set and stern. He didn't look as if killing the other man had affected him at all.

Maybe this wasn't the first time he'd killed.

She shivered at the thought. Only days ago she'd thought him a simple good guy, but he wasn't. He wasn't bad, he wasn't good, he was Sam—a man who'd had to make decisions, take actions that couldn't be categorized as black or white. She'd thought him naïve. She scoffed to herself.

Turned out she was the naïve one.

She should've known that no one was entirely good or bad. That people were complex human beings, capable of doing all sorts of things in order to survive. Even small-town cops.

Maybe that was part of what Sam had been trying to

tell her all along. She shivered again, because if Sam wasn't all white, then maybe Dyadya—and she—weren't all black.

She wasn't sure what to think about that.

They were at the edge of town now. The prairie stretched ahead, disappearing into the white-gray of the clouds and the snow-covered ground, and it was nearly impossible to tell where they met.

Maisa bowed her head, trying to shelter her face in the hood of her parka. She should've worn a scarf. Her cheeks and lips and nose were numb, ice freezing on her lashes. She blinked hard for a moment, and when she looked again a small, single-story cabin was right in front of them.

Sam waded to the door and bent and began brushing away snow from the step with his hands.

"What are you looking for?" she yelled into the wind.

In answer he stooped and pried at a stone frog the size of a cat. When it didn't move, he grunted and stood to kick it loose. The frog fell over and he picked it up. There was a hidden compartment underneath and he pulled off one glove with his teeth to open it with his fingers.

He took the key and unlocked the door.

The wind pushed them inside and Sam slammed the door.

For a moment Maisa panted in the dark room. The wind rattled the door.

"Stay here." Sam opened the door again and disappeared.

Maisa blinked, staring at the closed door. Where the hell was he going? Had he just left her here?

She pivoted, her boots scraping against worn linoleum. She stood in a tiny entryway, demarcated by a half moon

of linoleum. To the left was a living area with thin car-
peting. To the right was an open galley kitchen with an
ancient refrigerator, a narrow avocado-green stove, and a
chipped sink. The cabinets were dark wood.

A doormat to the side of the door held two pairs of
boots, neatly lined up. It was customary in winter in
Minnesota homes to take off snowy boots or shoes, but
now that she was out of the wind, she realized just how
cold the cabin was. Maisa settled for wiping off her boots
thoroughly.

She'd just stepped onto the living room carpet when
the door banged open behind her.

She jumped, startled, as Sam stamped in, his arms
laden with firewood, and nudged the door closed behind
him.

He glanced up and saw her staring. "See if you can
find some matches and newspaper. Magazines, if nothing
else."

Of course. She went to the kitchen and began opening
the cabinets. Behind her, she could hear Sam tossing the
logs down by the fireplace.

She finally found a box of matches in a cupboard over
the stove.

She took it back to where Sam knelt piling the logs
carefully in the fireplace. "I haven't found any newspapers yet."

"That's fine. There're some here." He gestured to a pile
of yellowing newspapers in a milk crate by the hearth.

She felt odd, standing over him when he was kneeling,
so she sat on the cold floor, her knees drawn up to her
chin. She watched as he crumpled newspaper and shoved
it under the logs.

"Will they light, when they're that wet?" she asked.

"There's just a little snow from me bringing them in. Hopkins keeps his firewood under a tarp." He was working as he talked, keeping his eyes on the fireplace.

She shivered. "You know the owner?"

He nodded. "Tony Hopkins, retired trucker. He takes a two-week trip to Las Vegas every January. Asks me to look after the place while he's gone."

Sam dusted off his hands and reached for the matches. He took one out, struck it on the box, and held the flame to the newspaper.

Maisa watched, nearly hypnotized, as the flames began to curl around the paper.

Sam fanned the tiny fire and it suddenly burst into a blaze.

She held out her hands to the fire. "Won't someone see the smoke from the chimney?"

He shrugged. "In this weather? I doubt it." He stood, gathering the wood he hadn't used in the fire and stacking the logs neatly to the side. "Even if they do, they won't be coming after us in this storm."

He still wasn't looking at her.

Maisa knit her brows thoughtfully and then rose herself, walking into the little kitchen. She went to the sink and turned the faucet handle but nothing happened.

"Water's off," Sam said from behind her.

Of course it was. Maisa rolled her eyes at herself and took down a pot from the cabinet before moving to the door.

"What are you—?"

The rest of Sam's question was cut off by the rush of the wind as Maisa opened the door. She leaned down and scooped snow into the pot, packing it down before shutting the door again.

When she turned back around, he was right behind her, frowning at the pot.

"Water." She gestured with the pot and went to place it on the hearth next to the fire.

"Why do you need—?"

She was already exploring a little corridor just past the living room. As she'd suspected, there were two bedrooms along with a bathroom. Piled neatly on a shelf next to the tub was a stack of towels. She selected two and went back to the living room.

Sam was rummaging in the cupboards. "Are you hungry? Hopkins has some canned stew and a couple jars of grape juice. Some V8 as well."

She winced at the thought of V8—or grape juice, for that matter, though since the water was off she might end up drinking that later. "I'm pretty full from Becky's breakfast."

"Yeah." He came back with a glass. "Do you want to pour your water in here?"

She shook her head. "It's not for drinking. Come sit here." She patted the raised brick hearth.

Sam looked directly at her for the first time since he'd shot the gunman. She expected some resistance, but he merely nodded and sat.

She tested the melted snow with a fingertip and found it tepid. Maisa took a washcloth, wet it, and leaned toward him.

Sam flinched and something within her crumbled. She didn't want to see Sam flinch away from anything—most particularly her. But she also knew that his reaction at the moment had very little to do with her. She took a deep breath. Time to put aside her own anxieties and concentrate on Sam.

She touched his cheek with the washcloth, gently wiping away the dried blood.

He held very still, staring at her face as she worked.

She cleared her throat. "Did the others make it?"

"Stu's fine. We got Dylan. Doug was shot—"

"Oh, my God!" She froze, looking at him in shock.

He shook his head. "Only in the arm. He should be okay."

She blew out her breath and rinsed out the washcloth before returning to her task. There were speckles of blood near his hairline and next to the outer corner of his left eye. "What about Karl and Molly?"

"I don't know." His voice rasped and he cleared his throat. "Karl was supposed to take Molly back to my cabin instead of meeting up. They should've both gotten away clear. At least I didn't see them."

He raised his eyebrows at her.

She shook her head. "Neither did I."

Leaning closer, she peered at the dots across the bridge of his nose. His eyes were neon blue, beautiful and watchful. Almost painful to meet.

She cleared her throat. "Why did you bring me?"

"To get the diamonds."

"I know that." She wrinkled her nose at him as she gently wiped his forehead. "I meant, why *me*? Why not Becky or Haley Anne or even Walkingtall?"

"Because I wanted you here," he said. "Because this is your town, too, now."

For a moment she stared at him, her hands arrested. Her town? Did he really think that?

Did she?

She sat back, focusing on her hands as she rinsed the washcloth again. The water had turned pink. "What will you do when the storm clears?"

"Go after Beridze."

"Alone?" She glanced up, worried. "Maybe if we just give him the stupid diamonds—"

A muscle flexed in his jaw. "No. Beridze isn't getting what he wants and he's not leaving my town."

"You'll kill him?"

"Not unless I have to," he said calmly. "I'm going to arrest him. Make sure he spends the rest of his life in prison."

She nodded. "Okay."

"Just like that?" he asked. "No arguments?"

"Nope." She shook her head. "I trust you to do what's best, Sam."

"Thanks. All done?"

"Just..." She dabbed at a smear on his chin, then nodded. "Yes."

"Good." He took the washcloth out of her hand and dropped it into the pot. Then he leaned forward and cradled her face between his palms and kissed her.

Chapter Thirty-Five

The blood on his face should've disgusted May—it had Sam, that was for sure. But instead of turning away from him, she'd heated water and washed him with a tender gentleness that had made his heart hurt.

May, his May, was sharp and pointy on the outside and so soft on the inside.

"I want you," he whispered against her lips. He didn't know how to tell her what she meant to him—what he wanted her to mean to him. What they could be together. So he only repeated what words he had: "I want you."

She didn't reply, but she opened her mouth beneath his and that was answer enough for the moment. He took what she offered: the slick, soft inside of her mouth, her sharp teeth, and the tongue that slid against his.

He shoved his fingers into her hair, pulling her closer, and felt the short strands alternately soft and bristling, against his palms. Like her.

Like her.

His cock was pulsing against his zipper and he wanted her. He laid her down on Hopkins's old carpet, shrugging out of his parka so she had something beneath her head.

She stared up at him, her eyes dark and mysterious, as he pulled off her boots and coat. She lifted her hips so he could tug down her jeans and the long underwear he'd lent her this morning. He smiled when he saw she was wearing sexy little red panties.

She sniffed, but then her eyes softened.

"Here," she whispered, hushed, like a little girl telling a secret.

She unbuttoned the chambray shirt she wore, eyes lowered, a smile flirting with her mouth.

He couldn't resist that mouth. He bent and kissed the corner, as she murmured in protest, "Wait a minute."

But he couldn't wait. He mouthed down the column of her neck as she fumbled with the buttons wriggling beneath him. He nearly laughed until her shirt parted and he realized she was wearing the tiny red bra that'd fallen out of her suitcase this morning.

He reared back to get a good look: May lying on his parka, waiting for him, wearing that sexy bra and a scowl on her face. The deep red of the bra made her skin look like new fallen snow—so pretty it made his eyes hurt.

He traced the upper edge of the bra where tiny little rhinestones sparkled. "My, my, Ms. Burnsey, what you wear beneath your clothes."

She scowled harder. "I like nice things. There's nothing wrong with—"

She gasped as he bent to run his tongue along her breast where it met the bra's edge, and he smiled against her silken skin to think he'd made her lose her words. He followed the bra cup down between her breasts. There was a thin little cord holding the two cups together, and on it was a little silver bow. He caught it between his teeth and tugged gently, but it didn't taste near as good as her skin, so he kissed back up the other breast, staying right outside the bra.

Her breasts quivered beneath his lips, warm and alive. That bra was pretty, all right, he couldn't deny it, but when he palmed one breast all he felt was foam and nylon. He traced up the red strap, so thin and delicate, to where her collarbone winged into her shoulder.

"Sam," she protested.

"Shhh," he replied. No point in hurrying this, and besides, he kind of liked the idea of teasing her.

Just a bit.

He slipped one finger beneath the strap, pulling it down her shoulder until it hung, useless on her arm. He was amused to see that the bra cup on that side moved not a bit.

"Bet they have NASA scientists design these things."

She blinked up at him adorably—though he was smart enough not to tell her. "What?"

"Never you mind," he whispered, running his tongue experimentally beneath the cup.

It was warm in there and he could taste the salt of her skin.

He slid the other bra strap down, then pushed the bra down beneath her breasts, cupping them in his hands.

Her nipples were already drawn tight.

He bent to suck one into his mouth and felt his cock jolt against his jeans. He reached down and unzipped and unbuttoned himself, shoving his jeans down a bit to let his dick free.

May moaned and clenched her thighs around his left leg, and he realized that he had no condom.

"Fuck."

"What?" Her cheeks were flushed, her eyes dazed.

"Nothing." He moved to her other nipple. He'd just make do because he sure as hell wasn't going to stop this.

He shoved his upper leg into her mound, grinding gently as he rubbed his bare cock against her thigh. He pulled back to look at her tits. Her nipples were a deep, rosy brown, gleaming wet in the firelight.

He took her hands and guided them to her breasts. "Pinch them for me."

She bit her lip, looking shy for once as she did as she was told.

He watched for a moment, feeling his blood pounding, his breaths deepening, then he slid down her body. Her belly was so smooth, so soft, as he mouthed around her belly button. He framed her hips, feeling his need growing. He could smell her core, and he knew if he told her that she'd be horrified, but the truth was the scent of her made him horny as hell.

He caught the sides of her panties with his fingertips and dragged them down her hips and off her legs. She was wet already, the black curls sodden.

"C'mon," he whispered, "make a place for me, darlin'."

She spread her legs wide and he could see her pussy now, dark red and glistening, her clitoris swollen, and he grinned, fierce and feral.

He gathered her legs in his arms, scooping them over his shoulders, and cradled her ass in his hands.

He glanced up once to see her watching him, her hands still, and he shook his head, unable to smile. "Keep pinching yourself."

She swallowed, her throat fluttering, and then he closed his eyes as he licked into the heart of May.

She moaned, and he felt the sound vibrate against his tongue. He kissed all around her clit, sloppy, open-mouthed kisses that smeared her slick over his face. He was rutting against the parka on the floor as he licked her, driven half insane by her smell, by the sounds she made as he ate her out, by his own want building. Her legs were moving restlessly on his shoulders, and he gripped them tight as he drove into her center, tongue-fucking her. She went completely rigid, trembling all around him, and then she screamed.

God damn.

He let down her legs gently and knelt up over her, hastily smearing his right hand in her come before fisting his cock. She was moaning continuously, her fingers still twisting her nipples, as she lay before him, her legs sprawled, her pussy sodden, and he'd never seen anything in his life so hot. But it wasn't until he saw the slit of her eyes, knew that she was watching him with his hand on his cock that he broke.

He bowed, the orgasm like a punch in his gut, and grunted, winded as his come streaked across her belly and thighs.

"God," he gasped, half-falling on her. He fumbled to clean the mess he'd made of her. She must think him a complete jerk, but his hand touched hers and he looked up.

Her eyes were half closed, and she had a wicked little smile curling her lips as she licked her fingers. It took him a minute—wasn't like his brain was functioning too well at the moment—but then he realized she was licking his come off her belly.

Jesus Christ, if he hadn't just come, he would've blown.

He bent to kiss her and tasted his own semen on her lips, which was kind of gross, but really hot, too. "You're going to kill me."

May laughed, her eyes crinkling, her face flushed, and he knew suddenly that he loved her. That he always had loved her and always would love her until the day he died.

He kissed her laughing mouth, wanting to keep this moment forever.

When he raised his head she was watching him, a puzzled look in her eyes. "Sam." She raised her hand and touched the side of his face. He wondered if she knew how much she revealed by that gesture alone—if she'd draw back if she knew.

Her hand dropped and the moment was gone. She shivered.

He got up and put himself back together then bent and picked up the pot of water. He went to the door and tossed it out before packing the pot with more snow.

When he turned, she was struggling with her bra.

He set the pot by the fire and knelt in front of her. "Here."

"I can do it," she snapped.

"I know." He gently batted her hands aside and bent to kiss each nipple. Then he pulled the cups of her bra up over her breasts.

When he glanced up, she was watching him.

She hastily looked away and reached for her panties.

"Wait." He grabbed one of the washcloths from the pile she'd brought out earlier and wet it in the melting snow. "Lay back down."

She arched an eyebrow, but she did as he said. There

was something he liked about May following his directions. She so rarely agreed with anything, the victory was all the sweeter when she did.

Carefully he wiped her thighs, ignoring her muffled exclamation. The water was cold, but he knew she'd appreciate it anyway. He washed her gently, this most delicate part of her. It made him feel good. Protective. When he was done he helped her into the shirt, socks, and long underwear again, but when he reached for her jeans, she shook her head.

"Leave them."

He looked at her.

"Just . . ." She held out her arms to him.

He lay down next to her on the hard floor and gathered her into his arms. He'd never felt more at peace.

Then she turned her head to look at him and said, "Tell me about Afghanistan?"

Chapter Thirty-Six

Maisa watched Sam. She knew that asking about Afghanistan was going to sink her deeper emotionally with this man.

But maybe that was okay.

Maybe for once she should stop thinking so much and just let things happen. That was kind of hard for her, actually. She was the type who liked lots of control, lots of information. Except what if she simply couldn't control this thing between them?

It was a scary thought.

And still she wanted to know what had happened to Sam in Afghanistan—even if it meant taking their relationship a step further. What made him look so haunted when she'd found that photo. Why she'd known, deep in her bones, that he'd needed to be comforted this afternoon after he'd killed that mafiya thug. Maybe she was wrong. Maybe the two weren't linked at all and had nothing to do with his stint in the army.

Oh, damn it. Forget all her reasons and reasonings. She just wanted to know.

Wanted to know Sam.

Her hand, laying on his chest, clenched at the thought, and Sam, who hadn't said anything this whole time, she realized now, covered it with his own.

"What do you want to know?" he asked, and his voice was dead flat.

Well, that was intimidating, but it wasn't like she was easily scared away or anything. She raised her head to look him in the eye. "I want to know if you killed anyone over there."

He blinked, maybe at her terrible bluntness. "Yes."

She laid her head back down on his shoulder so she could hear his heartbeat and know that he'd survived whatever had happened. "Tell me."

His hand tightened for a moment over hers and she wondered if he'd resist her.

Then he sighed. "It was a long time ago, May."

She kept silent, waiting.

"There were five of us," he began at last. "Well, five that went out. We were part of a larger unit, stationed in one of those valleys over there, but just five were sent to a little village, really just a bunch of huts. There were rumors that the Taliban had a cache of arms buried there." He brushed his free hand through his hair. "You have to understand. We would go looking for arms or insurgents and most of the time we'd just be scaring farmers—old men, women at home. People trying to go about their daily lives in a war zone. Usually we never found anything and ended up being screamed at by housewives."

She closed her eyes and listened to his heartbeat, strong and steady, because she knew the time he was talking about was different.

"There was Zippy and Enrico, Frisbee and King, and

me. I was in charge because I had rank as a lieutenant. It was my mission."

He paused and she could hear him swallow.

"What happened?" she asked softly.

"There was a farmhouse and a little corral with some goats, a few chickens, and a cow—an old, bony thing. A little boy came out to meet us. He knew 'Hi' and 'Okay,' and that was all of his English. I gave him a pack of gum. He followed us and we went to look at the outbuildings—really a bunch of sheds. Nothing there. Didn't expect any different."

He took another breath, slow and shaky.

"Enrico had been bitching about his feet all day—we'd had to hike forty-five minutes to get to that place—and he sat down to pull off his boots. They shot him with one boot off. Turned out there were Taliban in the farmhouse—I don't know if they were holed up there or if we'd surprised them or what—but they started shooting. Enrico was dead. Zippy got hit in the hip. Frisbee and King dragged him into one of the sheds while I radioed for help."

He stopped and she waited, but he didn't say anything more.

When she raised her face she saw that his eyes were wet. She swallowed, shocked. "Sam..."

"They all died. That's what you wanted to hear, isn't it?" His words were hostile, but his tone continued flat. "The shed wasn't worth a damn as cover—bullets went right through it. Frisbee was shot in the neck and died pretty much instantly. King was hit in the jaw. But Zippy, well, Zippy bled out. I put pressure on the wound, but it just kept on bleeding and it was too high for a tourniquet. Took him two hours."

"How did you survive?" She'd never tell him, but she

was happy—fiercely happy—that he *had* lived, even if his friends had not.

She felt him shrug. "Dumb luck, mostly. There really wasn't a good reason I made it out and not them. We were all trained well, all experienced soldiers. They got shot. I didn't."

His grip had loosened as he talked and she turned her hand taking his thumb between her fingers, rubbing it. He had callouses at the first knuckle and at the base.

"It got close to nightfall, and I figured they'd rush me when it got dark and I'd be gone, too, because there wasn't anywhere to go. I could try hiding in the hills, but it wasn't like it was my home turf—and in the dark? Nope. I was ready for it, too. Made my peace. Was going to make it damn hard for them if nothing else, and what do you think but backup arrived?" He inhaled and his voice got hard and she heard something in it she'd never heard from Sam: sarcasm. "Took out everyone in the farmhouse, probably the kid as well, and there I was not even a scratch on me and my CO thumping me on the back, telling me what a great job I'd done. Why, that farmhouse and the half-dozen Taliban were instrumental to the war. Turned out there wasn't any cache of arms, though. And in another month we left that valley. For all I know the Taliban took it back over."

He sounded...he sounded almost defeated, and that was just wrong. Sam West wasn't a man to be defeated.

She raised her head and kissed him on the jaw. "You did the job you were given, shitty as it was, you know that, right?"

His mouth twisted. "My CO, know what else he told me?"

"What?"

"He said sometimes you had to sacrifice to win." He turned his head to look her in the eye. "Sounds pretty vague, doesn't it? Sacrifice? But the sacrifice he was talking about was specific: it was Zippy and Enrico, Frisbee and King. It was their *lives* I sacrificed, not some abstraction."

"But it wasn't your fault. You were ordered—"

"May." He cut her off ruthlessly, his voice brooking no dissent. "They were under my command."

She stared at him helplessly. What could she say to a man who'd lost his men, his *friends*, and believed it was his fault because he'd led them?

"Sam, you did what you had to."

"I know." He turned to her, his expression resolute. "And I'm doing what I have to now. Doc says that you have to be willing to sacrifice a man in order to win, but he's wrong. Dead wrong. You sacrifice one of your own and the game's lost already, 'cause your *people* are what the whole damn game is about in the end. I'm not sacrificing anyone else ever again."

Chapter Thirty-Seven

Sam stroked May's hair and listened to the storm raging outside.

"We should get up," she murmured sleepily.

"No point." He glanced at the window where the snow blew against the glass. "We can't go anywhere."

"I suppose." She yawned. "How are we going to get back to your cabin after the storm?"

"Walk if we have to." He thought a moment. He was pretty sure there was an easier way.

"'Kay." She turned to snuggle against his side, and he wondered if he was ever going to recover from this. It was as if she'd shot a bolt through him, and only she could fill the hole.

"This's pretty great," he said carefully.

She snorted. "Being trapped in an unheated cabin on a hard floor with a storm outside? I'm especially appreciative of your friend Hopkins's taste in food."

"Be nice." He squeezed her. "I meant us."

She was quiet so long, he thought she might've fallen asleep. "Yeah."

He turned and brushed his lips against her forehead.

She began struggling. "We ought to get up."

"May—"

"At least be prepared for when the storm stops."

He turned and took her arms. "What are you doing?"

"Let me go."

"May." He waited until she glanced up at him, her eyebrows lowered ominously. But he wasn't going to be turned aside by her orneriness this time. "What are you doing?"

"I don't know what you mean."

She was so damned stubborn he just wanted to yell at her sometimes, but he knew that wouldn't get him anywhere. He wondered if that was her goal all along with her bitchiness: to distract and confuse him.

So that they never got to the important issue.

"We've got something good here." He squeezed her arms for emphasis. "Something that isn't real common. I don't know about you, but I've never felt it before."

She opened her mouth, but he gave her a look.

"Let me finish and then you can go off on me all you like." He lowered his voice. "If that's what you really want."

She pinched her lips together, but nodded jerkily.

"Okay." He took a breath. He'd never been much of a talker—wasn't real eloquent even at the best of times—and this was important. Maybe the most important thing to ever happen to him in his life. So he took another breath and tried to think of the words that might make her see things his way. "You've been running ever since I first pulled you over—what was that, summer before last?"

"May."

"What?" He blinked, confused.

She cleared her throat. "It was in May."

"Oh, okay." He smiled a bit and hoped she didn't see: she remembered the month they'd met in. She cared more than she let on. "So two years, come next May, then?"

"Yes."

"And the thing is, I've never quite known why."

"You do too know why," she said at once. "I'm not attracted to you."

He just let that sit for a space.

"That's not what I mean," she said gruffly. "Sex isn't the same thing."

"Well, I think it is," he said, not pushing it too hard, just stating it. "With you, anyway."

"I don't want... I don't need anything beyond this."

"You know, you act like you're a real good liar," he said. "And I suppose to most you are. But the fact is, I've gotten to know you a bit, and now? Now I can tell that you're not being honest with me."

He thought she'd fly into a rage, maybe yell or even hit him, but she gave a sigh instead, like all the air had gone out of her.

"I don't know if it can work, Sam," she said, and he got worried because May could get angry and sarcastic and even kind of evil, but she never got sad. "You're a cop and I'm... well, you know what Dyadya is."

"He's mafiya."

She nodded, her head down on his chest so he couldn't see her face. "Exactly. You're... not."

He chuckled then, even though he knew he shouldn't.

Her head snapped up so fast she nearly clipped him in the chin. Her glare could kill a man at thirty paces. "What's so funny?"

"Nothing. Nothing," he said hastily. "It's just... I never knew you were so romantic."

"What?"

He smiled down at her angry face. *This* was the May he knew. "Like Romeo and Juliet."

"What? No..." Her mouth opened, but no more words came out.

He threaded his fingers back through her hair just because he could. "Two star-crossed lovers kept apart because of family politics?"

"It's not the same at all." But she sounded uncertain.

"Nope," he agreed. "For one thing I'm pretty sure I wouldn't look good in tights."

She slapped at the hand he had laying on his chest, but then she wrapped her fingers around his, listening.

"And for another," he continued, his voice low, "I always thought it was kind of stupid they couldn't get together. I mean, they were teenagers, I know that. But we're not."

"They had everything against them," she said low. "Society, their families."

"Yeah, but we don't." She shook her head, but he talked over her. "I don't even have family, not really."

"You have this town."

Yeah, that was actually kind of true, now that he thought about it. He had Coot Lake. "Okay, and no one in this town is against you and me being together."

She twisted to look at him, her face skeptical. "Doc Meijers? I always got the feeling he isn't my biggest fan."

"Yeah, Doc isn't particularly happy about us being together. But see, here's the thing: I'm not a teenager. I'm not Romeo. I make my own decisions, and if I decide to be with you because—" he almost said the words, but then figured it was too soon "—because I want to be with you, then people have to kind of come to terms with that."

Her mouth twisted cynically. "And if they don't? Sam—"

"What makes you so sure everyone in this town is against you?" he asked. "Have you asked around? Have you gotten to know people here?"

"No, but people know Dyadya, and—"

"—and they *like* him."

"You don't," she whispered.

That took him aback. "Yeah, I do, actually. I don't like what he was, I don't like him bringing his past troubles to my town and endangering you and Coot Lake, but Old George himself? He's okay."

He peered at her, but she still seemed skeptical. "Look, I'm not saying everyone in this town would throw a party if we got together, but you haven't given them a chance yet, have you? You've decided all on your own that we won't work, and you've given up before we've even tried."

That made her brows draw together.

He smoothed a thumb over one. "Why don't we try? Not forever, nothing permanent, just for a little bit. See what happens."

"What . . ." She bit her lip and tried again. "What would 'trying' include?"

This was the most she'd ever given him, and it was more than he'd hoped for so soon, but he knew better than to let triumph show on his face. "You could let me take you out to dinner, for one. Come up here twice a month instead of once. I could come down to visit you in the Cities on my off days."

"That's all?" she asked softly, but her words were a challenge. "Just a couple of dates."

The hell with being cautious. He rolled, pinning her beneath him. "You know damn well I want more than just a couple of dates. I want more of *this*." He pressed his hips into her sweet warmth. "I want Saturday mornings with French toast, I want walks with Otter, I want to hear about your day and the clients you can't stand. I want you, Maisa Burnsey. I want you."

Chapter Thirty-Eight

Maisa lay underneath Sam and stared into his electric blue eyes, hearing the echo of his words: *I want you.*

The words gave her a cautious sort of hope. Because she wanted Sam, too, though she'd been burying the thought for a very long time.

"It won't work," she said, mindlessly repeating the protest she'd had all along. She wasn't used to hope and was of suspicious of it.

But Sam must've given up persuading her with words. He bent and claimed her mouth. That really was the only word for it—the hard, possessive press of his lips, the deep penetration of his tongue. The force of his kiss bent her head back over his arm. She submitted at once, almost as if her body knew something her mind didn't yet. The action should've irritated her.

Instead she gave herself, without thought, without hesitation, without worry for the future. She let herself go, running her hands through his short hair, arching beneath him, widening her legs. He ground down, and she wished they hadn't dressed again. His cock was hard again behind his jeans. She rubbed up against it, wanting him there.

He groaned and broke their kiss, nipping along her bottom lip. "Say yes, May. Say yes to me, say yes to us."

"Come back here," she muttered, pulling at him.

"Say yes first." He suddenly raised himself on straight arms above her, his pelvis still pressed to hers, still grinding against her.

"That's blackmail." She pouted.

"Damn straight it is." He grinned and she caught her breath, he was so beautiful. Here in this dingy little cabin, the snow beating against the windows, and the cold, hard floor only covered with a thin carpet. The firelight gilded his hair, lit the side of his face, and made his eyes nearly glow. This man, this beautiful, stubborn, good, *kind* man, a man who knew who he was, who was respected by all who knew him, this man, this wonderful man wanted her. Wanted a relationship with her.

There was no way she could refuse, and truth be told, she was tired of trying.

"Yes," she said, and then louder, "Yes!"

He threw his head back and laughed, his throat clean and strong, and she felt joy.

Pure joy.

Chapter Thirty-Nine

❧❧

Karl squinted into the snow. His eyelashes were frosted, his cheeks burned, and his fingers had gone numb at least half an hour ago. Thankfully, though, his frozen hands still gripped the sled rail. Actually, he wasn't too sure he could let the rail go even if he wanted to.

"How's she doing?" he yelled into the wind.

"She's holding on," Molly hollered back.

She sat in the basket with nearly seventy-five pounds of Cookie sprawled over her lap and chest. The bullet had hit her in the side and she was bleeding bad, but she was still alert. Molly didn't seem bothered by the fact that her winter coat was covered in dog blood and Karl felt a well of emotion for the woman who understood how much that damned bitch meant to him. He'd raised Cookie since she'd been three months old, an adorable ball of terror. He wasn't sure what he'd do if he lost her.

Cookie growled at Molly's voice, and without missing a beat Molly tapped her on the nose and murmured, "Hush."

Cookie lowered her head with a little whine and Karl marveled. Never in all the time that he'd known Cookie had she done anything he'd asked of her unless *she* wanted to. Molly was obviously some kind of dog goddess.

Or just a goddess.

He looked down longingly at the back of her hood-covered head, which wasn't easy, what with the frosted eyelashes. Molly and he had been friends since the first grade, when he'd noticed her lecturing Scott Henderson on the proper way to color in a banana—always outline first was Molly's policy. He'd come over and backed up Molly's philosophy, even though at seven he hadn't yet formed any personal coloring guidelines. And when Scott had shoved Molly in inarticulate anger over being lectured on coloring, Karl had kicked him in the shins. Kind of like a knight of old championing his lady fair. That had led to a time-out and an awkward letter home to his mom, but seven-year-old Karl figured it'd been more than worth it.

Molly Jasper had had the biggest, brownest eyes Karl had ever seen.

After that Molly had regularly instructed Karl on such things as Why Ding Dongs Weren't Health Food and How He-Man Wasn't a Real Name—Karl secretly still wasn't entirely convinced on that one. He'd learned how to write cursive with her in third grade. In fifth grade, he'd given her an awesome Spider-Man valentine with a bonus Swedish fish insert—only a little smashed. In eighth grade, he'd asked her to the winter dance—which she'd declined, due to stupid Dave Beaulieu asking her first, but he had danced with her and later kicked Dave in the shins in the boys' restroom. And when Karl had joined the army and left the rez, Molly had e-mailed him and sent him care packages of wild rice and Swedish fish.

They'd always been friends and somehow Karl had figured that, you know, they'd end up together.

Married. Maybe with tiny Karls going ice-fishing with him and tiny Mollys lecturing him on his caffeine consumption.

But now there was that dickhead Walkingtall, looking so serious—just like Molly—and college educated, and even Karl—who had to admit he wasn't always the quickest on the uptake—could see they kind of *matched*. And Molly was mad at him because of the stupid arrowheads and he hadn't had time to explain yet, and now Cookie was covered in a terrifying amount of blood and they were in a blizzard and he couldn't see Bug, who was taking lead from Cookie, and Bug wasn't the brightest dog in the world and for all Karl knew they were headed to Canada, and really?

Things had kind of gone down the shitter.

"Maybe we should've stopped," he said to Molly. "Maybe we should've found a cabin and broken in and made a fire and, I dunno, brought all the dogs in and gotten Cookie warm."

Molly didn't say anything and Karl actually felt his heart sink. There were times, late at night with all the lights off, that Karl had to admit that he was sort of a screw-up. He had the feeling Molly thought so, too.

The wind howled, beating against him, beating against the sled and the dogs, and Karl wondered if they were going to die out here, him and Molly and his sweet, psychotic Cookie and all the rest of the dogs who only wanted to run and chew on the special rawhides he bought in bulk at the feed store.

He might've sobbed.

And then...and then he saw the sign for Sam's road, suddenly *there* in the white.

Karl whooped and yelled "Haw!" at Bug, and Bug, that big bundle of dumb mutt, swung left, just like he was supposed to, and they raced down the road and then there was Sam's cabin and Karl whooped again and yelled, "Whoa!"

So, okay, Bug went a little past the cabin, but Karl got him turned around and then they were there and he looked at Molly as he set the brake and grinned. "We made it."

She gazed at him a little puzzled. "Of course we did. You were driving."

Her simple faith in him caught him unawares and made his heart suddenly leap up and soar. He came around the sled and bent and kissed her, frozen-mouthed and hot-tongued. Cookie tried to nip him, probably because she was sort of squished between them, but Karl was too busy being relieved and happy and kind of glorying in Molly's sexy mouth.

Which was when someone cleared their throat.

He looked up.

Walkingtall stood in the doorway to Sam's house, pinch-faced and too tall and said, "Doug's been shot, Doc's got a fever, Sam and Maisa haven't returned, and George Johnson's disappeared. That dog is covered in blood. Is she dying? You want to come in? It's freezing out here."

Karl kind of wanted to kick him in the shins.

Chapter Forty

By the time Sam and May caught sight of his cabin, dusk was closing in. They'd had to wait until the storm had let up to even set out. Sam had found Hopkins's ancient snowshoes—fortunately he still had his late wife's shoes stored away as well—and showed May how to strap them on. Then it'd just been a matter of walking to his cabin. But snowshoeing, though effective on deep snow, was slow going. It'd taken them hours, and May had started lagging the last mile or so, her face tired and drawn.

All in all, he was damned happy to see his front door.

Some of the sled dogs staked out in his yard stood and greeted them with yaps, though most didn't bother uncurling from their balls of warm fur. He could hear Otter, though, inside the house, racing to the door and barking his head off.

"We'll get some hot soup in you," Sam murmured to May as he led her to the door. "And a shower. That'll warm you up."

She only nodded at him, which made him worry more, because a May without a snappy comeback was a very cold and tired May.

He tried the handle to his own door, realized it was locked, realized further that he hadn't brought his keys on the raid on Beridze, and knocked.

The door cracked and Karl and a shotgun barrel peered out.

"It's us," Sam said, too tired to even protest being held at gunpoint on his own front step.

"Oh, thank God, dude!" Karl said and flung open the door.

Sam helped May in, an arm around her shoulders, as Otter leaped at his knees. The little dog was nearly beside himself, panting anxiously as Sam gently shoved him aside so he could shut the door.

"We didn't know what was up when you didn't come back," Karl said, his expression uncharacteristically serious. "Doug's been shot."

"Yeah, I know." Sam helped May take off her snowshoes, propping them next to his by the door. There was a big duffel that hadn't been there before, and he stared at it a moment before leading May into the kitchen and sat her on one of the stools by the island.

Becky, Haley Anne, and Molly were already gathered. Ilya glanced up from where he slumped in one of the chairs by the windows. In the chair next to him was Jim Gustafson of all people. Becky took one look at them and put a kettle on.

"What're you doing here, Jim?" Sam asked

Jim shrugged. "I was in town at Sarah Milton's place. We...ah, we have kind of a thing going."

"Yeah?" Karl asked, sounding interested.

Jim turned a little red. "Yeah, so we heard the shooting and the phone lines were down this morning." Jim shrugged. "Thought I should come see what was going on. If Sam needed help or anything."

"Appreciate that," Sam said. "May lost her skis and we got caught by the storm. Had to hole up in Tony Hopkins's cabin."

"Thank God you made it there," Becky said quietly. She was sticking something in the microwave to heat.

"Yeah," Sam said. "Everyone else make it back?"

Becky nodded to the downstairs bedroom. "They're all in there, still sleeping. We patched Doug up, but he needs a doctor. He's lost a lot of blood."

"What about Doc?"

The lines deepened in her face. "He's got a low fever. I think he's okay for now, but we need to get him to a hospital as soon as we can, Sam."

"Noted," Sam said grimly as he shucked his parka. He threw it over a chair. "How'd you get here, Jim?"

"Snowmobile," Jim said, short and succinct.

Sam nodded. "Anyone try the phones?"

"Still not working," Becky answered.

The microwave beeped at the same time the kettle began whistling, and Sam walked around the island to help get out some silverware. He noticed then that a big grey-and-black sled dog was curled on Otter's dog bed, a bandage on her side. The bandage was bleeding through and Otter had gone to sniff at it. The bigger dog opened her eyes and lifted her lip in a silent snarl to warn Otter. He sat on his butt and lowered his head to the floor in submission.

"What's going on?" Sam asked.

"That's Cookie, my lead dog," Karl said from behind him. "Got shot. She's..."

He broke off, gulping.

"She's not doing well," Molly said gravely, her eyes on Karl. "But she's strong. She'll last until we can get her to a vet."

She put her hand on Karl's shoulder and he looked at her gratefully.

A toilet flushed and Walkingtall came out of the downstairs bathroom. "Did they tell you?"

"Tell me what?" Sam frowned as he took down a package of herbal tea from the cupboard. It was left over from an old girlfriend and was probably two years old or more, but it would be hot.

"George is gone."

Sam froze, his hand on the teakettle. He looked at May.

She'd straightened, her face stricken. "What? What do you mean?"

For a second Sam wished he could've just decked Walkingtall.

Karl looked like he had the same idea. "Apparently one of the SUVs showed up down the road, cruising slow like it was searching. Fortunately, Becky was watching with your binoculars, Sam. She spotted them before they got too close and saw the tracks out front of your house."

"What happened to my uncle?" May asked. Her face had gone white.

Becky brought over two plates of some kind of casserole with canned green beans on the side. "George said he was going out to talk to them before they came closer down the lane and figured out which cabin we were in. He took one of the suitcases, went out the back, and walked through the woods by the lake before coming out on the road."

Karl nodded. "Becky saw him get in the SUV. Next thing we knew they were gone."

"Oh, God," May said.

Tears sparkled in her eyes and Sam went to her, putting his arm around her shoulders. She sagged against him and that more than anything worried the hell out of him. May wasn't a quitter. She never gave up, never gave in. She was tough as nails and as ornery as a mad badger, and it made him sick to see her head bowed into his shoulder.

Sam looked at Stu. "So George kept them from discovering you all."

Stu nodded grimly.

"That was brave of him," Sam said. He looked at Karl. "When was this?"

But it was Stu who replied. "Before the storm." He closed the door to the downstairs bedroom quietly behind him. "We got back just after."

Karl shook his head. "No way they could've made it back to town before the storm hit. They were moving slow—it's a wonder they could get that SUV through the snow at all. Might've stuck on the way back for all we know."

May inhaled.

Sam squeezed her shoulder. "That's a good thing. If they've gotten stuck or had to stop, they're vulnerable."

May stood, her stool screeching back behind her. "We have to go after them."

She was still wearing her parka so Sam unzipped her and pulled it from her shoulders. He placed the parka over a kitchen chair, and as he did so he felt the lump in her right pocket.

Karl glanced out the window. "It's dark."

May looked as well, and as she did so, Sam took the diamonds out of her parka pocket and slipped them in his jeans pocket.

Stu shook his big, shaggy head. "No way. It's too dangerous. We don't know the route they took back to town, and besides, the dogs are pooped. They need to rest before they go out again."

Jim Gustafson stirred. "I've got my snowmobile."

Stu shot him a look.

Jim shrugged. "But, yeah, it'd be stupid to go out now. Might get lost. Freeze to death."

May turned on Sam fiercely. "I'll go after Dyadya myself if you won't go. You don't understand. He testified at Beridze's uncle's trial. Dyadya is the reason his uncle will be in prison for the rest of his life. Beridze *can't* get his hands on Dyadya!"

Sam gripped her shoulders, trying to tamp down his own worry, trying to channel all his strength and calm through his hands into her body. "It's dark and we're tired. We can't go up against them without a plan."

She wrenched against his hands, trying to fly away. "You don't understand—"

"I *do* understand," he said, gripping her shoulders. "He means the world to you. He's the father you never had. You can't lose him."

She stopped and stared up at him, her eyes wide.

He rubbed her arms with his thumbs. "I understand, May, I do, and I promise, I *promise* on everything I hold dear—on this town and us—I promise I'll get your uncle back for you."

Chapter Forty-One

The police station was cold—so cold that Jabba's feet ached as they hadn't since he'd been a very small boy in Moscow. The fucking townspeople had blown up the small electrical generator in the parking lot. Smoke still trailed sluggishly from the remains of the shed.

He'd lost his hostages. Lost one of his SUVs to the lake's ice. Nearly lost Sasha in the water of the lake.

And he still didn't have his diamonds.

"I do not understand why I cannot go shoot up this fucking town," Jabba said, peering through the window to the darkened street below. Nothing moved. Maybe all the townspeople had frozen to death.

"You know," Sasha said. "We wait for the last SUV. Without it we cannot escape."

Jabba jerked his chin at him. "You think I was stupid to send Rocky to find that policeman's house. The policeman who is in charge."

He had ordered Rocky out before the police station had been attacked. Because Rocky had been out, they'd been short of manpower. When the fucking dog sleds had shown up and then a sniper appeared on the roof opposite,

Jabba had taken Sasha and two other men outside and split up to find that sniper.

Instead he'd lost two men outside, four inside, and the fucking SUV when it'd gone through the ice. If Sasha hadn't pulled himself and Nicky out of the SUV, Jabba would have been entirely alone in the police station.

"It is not my job to think, Boss." Sasha said flatly. "But we're running out of time. By now the FBI will be alerted and will be looking for us. We need to leave the country."

He looked at Sasha. Sometimes Jabba wondered if he should kill him. Sasha was the only one who did not fear him, and Jabba thought this was not good.

On the other hand, Sasha was very useful.

"Truck," barked Nicky. He was looking out the back window. "Ours."

"Rocky?" Sasha asked.

"Rocky and Ivan," Nicky said. "And they have another with them."

Jabba looked at the door as they heard the footsteps on the stairs.

Sasha rose, his gun pointed at the door. He gestured to the remaining two men to do the same.

Rocky opened the door, his expression cautious.

Behind him was George Rapava.

Jabba cocked his head. "Have you come to visit me, my old friend George?"

George Rapava was a mafiya of old—those who showed fear did not last long in the gulag. He sauntered in, his back a little bent, his hands clasped before him like an old man. He was an old man—over seventy, most likely—yet he was dangerous as well. None of the old mafiya, the ones from Mother Russia, were entirely safe, even in old age.

Old George smiled, a thin smile such as a snake would give, and said, "I have come at the invitation of your men, Jabba."

Jabba stretched wide his arms. "My house is yours, I assure you, dear George. I hope you do not mind, it is perhaps rather cold because your friends have destroyed the power."

George shrugged. "I have survived Siberia. This? This is nothing. Although"—he glanced about—"there are far less of your men here than I was led to believe."

For a moment Jabba felt the rage rise within him, firing his blood, boiling the thoughts from his brain.

And then he was controlled again. Serene and complacent. He looked at the black suitcase one of his men carried. "Have you brought me a present?"

"For you? Naturally," George rumbled.

"There's a bomb inside," Rocky said.

"You brought a bomb to us?" Sasha snarled. His gun, which had never lowered, swung to point at Rocky's face.

George Rapava chuckled.

Jabba felt his lip curl as he strode forward and took the suitcase from his man's hand. He laid it on one of the policemen's desks.

"Boss," Sasha warned. "He was known for his explosives in Russia."

Jabba looked and saw the pathetic piece of tape closing the zipper, the childish warning: *BOMB. DO NOT OPEN.*

In one motion Jabba unzipped the suitcase and flung open the lid.

Rocky and those behind him jerked away, their arms

raised as if to shield their faces. Sasha stood his ground, but flinched.

Only George and Jabba did not move.

Inside the suitcase were a few old magazines, some towels, nothing else.

"A foolish trick," Jabba said contemptuously, shoving the suitcase off the desk. It fell to the floor, spilling its contents. "Perhaps you have grown weak in your old age, George my dear friend, to think this would deceive me?"

Old George shrugged, his smile never wavering. "I thought it would make you laugh only."

"Yes? This is so?" Jabba perched on the corner of the desk. "But if you seek to amuse me, this is easy enough to do."

George's smile faded.

"Very easy," Jabba continued, taking a knife from his pocket. He flicked it open with his thumb, the razor-sharp blade gleaming dully. "You will tell me where Ilya the thief is, where my diamonds are, and you will do this very quickly."

"Ah." George shook his head in sorrow, smiling wryly. "And yet I am afraid I must disappoint you, my friend Jabba, because I can do neither."

Jabba had been expecting this answer and his smile answered George's as he said softly, "Then I will have to find my amusement another way, eh?"

Chapter Forty-Two

Maisa closed her eyes, inhaling the scent of Sam from his sweater. She knew he was perfectly sincere. That he really would do all he could to bring back Dyadya to her. Except that Beridze had shot Doc, and if it meant giving the diamonds to Beridze and letting him go, she wasn't sure Sam would do that. He hadn't said so explicitly, but she knew damned well that Sam wanted to avenge Doc. Avenge his town. And beyond that, Sam was on the side of law and order. He wasn't going to let a murderer, a psychopathic gangster, go free. If it came right down to it, she was afraid that he'd choose capturing Beridze over rescuing Dyadya.

She took a breath, trying to calm her shaking. This was it: the event that would tear them apart. She'd known it was coming, she just hadn't realized that it would arrive so quickly.

"Okay." She raised her head, looking into his gorgeous blue eyes, and she was able, finally, now that it was too late, to acknowledge to herself that she loved him. Completely, utterly, and awfully, she loved Sam West, and she suspected she always would. "Okay, I'll wait."

The relief that swept his features eased the lines around his eyes and mouth. He was almost as tired as she from their trek and the events of the last few days. She wished she could comfort him, just spend a little time savoring this man.

"We'll find your uncle," he assured her, low.

"Yeah, we will," Stu said. "Doug's out, but we have Jim's snowmobile and the three sleds still, plus me, Karl, and this guy here." He jerked his head at Walkingtall, who looked suddenly alarmed.

"Us, too," Becky spoke for both her and Haley Anne.

"And me," Molly Jasper said quietly. Maisa remembered how the petite woman had given them all cover from the roof of the antique shop.

"Oh yeah, and me and Molly took out one of the SUVs," Karl said, perking up.

Sam swung on him, intent. "What?"

Karl beamed. "Yup. Led them out on the ice on Lake Moosehead and over that spot where Gopher Creek lets on the lake. Ice's thin there. They went right in. Coolest thing I've ever seen."

"Damn," Stu said, admiration in his voice.

"That means they're down to one SUV," Sam said. "Did you see how many men were in the truck?"

Karl shrugged. "At least two."

Sam nodded absently, his eyes narrowed. He was probably calculating odds and the number of enemy still left.

Maisa just felt tired. She needed some rest if she was going to accomplish what she needed to do. She looked down at the macaroni, ground beef, and cheese hot dish Becky had set on the table, and her stomach rolled. She placed her palm on Sam's chest and pushed gently.

Immediately his arms tightened and his gaze focused on her.

"I need a shower," she murmured.

He nodded and his arms opened, letting her go, though his eyes were speculative as he watched her. "Go on. I'll be up in a bit after I check on Doc."

She felt her cheeks heat. It seemed sort of ridiculous to be self-conscious now, but she was suddenly aware that everyone must know she was sleeping with Sam. She walked around the island, past Stu as he moved aside, and grabbed her suitcase—the *right* suitcase this time—from the kitchen closet.

"Let me take that," Sam said, as she came back by him.

She shook her head. "It's okay."

He nodded, but his eyes narrowed as she turned away. She'd need to be careful if she was going to go through with her plan to rescue Dyadya and betray Sam.

Her Sam wasn't stupid.

Otter trotted after her as she mounted the stairs to the loft above.

It was dim up here in Sam's personal space, dark but cozy, with the warm air rising to fill the loft. She set her suitcase on a straight-backed chair next to his bureau, and for a moment just stood there, staring at nothing. It was nice to be alone. To have a minute to gather her thoughts apart from anyone else. Fine tremors were shaking her arms, and a part of her marveled at them in a detached way.

She frowned and bent to open her suitcase.

She picked out fresh underwear and the sleep pants and long-sleeved T she'd packed almost a week ago. They weren't at all sexy, but they were all she had.

She'd noticed that first day that Sam's bathroom was pretty small, but nice. He must've put it in himself, because the toilet and pedestal sink were newer, and the shower was lined in light terra-cotta tile. No bath, but the shower was roomy. She started the water as she stripped out of her clothes, then tested it before stepping under the spray. It was nice and hot, and she nearly moaned as the water hit her sore muscles. She'd never been snowshoeing, and the exercise had used muscles that she hadn't known she possessed.

She closed her eyes, letting the water stream over her face, flattening her hair. She felt as if she needed to wash away more than sweat and grime.

The shower door opened behind her and she didn't even look, because she'd been half-expecting him.

And anyway she was so very glad he'd come.

"Want me to wash your back?" he murmured in her ear. His smoky voice sent shivers down her neck, making her nipples peak even under the hot spray.

"Yes."

He kneaded soapy hands down her back, his thumbs digging small circles on either side of her spine. She bowed her head and this time she did moan aloud, not caring if anyone else heard her in the house. He moved back up her spine and then over her shoulders, loosening her muscles, turning her to putty. He rinsed her back and she started to turn around, but he halted her with a touch.

"Don't move."

She waited, not even caring what he meant to do next, she was so relaxed, so tired emotionally and physically.

Then she felt the touch of his fingers in her hair, working shampoo in. He massaged gently over her temples and at the base of her head where she hadn't even known the muscles were tight, and then he tipped her head back so that she rested against his shoulder. Carefully, cupping his hand against her forehead to prevent the soap from streaming in her eyes, he rinsed her hair.

She could feel the brush, now and again, of his erection as he moved behind her. It was a peripheral reminder, not urgent or rude, that he wanted her. Tears gathered in her eyes, surprising her with her defenses down. This was nice. This was actually wonderful... and she wouldn't have it soon.

But she brushed aside the moisture, letting the salt mix with the hot running water, before he could notice. She wasn't going to spoil tonight.

It would be their last.

He reached around her, and she could see him soap his hands up. He caught her hands with his, lacing their soapy fingers together. He stepped forward so that he stood against her back. She could feel his chest against her shoulders, his belly against the small of her back, his cock against the crease of her buttocks, and still there was no pressure. They were simply a man and a woman, standing nude together, the water hitting her chest.

He unlaced their fingers and trailed his fingertips up her arms, a marionette under the thrall of a puppet master.

"Lift," he whispered in her ear, and she obeyed.

He soaped under her arms and let the running water rinse the bubbles away. She watched as he soaped again and then lifted his hands to her breasts.

She groaned and let her head fall to his shoulder when he touched her.

He circled her breasts with just his fingertips, the light,

tantalizing touch in contrast to the heavy beat of the shower. When he at last circled in to her nipples, they were tight and aching. He pinched them between thumb and forefinger, both at once, and made her gasp. She felt the brush of his lips against the side of her neck, and she tilted her head to give him better access. His penis was hard and wedged into her bottom now, thrusting just slightly, hardly noticeable, really, but it made her knees weak.

His hands left her and she watched, hypnotized, her eyes half-lidded, her breath coming faster, as he soaped them for a third time. Now he laid them on her belly, making gentle, maddening circles around her navel as his hips thrust behind her.

Her hands had been hanging by her side, but now she broke, too impatient to wait for whatever he planned. She gripped his forearms and pushed down and she heard his chuckle in her ear as he let her guide his hands to her bush and below.

He threaded his fingers into her wet curls, gently exploring, and she widened her legs to encourage him. His other hand traced tickling patterns on the insides of her thighs. His middle finger found her clitoris and she arched into his hand, gasping, as he tapped it.

He twisted his right hand free suddenly and reached behind her as at the same time he bent his knees. And then she felt his cock pushing through her legs, rubbing against the wet of her folds.

"Close your thighs," he said, hot and urgent in her ear, and she did, trapping his penis between them.

She rocked slightly, feeling the slide, so close to her center.

He wrapped his arms around her again, pushing against

her, his breath hot on her neck. Then he twisted his right hand down, seeking out her clit while his left flicked at her nipples. It was so much, all the disparate sensations all at once, and she had to hold on to something. So she gripped his arm with both hands as he played with her. She felt swollen, engorged with heat and want, and her hips jerked helplessly. The head of his cock was shoving up against her clit from below while he pressed gently down with his finger from above. She mewled, arching back against him.

"Shh," he murmured into her ear. "You're so hot right now. If I had a condom, I'd put my prick in you and fuck you up against the shower wall. Fuck you until your legs gave out and you screamed for me, May, my May. Come. Come now, so I can feel your slick on my cock. I want to bathe in you. I want to suck the come from your pretty little pussy, tongue you until you go insane."

She gasped at his words and he pressed hard, circling his finger. She saw stars, bursting behind her eyelids, her legs shaking uncontrollably as heat raced through her limbs.

She was still panting, her orgasm still sparking within her, when he slapped off the shower. He grabbed a towel, wrapped it around her, and picked her up, striding into his bedroom without bothering to dry off.

Her eyes widened when he put her on the bed.

She watched him impatiently fish a condom out from between the mattresses and curse steadily to himself as he rolled it on. Her mouth curved uncontrollably, a giggle bubbling at her lips at his swift movements.

But all desire to laugh left her when he climbed on the bed and on top of her. He looked her in the eye and thrust into her at the same time without preamble.

She gasped. The sensation—the *pleasure*—was so exquisitely sharp it was nearly painful. He forced his way into her swollen, sensitive flesh, burrowing, filling her. Claiming her—or so it felt. A complete possession, irrevocable and final. He held her gaze as he pushed into her without hesitation.

In command.

In command of her. Her eyes filled with tears with the thought. He was everything she wanted, though she'd been denying it for so long. And now . . . and now that it was too late she could at last admit it: He was her mate, her companion, her opposite, the man who should be by her side for the rest of their lives.

And he would not.

Not after what she would do to him.

He had no sympathy for her tears. If anything his face became sterner as he lay fully on her, making her accept his weight. She welcomed him, though, reaching up to wrap her arms and her legs around him.

She'd wrap her soul around him, too, if it were possible.

He withdrew and shoved back into her, hard. Hard and almost cruel. He was telling her something with this lovemaking. Making a point that she couldn't miss—but that she had to ignore anyway.

When he bent to open her mouth beneath his, she let him. Because she doubted she could deny this man anything now. Well, anything but the one thing he wanted.

She sobbed and lifted against him, suddenly mad. It wasn't fair. He shouldn't expect the impossible from her, she told him from the very beginning that this wouldn't work. That it could never last.

He raised his head and watched her as she struggled

under him, her hips meeting his almost brutally. He was rubbing against her with each close thrust, driving her higher as she stared, defiant, angry, and bereaved beneath him. She was his match, God damn it, and if nothing else, he would remember her until the day he died.

She'd leave her mark on him, burn it into his very soul.

It hit her hard. Without warning or buildup. Her orgasm bent her spine in a bow of agonized sweetness. She gasped, her breath knocked from her body, black spots dancing in front of her eyes, and somewhere in the midst of her turmoil she heard him groan, loud and awful, and knew he was with her.

Together they died.

Together they lived.

Chapter Forty-Three

DAY FOUR

Sam woke to the sound of dozens of dogs barking and a shout from downstairs. He cursed himself, rolling off the bed and fumbling in the dark for his gun. Beridze's men had been searching for his cabin yesterday. There was nothing to stop them from coming back with reinforcements and maybe finding it this time. He'd been so concerned with May that he'd let his guard down, failed to defend the perimeter.

Put everyone at risk.

He pulled on his jeans and, gun in hand, clattered down the stairs.

"Sam!" Dylan had a shotgun aimed out the front door.

"What's going on, Dylan?" Sam shouted. The dogs were nearly deafening.

Dylan answered without looking away from the door. "We've got someone walking up. He's holding a white flag."

"What the hell?" Karl was barefoot and wearing the

same clothes from yesterday. "He's never gonna make it through that sled dog minefield."

"Shit, he's throwing something!" Dylan ducked inside just as the dog barks reached a peak.

Something thumped against the door.

"Well, what was it?" Karl hustled to the door. "He better not've hurt one of my dogs."

But Sam held out his arm, pushing Karl back. "Let me look first."

He opened the door cautiously, watching for an ambush. The only thing he saw was the figure retreating in the distance. Even the dogs' barking had died down. On his front step was a rock wrapped in plastic.

"What is it?" Karl reached past him and picked it up. "Hey! It's a note."

Sam sighed and shut the door. "Might as well bring it in."

Karl was already untaping the rock when he turned. Karl fished out a piece of paper. "It's from the crazy Russian. He wants to make a trade: George for the diamonds. Middle of Coot Lake, high noon."

Sam frowned, thinking logistics. "Middle of the lake? He must be worried we'd set Molly and her rifle on him again. What—?"

"Oh, shit!" Karl cried dropping the rock.

"What?"

Karl bent to pick up the rock again, looking suddenly green. "There's something else." He opened the plastic bag fully.

"Sam?" May stood on the stairs, wrapped in one of his old shirts, her feet bare. He started for her when her eyes widened. "Oh, my God, what's that?"

He turned back to see that Karl held something fleshy on a blood-soaked scrap of cloth in the middle of the opened plastic bag.

"It's the tip of a finger," Karl croaked. "George's finger." He looked up, his usually cheerful face stricken. "Beridze is going to send him back in pieces if you're not at the lake at noon, Sam."

Chapter Forty-Four

Maisa couldn't take her eyes off that ghastly fingertip. The room was moving sideways and she couldn't think.

Then Sam was there, catching her, helping her to sit down. He was telling Dylan to put away the damned finger and Becky was handing her a glass of water. Maisa felt sick to her stomach, but she sipped the water like Becky instructed.

All she could think about was that fingertip. How much it must've hurt Dyadya to have it chopped from his hand. He was an old man. A bent old man with gnarled, tattooed fingers and sweaters that had tea stains on them. He never should've been in danger. She should've kept him safe.

Something dripped on her hands, and she raised them to feel moisture on her face. She was crying and hadn't even known.

Sam took her hands in his own. He was squatting in front of her, bare-chested in the morning cold, his hair rumpled from sleep, and he was telling her in his steady, strong, deep voice that it would be okay. That he would bring Dyadya back to her.

"We have to give him the diamonds," she said. "We have to."

"No." He shook his head. "Beridze gets the diamonds and he disappears scot-free. I'll get your uncle for you, but I'm not giving that maniac what he wants."

"Sam—"

"Trust me, May." He looked a little desperate. "Can't you trust me to do this for you?"

No. That was the real problem, wasn't it? In the end, she could trust only herself.

She smiled at him and he stopped talking, looking at her warily. She needed to be cautious, to be sly and deceptive, because she loved this man—loved him with all her being and always would—but she trusted only herself to save Dyadya.

Only she could bring him home whole.

So she bowed her head, listening as he turned to Dylan, Karl, and Stu, and made plans. The old farmer, Jim, sat drinking coffee across from her, and she remembered that he had a snowmobile. All she needed was the keys.

She glanced from under her eyelashes at the front door, where all the coats were hung or piled. Somewhere in there would be his parka.

"I need to get dressed," she murmured, standing, deliberately keeping her voice weak and thin.

Even so, Sam shot her a suspicious glance. He knew her far too well.

She met his eyes. "I'll be quick. Don't make plans without me."

That indication that she wanted to know what they would do seemed to reassure him. He nodded and stood, moving close, brushing her cheekbone with his thumb. "You okay?"

"No." She didn't have to feign the tremor in her voice. "Not at all."

He kissed her, frowning, and then nodded at the stairs.

She turned and made her steps slow, though she wanted to run. Beridze had her uncle, and Beridze was insane. There was no guarantee that he would even keep Dyadya alive until noon and the planned exchange.

She had to hurry.

Upstairs she dressed in her borrowed long underwear and sweaters, jamming her feet into boots, and picking up the little gun that Sam had given her yesterday. She'd fired two shots out of it while the mafiya gunman had been chasing her. She wasn't sure how to check the remaining bullets, but she figured she had at least four left.

If she was lucky, that would be more than enough.

She shoved the gun into the waistband of her jeans, pulled her sweater over it, and glanced one more time around Sam's bedroom, trying to think if she needed anything else. The most important things—the diamonds—were still in her parka downstairs. She'd never taken them out last night. She took a deep breath. This would be the last time she'd ever stand here in Sam's bedroom.

She left without a backward glance.

Downstairs, the men were huddled together. She went over to them and placed a hand on Sam's shoulder. He covered it with his own and she stood there for a moment, leaning against his back, absorbing his warmth. They were talking about a complicated plan involving dog sleds and Molly's rifle. Naturally Sam was reluctant to just give the diamonds to Beridze in exchange for Dyadya. He wanted to trap him somehow.

All she wanted was her uncle alive.

Otter came to sniff her hand and she bent to him,

rubbing her hands in his floppy ears. "Do you have to go out, Otter?"

He yipped at the word *out*, and she led him to the front door, murmuring nonsense to him. She glanced behind them, but no one was paying her attention, and she quickly slipped her hands into the pockets of one coat after another.

"Don't go far," Sam called, making her jump.

"We won't." Her fingers closed around a set of keys inside the pocket of a huge old coverall. She kept searching in case she had the wrong ones, but none of the other coats held keys.

She put on her own parka, zipping it up tight, the keys hidden in her fist, and opened the door.

Otter flung himself into the bright, cold air, barking at the lumps of sled dogs, curled into balls in the snow. A couple stood and shook themselves, looking curiously at the funny little terrier, bounding from drift to drift and occasionally sinking neck deep.

The snowmobile was parked behind the truck in the drive. Maisa walked to it as quickly as she could in the snow.

She straddled the huge machine, glancing nervously at Sam's front door before trying one of the keys on the loop she held. There were three keys. The first wouldn't go into the ignition. She shuffled keys in her cold fingers and tried another.

The key slid in and she turned it. Nothing happened.

"May!"

Sam was at the front door.

She gasped and saw the choke, flipping it.

"God damn it, May!"

There was a cord, like a lawn mower. She pulled it and the snowmobile roared to life.

Otter was barking frantically. She clenched the gas on the handlebar and the snowmobile raced away.

She glanced back just once.

Sam was running after her through the deep snow, but as she gunned the snowmobile he stopped.

Chapter Forty-Five

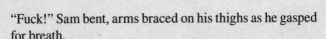

"Fuck!" Sam bent, arms braced on his thighs as he gasped for breath.

He straightened. May was no longer in sight. "God damn it. *Fuck!*"

"She gone?"

He turned, looking back at the cabin. Karl stood in the doorway. Otter was struggling to leap from footprint to footprint in Sam's wake. He started back, his feet burning. He'd run barefoot into the snow.

Otter stood, hesitating in one of the footprint hollows, unsure which way they were headed.

Sam scooped him up as he passed, holding the terrier under his arm like a football. Otter hung there, panting happily. He had no idea of the disaster that'd just happened.

"She's got the snowmobile," Sam told Karl as he made the porch.

Karl stepped back, letting him inside. "I saw. You think she's headed to Beridze?"

"I *know* she's headed to Beridze," Sam said.

Becky came around the corner of the kitchen island,

caught sight of Sam's feet, and made a horrified sound. She turned back to the kitchen.

Sam let Otter down.

"Does she have the diamonds?" Karl asked, running his hand through his hair. "Dude. We're screwed if she does."

The microwave beeped in the kitchen and Becky took out a towel.

"That's just it," Sam said, frustrated, angry, and worried as hell about May. When he got his hands on her... "She *doesn't* have them."

"What?" Karl asked as at the same time, Becky barked, "Sam, sit down."

He sat because Becky was looking kind of militant. She immediately began wrapping his feet in warm towels.

His feet tingled as they warmed.

"What do you mean May doesn't have the diamonds?" Karl demanded. His hair was sticking straight on end. "I thought you said she got them from the café."

"She did." Otter came over and put his wet front paws on Sam's knee. He ruffled the dog's wiry fur. "She had them in her pocket the entire time yesterday, but last night I took them out of her coat pocket. She must've been so damned concerned with getting away from me that she didn't even check her own pocket."

She was walking into a meet with a psychotic mafiya boss with no assets, and it was all Sam's fault. He should've told her he'd taken the diamonds, should've confessed that he didn't completely trust her when it came to her uncle. But he hadn't wanted to start an argument, to start fighting again over how to handle Beridze and get Old George back. They'd been so close for once, he thought it all could wait for just one night.

Shit. He'd chosen his cock over May's safety.

He gripped his head in his hand, trying to *think*. May had the snowmobile. They had two dog sleds and a truck with a plow blade—none of them anywhere as fast as a snowmobile. And even if he could catch up with May, what was he going to do? Hand over the diamonds and hope Beridze would suddenly grow some morality and give back both May and her uncle?

Fuck. He was just fucked.

"Breathe, Sam," Becky murmured, kneeling at his feet. She'd brought over another batch of warm towels.

"Sam?"

He looked up at the croak. Doc was in the doorway to the spare room, leaning hard on Dylan. "Jesus, Doc, you need to be lying down."

Doc looked pale as death, but a corner of his mouth twitched up. "Kind of hard to sleep with all the commotion out here. What's your plan?"

Sam stared at him, his mind blank.

But Doc simply nodded his head, no trace of worry in his face. "You can do it. You'll make a plan, save Maisa and George. Town's counting on you, son. I am, too."

And with that Doc turned and limped back into the spare room with Dylan.

Sam inhaled and glanced around. They were all looking at him, Karl, Molly, and Haley Anne. Stu, Walkingtall, and Jim were on the other side of the kitchen island, Ilya was still huddled in his chair, and even Doug was propped in the doorway to the spare bedroom. They all expected him to know the answers, to save them from catastrophe, to get them out of the hopeless situation.

You play afraid and you'll never win, Doc had said so long ago at Ed's.

Sam stood. "Okay. We're going to toss these assholes out of our town once and for all."

Relief swept Becky's face, but Walkingtall merely grunted. "How?"

Sam stared him in the eye a beat and then looked one, by one, at everyone else. He needed them all behind him for this. "We need to find a way to surprise Beridze. Something he won't expect."

Jim cleared his throat. "Would explosives help?"

Everyone turned to stare at him.

Sam blinked. "Yeah, Jim, I'd say explosives would be very helpful."

Chapter Forty-Six

She was small and dark, this niece of George Rapava, and what was more, George was very fond of her.

Jabba watched as the old man tried and failed to hide his anxiety over the woman. Of course George was most likely in quite some pain, which may've made it harder for him to conceal his emotions. Jabba had amused himself the night before tracing the tattoos on George's chest with his knife. Shallow cuts, not deep enough to do any lethal harm. And then he'd cut off George's little fingertip, and George had screamed and Jabba had thought that perhaps he should stop there.

It would not do to kill him too soon.

But now he had this niece who had so kindly walked into the middle of the town street and shouted that she had the diamonds. He had had her brought to him and she stood defiantly before him, her gaze calm and unafraid.

"So," Jabba said, lighting a cigarillo. "You have the diamonds."

"Yes," the niece said. "Send my uncle out and I'll give them to you."

"Or—" Jabba sucked on the cigarillo "—I have my

men kill you and I take the diamonds from your dead body." He exhaled smoke through his smile.

She shook her head. "I'm not stupid. I don't have them on me. Let my uncle go and I'll lead you to where I hid them."

Jabba thought about torturing the niece to find out where the diamonds lay. It would be simple enough with his men here. But he grew bored easily. More torture—even of a woman—seemed tedious.

He caught a movement from the corner of his eye, and then he had a new idea. George Rapava seemed truly afraid for the first time since he'd stepped into the police station.

Afraid not for himself, but for his niece.

"Very well," Jabba said. "You've convinced me with your words. I shall let your uncle free."

"No!" George lunged forward.

Rocky casually kicked him in the hip and the old man went down, groaning.

The niece looked down at the uncle writing in pain on the floor and then up at Jabba. "Are you finished?"

Ah, now this was interesting. She'd risked her life to save the uncle, yet she was uninterested in his pain.

Jabba cocked his head. "Should I be?"

She sighed as if weary of him. "I think so. You do want those diamonds, don't you?"

"Oh, indeed I do." He stepped close to her, and raised a hand to trail his forefinger over her cheek. "Perhaps I want other things as well."

She slapped his hand away. "I bet you already have plenty of women for that. I have something else you need."

He narrowed his eyes, intrigued. "And what is that?"

She smiled, her lips curving prettily. "You want to get out of here alive, don't you?"

"Most assuredly."

"Then you're going to need a hostage."

Jabba smiled. "And you offer yourself in exchange for George here? The niece of a notorious mafiya?"

"No," she said, her eyes hard. "I offer myself. The daughter of a notorious Minneapolis prosecutor."

Chapter Forty-Seven

Maisa was so busy staring Jabba Beridze down and trying not to look at Dyadya that when at first her cell phone rang she didn't even notice.

In fact, it was one of Beridze's men, Rocky, the one who'd brought her in who said in a thick Russian accent, "Boss? Do you hear a cell?"

Everyone patted their pockets.

Maisa took the opportunity to glance at Dyadya. He still lay on the floor, but when she looked, he winked at her, which made her feel a lot better.

"It is yours," Beridze said.

Maisa took her cell out and stared at it. After being a useless piece of plastic and glass for last couple of days it had suddenly come alive again. And she didn't recognize the number on the screen.

"Answer it," Beridze said.

She swiped the screen and held it to her ear. "Hello?"

"Sweetheart." Sam's voice was rich and deep and oh, so wonderful.

Her heartbeat started doing triple time. He must hate

her right now. She didn't say anything because there was nothing to say, not really.

"Are you all right, May?" His voice held impatience now.

"I'm perfectly fine," she said. "I'm discussing hostages with Mr. Beridze."

That earned her a short pause. "Can they hear me?"

"Not right now."

"Good. Do you know that you don't have the diamonds?"

"Yes." She'd made that unpleasant discovery when she'd gotten off the snowmobile in front of the police station, much too late to change her strategy.

"Okay, put me on speaker."

She blinked, feeling almost hurt that he was so brusque. Silently, she held the phone out and pressed the icon for Speaker. "Everyone can hear you now."

"Beridze."

The mobster raised his eyebrows and stepped closer, peering curiously at the phone. "Officer Sam West, am I not right?"

"Correct," Sam said. "I don't know what Maisa Burnsey told you, but she doesn't have the diamonds. I do."

Maisa felt her blood turn to ice crystals in her veins.

She looked up and met Beridze's amused lizard eyes. "Oh, yes?"

"Yeah," Sam drawled, sounding as relaxed as if he were lounging in front of a football game. "You want 'em or not?"

Beridze's eyes narrowed. "You know I do."

"Good. Then bring both Ms. Burnsey and George to the lake at noon. I want them safe and I want them alive. I see either of them hurt or if you leave one behind, I'll throw these lovely pink hearts into the lake. We make the exchange there and then I want you out of my town. Deal?"

"And why should I make any deals with you, Mr. West?"

"Because the cell towers are back up," Sam said. "We have reception and soon we'll have a boatload of FBI and police, all tearing into my town looking for you. And Beridze? You might not like my deal, but I assure you the FBI won't be making any deals at all. This's your last chance to get out of my town alive. Take it or leave it."

The phone clicked and the screen read, *CALL ENDED*.

Maisa looked up into eyes that had all the humanity of a dead lizard.

"You lied to me," Beridze said.

"Yes." Maisa swallowed drily. "And I lied to him, too. I'm like that and so are you. But Sam West? I don't think he's ever lied in his life. If he says this is your last chance, then you'd better take it."

Chapter Forty-Eight

It had been a good long while since Sam had smoked. Maybe once or twice when he'd been stupid and fifteen. A couple more times when he'd been in bars on leave in the army. Not since then.

He fought the urge to cough as he squinted through the thin stream of smoke from the cigarette between his lips. His main worry was that it would burn down before he needed it.

He stood on the side of the lake where Stu had dropped him off earlier. The sun shone blindingly, reflecting white off millions of snow crystals.

In the center of a sheet of white stood four people: Beridze, one of his henchmen, Maisa, and George.

Sam took a breath and started out. He had to have faith that Karl, Molly, Dylan, and Stu could take out whatever of Beridze's men still remained.

Of course Beridze would expect that, too.

The black suitcase was heavy in Sam's hand, but he made an effort to carry it lightly.

As if it only held clothes.

"West!" Beridze's voice carried across the ice. He

sounded happy. But then he *was* a psychopath. "Stop right there. I have men with guns aimed at you."

Sam sure as hell hoped not, but he stopped as instructed. He could see May, shorter than the men. He couldn't make out her expression at this distance, but she had to be scared out of her wits.

The odds of them both making it out of this alive were slim.

He should've told her that he loved her when he'd had the chance.

"What now?" he shouted at the lunatic.

Beridze actually laughed. "Toss me the diamonds."

Sam shook his head. "Too far. Let me come closer."

Beridze nodded and waved him forward.

Even in the cold, sweat was gathering under his armpits and sliding down the small of his back as Sam walked toward the group.

"Tell me, Officer West," Beridze said, "you have killed eight of my men, wrecked two of my vehicles, and made me very, very angry. Why should I not have my men shoot you dead right there?"

Sam felt his shoulder blades crawl, but he refused to look around for the glint of a gun barrel. "Yeah, well, your men shot Doc Meijers in the leg, and his leg is worth a sight more than all of your men put together, so if anyone ought to be pissed, I think it should be me."

"And yet you intend to let me go with my diamonds," Beridze said. "That's far enough."

Sam nodded. He stood fifty feet away now. "Let them go."

"Let me see the diamonds first," Beridze said.

Sam eyed him. Beridze's eyes were sparkling and he was showing too much teeth. He sighed. The asshole was going to try and double-cross him. Sam sucked on the cigarette, making the end glow bright orange, and squatted in front of the suitcase. He held the cigarette between his first two fingers as he unzipped the suitcase. The diamonds lay in their bag right on top and he lifted them, pausing only a split second to light the fuse. He rezipped the suitcase with the fuse sticking out where the zip met the corner, not quite shut. The fuse smoldered and Sam felt sweat start at his hairline.

"Got 'em." He held up the bag of pink jewels.

"Oh, very good," Beridze drawled. "Now, Maisa and George, run toward your savior. West, throw the diamonds to me. If I don't have them by the time your friends reach you, Sasha will shoot all three of you."

May gasped and took her uncle's hand, hurrying him forward. The old man must be injured from more than just his hand, because he sure wasn't moving fast.

Sam's gaze dropped to the suitcase full of explosives at his feet. The fuse had nearly disappeared inside. He was no expert. He probably had about a minute.

Give or take.

May and George were halfway to him now.

Sam took a step back and threw the bag of diamonds at Beridze.

For a moment, the asshole's attention was in the air, tracking the diamonds.

Sam bent, picked up the suitcase and, swinging it like a discus thrower, hurled it at Beridze and his man.

The suitcase thumped down at their feet just as Beridze caught the bag of diamonds.

"Shoot him!" Beridze said, nearly giving Sam a heart attack.

Beridze's henchman began to raise his handgun but before he could fire, he staggered back.

A gunshot echoed across the lake.

May. May was in a shooter's stance. She'd brought the little handgun Sam had given her yesterday. As Sam watched she fired three more times.

The henchman went down and stayed down.

Sam was pretty impressed. As far as he could tell, all her shots hit her targets.

"You...you fucking *jerk*," she screamed at Beridze and the gun in her hand began to shake.

"May," Sam said.

"Tiny-pricked *asshole*!"

Sam took her arm, trying to drag her back. "There's a bomb in the suitcase."

She turned to him, wide-eyed, mouth open. "What?"

He had May's arm in one hand and George's arm in the other and started hustling to the shore.

Behind them, Beridze was laughing like a hyena. "Do you think to play the same trick *twice*—"

BOOM!

The blast threw Sam onto his stomach, knocking the air from his lungs, bruising his hands, elbows, and knees. For a moment he just lay there, wheezing, fighting the familiar panic of not being able to draw breath. Beside him, he could hear May swearing and the sound sent a wash of relief through him. He gasped, the air whistling as his lungs, pain blossoming at his side. He wondered if he'd broken a rib or two.

Sam sat up and looked at George.

The old man was gazing up at the sky with wonder, but as Sam leaned over him, he smiled. "Thank you."

Sam inhaled painfully. "No problem."

He looked at May, but she wasn't waiting to let him see if she was okay. She threw herself against him, knocking him back in the snow and making him grunt with pain from his bruised ribs and lungs.

Not that he cared.

May was kissing him, alive and warm and safe, and frankly he could take a few aches and pains to have that.

He kissed her back, letting her straddle him, not caring about the cold or the fucking diamonds or really anything else but May's lips and May's weight and May's fingers in his hair.

Until someone cleared their throat above them.

May broke away to look up.

Sam tilted his head to see Molly Jasper staring down at him, disapprovingly, her rifle slung under her arm.

Beside her, Karl was staring at the lake. Sam struggled up, May still astride him, and looked, too.

There was a smoking, jagged hole with water bubbling up where both Sasha and Beridze had been.

"Dude," Karl said in wonder. "What do you suppose happened to the diamonds?"

Chapter Forty-Nine

She had to leave.

That was the one thought that kept running through Maisa's mind. After the gunfire, after patching Dyadya up, after the hugging and exclamations of relief when they got back. After things began to run down, and Sam had gone to secure the police station and the two remaining mafiya thugs. She couldn't face him after what she'd done.

It was over and the urge to run was nearly overwhelming.

Maisa slowly wiped down Sam's kitchen table. Everyone had scattered after lunch, either to take much-needed naps or to help with the cleanup of the town.

Everyone but Maisa and Becky.

"Are you going to talk to him?" Becky asked.

"What?"

"Sam," Becky said impatiently. "You need to talk to him."

"I..." Maisa shook her head. "I need to get Dyadya to the hospital, and Sam's busy with all the police work. I don't suppose we'll have a chance to talk before I leave. Probably that's best."

Becky threw the dishcloth she'd been using into the

sink and propped a hand against her hip. "What's that supposed to mean?"

Maisa watched her hand going around and around on the already clean counter. She shrugged.

"Maisa Burnsey—"

"I betrayed him, okay?" Maisa threw down her own cloth, frowning fiercely so she wouldn't cry. "When he most needed me, I left him. I didn't trust him to get Dyadya safely away, and because of that I nearly got us all killed."

"Yeah, that was a shit move," Becky said. "But keeping your worries to yourself isn't going to solve anything."

Maisa shook her head. "There isn't anything to solve, all right? I...I just don't belong here. I don't belong with Sam."

"Bullshit," Becky snorted. "Me and half the town have watched that man chase you for most of the year. Just stop running, why don't you?"

"Because he wouldn't be happy with me!" Otter looked up at her shout. Karl and Molly had taken Cookie to a local vet in the sled, and the little terrier seemed lonely without his bedmate. Maisa lowered her voice. "I just...it'd be better to leave him alone."

Becky looked at her and took a deep breath. "I'm going to say this only once, Maisa Burnsey. I always thought there'd be time for Doc and me. That there wasn't any hurry, no need to figure out anything between us." She let out a breath, a tear trickling down her tough face. "But we nearly ran out of time. Don't be a dumbass."

Becky stalked out of the kitchen and into the downstairs bath.

Maisa was left staring down at her hands, wondering which would be the bigger mistake:

Staying for Sam.

Or leaving him.

Maisa sighed and threw the dishrag in the sink before wearily tramping up the stairs to Sam's bedroom.

"Masha mine," Dyadya rumbled from Sam's bed—the only place left to put him when they'd got back. "What worries you?"

"Nothing." Maisa tried for a smile, but it wasn't working. "Now that Beridze is gone, everything's back to normal. We just have to wait for the roads to clear and we'll be out of here."

" 'We'?" Dyadya's voice was sharp. "I had the idea that you might be staying here with Sam West."

"No." Maisa took a breath, steadying herself. "You don't have to worry about that. You were right: there's too much difference between us."

"You are sure of this, Masha mine?" His words were so gentle she nearly sobbed.

She sank suddenly onto the side of the bed. "I really don't see how he can forgive me, Dyadya."

The old man's hand moved and then it was covering hers. He sighed.

"You were right. We're too far apart," she whispered. "We wouldn't have worked out any more than Mama and Jonathan."

"Such melodrama," he chided gently. "Do you remember when I told you that sometimes as a man grows older, he regrets decisions he made in his youth?"

She twisted to look at him. Despite his injuries, Dyadya was looking alert as he lay in Sam's bed. "Yes?"

"Well, Masha mine, I fear I have begun to regret things I have done—and not done."

She raised her eyebrows. She'd never heard Dyadya voice remorse for his bloody past.

"Oh, not *those* actions." Dyadya waved a hand, dismissing his years as a Russian mafiya. "No, I regret that I never fully told you *why* your father forced me to testify against Gigo Meskhi."

Maisa moved restlessly. "Dyadya—"

"No, my Masha," Dyadya said sternly. "You will listen this time, I think. Jonathan Burnsey did not like my closeness to you and your mother, but it was not for the reason you imagine. He worried less for his career and more for *your* safety."

"That's ridiculous."

"Is it?" He asked softly. "You have years of prejudice, but think as a woman, not a child. I worked for the most powerful mafiya *pakhan* in the U.S. Is it not natural, then, that a father should fear such a connection? When he forced me to testify, he removed not only Meskhi from you and your mother's life, but me as well. And I was the original source of this danger, was I not?"

"But..." Her mind struggled to understand this new view of her history, her life. "But why didn't he tell me?"

"Perhaps he knew you wouldn't listen." Dyadya shook his head. "I do not know, but I think it is past time for you to talk to your father, Masha mine. You may find that he is not entirely the monster you think him. People rarely are. Too, I think nothing good comes from avoiding discussions such as these. Misunderstandings can live for years, can they not? All avoidable if one has but a little courage to talk over things, eh?"

Maisa stared at her beloved uncle, too confused to respond for a moment.

Then someone whooped from downstairs.

Maisa rose and went to the head of the stairs to look.

Downstairs Dylan turned from the front door. "There's a plow coming through. We're out!"

She nodded and returned to Dyadya, her mind made up. "We need to get you, Doc, and Doug to a hospital."

Chapter Fifty

❧

"But you wanted me to get a job," Karl said, wincing as his voice edged toward a whine.

"Not by stealing our cultural heritage!" Molly had her lower lip outthrust, which wasn't helping Karl with his thinking, because he just wanted to bite it. Main Street was deserted and the going was slow in the deep snow.

They'd already brought Cookie to Frannie McIntyre, the local vet who lived just outside town. Frannie had a back-up generator on her little clinic and had assured Karl she could patch up Cookie, even as the bitch had been growling nastily at the vet. Good thing Frannie kept a supply of extra strong muzzles just for the sled dogs.

He sighed heavily as they crossed the street to the Laughing Loon Café, which was missing its front window. Marie was going to be real pissed about that. Sam had asked them to rummage up whatever supplies remained so they could feed their prisoners and possibly keep them from freezing. Karl was of the opinion that freezing mafiya thugs wouldn't be such a bad thing, but he wasn't the police, so...

They both looked up as a white pickup steered slowly

around the corner of Fourth and onto Main. It drew to a stop before the Laughing Loon Café. Tick opened the front passenger door and jumped down next to them.

He slammed the door shut and thumped it. "Thanks!"

The driver, wearing a baclava and brown insulated coveralls, waved a leather mitten-clad hand and pulled away.

Karl stared at Tick. "Where the hell have you been, man?"

"Got stuck out past 52, spent two nights in the squad car, and then hitched a ride into town. You cannot believe the crap forty-eight hours I've had. Only half a Snickers and an old granola bar to eat, melted snow to drink. Right out of one of those survival shows." Tick shook his head. "Hey, what happened to the window of Tracy's Antique Shop?" He glanced around across the street and did a classic double take. "What. The. Hell?"

Karl grinned. The municipal building—and indeed most of Main—*was* looking the worst for wear. "We've had a bit of trouble ourselves. Better check on Sam, he'll fill you in. He's in the police station."

"Uh . . . sure," Tick said faintly. He stumbled across the street.

Karl pushed open the door to the Laughing Loon Café and got back to important business. "I didn't steal any cultural heritage," he patiently explained—*again*. "I made the arrowheads myself, which means—Hey! I'm actually *promoting* our Native American heritage by making the tools of our ancestors."

He turned to grin in triumph at Molly, only to be met by the Stare of Exasperation, which, sadly, he had quite the experience with. "Karl, you're not promoting anything by making fake arrowheads. It's got to be breaking some kind of law to sell fake artifacts under pretenses."

"I never actually *say* the arrowheads are artifacts," Karl pointed out. "Is it my fault that people on eBay see my ad and think the arrowheads are ancient?"

"Yes," Molly said decisively. She stepped into the kitchen and began going through drawers, although how she was going to find crackers in there, he didn't know.

Karl kicked the floor, which only hurt his toe. "It took me a lot of practice to make those arrowheads. It's, like, a true talent. Do you want to suppress my natural creativity?"

She snorted at that, not even bothering to look around.

He watched her a minute, her hands working neatly and swiftly, as she rummaged through the drawers. A sort of longing welled up in him. He'd give away everything he had—his trailer, his truck, and his dogs—just to have Molly in his life. She was all he'd ever wanted, really.

"Molly," he said softly, creeping up behind her. His hands hovered over her shoulders. He wanted to touch her but was afraid of her reaction. "Molly, 'member when we were kids and you showed me how to bait a hook? And I showed you how to catch crayfish in the rocks? Do you remember laying out under the stars and you could name every one?"

She'd stopped rummaging, stilling as she listened to him. "Not *every* star."

"It seemed like every star to me," he said low and he dared to lay his hands on her shoulders. They were just the right height. "You knew the planets and the constellations and...and everything, Molly."

She breathed quietly under his hands.

"You're the prettiest woman on the reservation. Or even outside it," he said, going all out. "The prettiest woman I've ever seen."

She turned, her brows knit and her voice sounded impatient. "No, I'm not."

"Yes," he breathed. "Yes, you are to me."

Her eyes widened, and he felt for the first time in days that she was actually listening to him.

"I'm not educated like Walkingtall," he admitted. "And I'm not as tall as he is—"

She snorted again. "I don't care about that."

He smiled. "Good. I know I'm not everything you want me to be, but Molly, I can try to be. For you."

She looked distressed at that, and he wondered what he'd said wrong until she laid her mittened hands on his chest and said, "You don't have to change for me. I just want you to live up to your full potential."

"But I am," he said, very earnestly, because maybe she didn't see. "I know I don't make a whole lot of money, and I probably never will, but I help out. I fixed Mrs. Thompson's kitchen sink and didn't charge a dime, although I did eat the stew she made for me. I brought Crazy Ole a mess of sunnies just last week and even stayed to hear his war stories. I volunteer-coach midget hockey, and we might even win a game this year. I might not be a lawyer or a doctor, but I don't know that the rez needs more lawyers or doctors. Maybe it just needs people to help out. People like me."

"Oh, Karl," Molly said, sounding helpless and tender.

And he brought it home, leaning in to whisper, "I'll give up my arrowhead making, I'll give back the twenty-five thousand to that guy I already sold a couple of arrowheads to. Hell, Molly, I'll even give up my mushing if you want. Just...just give me a chance."

He kissed her and it was just like in the movies, if the movies took place in a back kitchen without any heat, but that didn't matter because between them they made heat, Molly and him. He saw stars, he heard trumpets, and he was pretty sure he was on his way to heaven when Molly pulled back.

"*How* much did you sell those arrowheads for?"

Chapter Fifty-One

"What do you mean she's gone?" Sam stared, stunned, at Becky.

Becky shrugged as she laid some kind of reheated hotdish in front of him. He was dog-tired. He'd spent the remainder of the day on paperwork and talking to bureaucrats who wanted to know how one of the most notorious Russian gangsters had ended up blown to pieces in a small-town Minnesota lake. He'd arrived back at his cabin hoping to spend some time with May.

Only to find that she'd up and left.

"She and Stu took them all to the hospital up in Alexandria," Becky said softly, pouring him coffee. He never drank coffee for dinner. "I would've gone, too, but there was no more room in Stu's truck. 'Spect I'll go up tomorrow when the roads are clearer. Maisa called and said Doc was resting comfortably. They've got him on an antibiotic IV and he's well enough to complain about the food. Apparently Doug actually likes hospital food, so Stu says he's happy."

"Well, why didn't she call me?" Sam pushed the plate away.

Becky shrugged. "I don't know, Sam."

He laughed. "She's running again. God damn it, I thought we were over this."

Becky frowned. "A lot has happened in the last couple of days."

"Yeah, it has," he snapped back. "I thought I'd started a relationship."

"Give her time, Sam."

He liked Becky, but he couldn't help scoffing at that.

Otter came over and pushed his nose into Sam's palm.

Becky moved quietly around the kitchen.

Sam didn't know where everyone else had got to—probably home, now that some of the roads had been cleared. All except Ilya, still dozing in his chair. Damn. Maybe he'd ended up with a permanent Russian mobster roommate. Except he was pretty certain that the government types he'd been talking to all afternoon had plans to make Ilya turn state's evidence.

"I'm sorry, Becky," Sam sighed. The older woman hadn't needed to stay and make him dinner, and he'd thanked her by taking out his anger over May on her.

"How you doin', Sam?"

"Fine." He took a half-hearted bite of the hotdish. God, he was tired. "This's good."

She gave him a look. "You're gonna have to go after her."

"Yeah, well, I've done that before and it doesn't seem to've made a difference," he said, not bothering to hide the bitterness in his voice.

"She's scared, Sam."

He laughed at that. "May's the least scared person I've ever met. She faced down a crazy Russian mobster today."

"Yes, she did," Becky said. "That's a woman worth working for."

"I have worked for her," Sam said hard and low. "She said she'd work on this with me, and now she's gone again. And I've reached my limit. If May wants this, she'll have to come after me this time."

Chapter Fifty-Two

❦

It was well past midnight by the time Maisa made it back to Sam's cabin and all the windows were dark. She sat in Stu's borrowed pickup for a moment, gathering her nerve. The sled dogs were gone, the other vehicles missing. Only Sam's big truck sat in the driveway. As far as she could see everyone else had gone home.

It was just the two of them now.

Okay. She could do this.

Maisa got out of the truck and trudged up the drive to the door. She'd swiped one of the spare keys on the hook by the door when she'd left for the hospital, and now she tried it in the lock.

The key turned easily and she opened the door to find Otter dancing on the other side, his tail wagging madly.

"I've only been gone a couple of hours," Maisa whispered to him, but his enthusiastic greeting made her feel better.

That is until she looked up and found Otter's owner staring at her. Sam wore a pair of boxer briefs and nothing else. Well, beside the gun he held by his side. "What're you doing here, May?"

Not exactly welcoming.

Maisa carefully hung the keys by the front door. "I wanted to talk to you."

He gave her a look and then turned and walked back upstairs.

At least he hadn't tossed her out. She shed her coat and boots and followed him up. Otter, too.

When she got to his bedroom, he'd donned his jeans and turned on the lamp. He was sitting, propped up on the bed's headboard. "Why'd you leave without talking to me, May?"

"Because I was scared." She shifted from one foot to another, then thought, *The hell with it*, and crossed to sit on the bed next to him. "You have to understand, I've only had my mother and Dyadya for such a long time…it's like I've forgotten how to let other people in."

He didn't say anything, just watched her.

She inhaled. "And I was ashamed of how I treated you this morning. I…I didn't trust you to save Dyadya. I stole the diamonds—or thought I did."

He looked away at that. "Yeah, well, I guess I see it from the other end: I took the diamonds from you because I didn't trust you not to do something stupid."

She winced at the *stupid* but raised her chin. "And you were right. I betrayed your trust."

"Did you?" For the first time he smiled, a small, wry twist of his lips. "Here's the thing: I don't know if I consider it a betrayal for you to love your uncle so much that you did everything in your power to save him. Sure, if you were a heroine in some old movie, one that never swore and never did anything wrong at all, then it might be a betrayal. But you're not some made-up character. You're

May, sweet and sharp and abrasive and gentle and *real*."
He took a breath, running his hand through his short hair.
"Maybe I'm the one in the wrong. I almost let my rage at
Beridze, my wrong-headedness over not letting him get
those damned diamonds, get the better of me." He looked
up at her. "It was never the diamonds, May, you know
that, right? I love you. That was the only thing I could
think about out there on that ice. I love you and I'd let
Beridze walk away a thousand times over if—"

But she couldn't wait to let him finish. Maisa launched
herself at him, catching his face, pulling it to hers. "I love
you." She kissed him, trying to convey all the power of
her emotion, because three simple words weren't going to
do it.

He wrapped his arms around her and pulled her tight,
his face angling under hers, his lips hot and possessive.

When she pulled back to gasp for breath, he made to
chase her lips, but she placed her fingers on his mouth,
forestalling him. "I need to tell you. I've stopped running,
Sam. I'm going to stay here and stick it out for whatever
this is between us, but I know I'm not going to get any
easier. I've got a temper and I'm going to say or do the
wrong thing sometime in the future, and I'm sorry—"

But he was already shaking his head. "As long as you
stay. As long as you let me talk it out with you. We're
going to be good."

"No," she whispered against his lips. "We're going to
be *wonderful*."

Chapter Fifty-Three

Sam West sighed as he pulled his cruiser tight behind the black Volkswagen Beetle and got out. Death, taxes, and speeders up on 52—some things were eternal.

Especially this speeder.

He strolled to the Beetle's side, motioning for the driver to roll down her window.

The window opened to reveal Maisa Burnsey peering at him over the top of her cat-eyes sunglasses. "Is there a problem, Officer?"

He fought to keep his lips straight. "I'm afraid so, ma'am. You were speeding."

She widened her eyes in exaggerated shock. "Was I?"

"Yup. You were driving over the speed limit. *Well* over," he replied drily, pulling down his own sunglasses to give her a look.

She reached out her hand and stroked a red-tipped fingernail slowly down his pants zipper. "Gosh, is there any way I can make this go away?"

He had to clear his throat and even then his voice came

out hoarse. "Damn it, May, how many times have I told you—"

He stopped speaking when she put out her palm. "Ask me what my hurry was."

"What's the hurry?"

"Well, as you know I'm marrying the love of my life tomorrow."

"I do know," he said softly. "I'm doing the same."

She bit her lip for a moment and it was all he could do to stop himself from bending down and kissing her right there.

But then she sobered. "I have a rehearsal dinner to get to tonight."

"Me, too," he said, his eyes narrowing. "And I need to shower first because Karl's idea of a bachelor party is fishing until three a.m. on Moosehead Lake."

That got him a mock sympathetic look. "No strippers?"

"You know damn well I would've vetoed strippers."

She grinned, because he was pretty certain she *did* know. "What's wrong with fishing?"

"Nothing. Just not twelve damned hours of it." He shook his head. "Karl's convinced that if he catches enough walleye, he'll eventually get one that swallowed a pink diamond."

She outright laughed at that.

He raised his eyebrows. "You gonna tell me your half-baked excuse for speeding?"

"It's not half-baked!"

"May," he warned, "if either of us is late to this rehearsal dinner tonight, Becky will have our hides. She's been planning this thing for *months*. But it's hours away. Why—"

"I have it on good authority that a certain newly promoted deputy police chief will be off duty in, oh—" she glanced at her wristwatch "—twenty minutes."

He leaned his hip against the car door. "Say that's true. What's it got to do with you speeding?"

"We-ell," she said, drawing the word out, "if I were at that certain deputy police chief's cabin when he got home, he might find himself getting lucky in the couple of hours before that rehearsal dinner."

Sam gave up trying to resist. He put his hands on either side of her open car window, leaned down, and caught her mouth in a kiss.

May gasped, opening her lips, and for a moment he forgot that they were on the side of 52 in broad daylight and in view of any passing motorist. He kissed May Burnsey like she was the most important thing in his life.

Which she kind of was.

Then he remembered. Sam broke the kiss just enough to whisper against May's lips. "You better get running, then, sweetheart."

He stepped back and watched as she pulled out onto 52, doing maybe just under the speed limit. And he wasn't at all worried as her taillights vanished into the distance. Because May Burnsey might run, but nowadays?

Sam West *always* caught his woman.

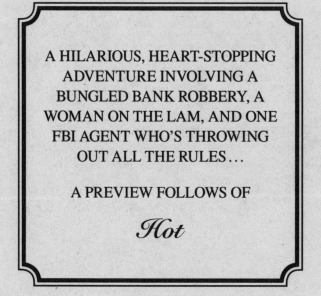

A HILARIOUS, HEART-STOPPING
ADVENTURE INVOLVING A
BUNGLED BANK ROBBERY, A
WOMAN ON THE LAM, AND ONE
FBI AGENT WHO'S THROWING
OUT ALL THE RULES...

A PREVIEW FOLLOWS OF

Hot

Chapter One

In Turner Hastings' opinion, the bank robbery didn't go truly bad until Yoda shot out the skylight. Which was not to say that the robbery hadn't had its problems up until that point.

It started out as a typically busy Saturday. Turner was working the drive-through teller station, peering out the bullet-proof glass at the customers in cars. It was almost noon—closing time for the First Wisconsin Bank of Winosha. Nasty old Mr. Johnson had just pulled up and begun fumbling with the plastic canister in the pneumatic tube when she heard the commotion behind her. She glanced over her shoulder in time to see two men rush the bank counter.

One was tall and spindly in that way some guys are. The kind of skinny where you can't help but wonder what, exactly, is holding up their jeans because they have no rear end to speak of. He was wearing a black Eminem T-shirt and a Yoda mask, and clutching a sawed-off shotgun in an uncertain way, as if he'd never held one before. The second man was short and hairy. He had the thick black stuff growing on his arms, the backs of his hands, his fingers, and of course, his chest. Unfortunately, he'd chosen to wear a yellow mesh tank, which only served to highlight all that abundance of fur. Perhaps he'd wanted to coordinate with the cheery yellow of his SpongeBob SquarePants mask. He held his shotgun with a bit more knowledge than Yoda, but under the present circumstances, that wasn't nearly as reassuring as it should have been.

"This is a floor! Everybody on the stickup!" SpongeBob screamed in a disconcertingly hoarse voice, little tube-socked SpongeBob legs swinging back and forth on the mask.

Everyone in the small bank paused, trying to digest those two sentences. Turner opened her mouth, thought better about it, and shut it again.

Marge, the only customer inside the bank if you didn't count the robbers, had no such inhibitions. "This is a *stickup*. Everybody on the *floor*."

And you really couldn't fault her, because she was right. Marge was short and bottom-heavy and wearing turquoise stretch capri pants with a big T-shirt that had glittery pink and orange flamingos on it. She was in her late fifties, which was an age, as she liked to tell anyone who'd listen, when she no longer had to put up with guff from men or boys.

Her correction seemed to make the robbers irritable.

"On the floor! On the floor! On the floor!" Yoda yelled redundantly, the mask's little sticky-out ears flapping.

Turner flattened herself to the floor behind the counter because, really, it seemed to be a good idea.

But that only made SpongeBob upset. "No, dickhead! They'll hit the police alarm back there," he told Yoda. "We need to get them out here in the lobby."

"Okay. Yeah. Okay," Yoda said. "Come on out here, *then* get on the floor."

Turner crawled out after Ashley, the other Saturday teller. Ashley was looking peeved. Before the robbery had started, she'd been talking about her new leaf-green summer pantsuit. She'd found it on sale at the Wal-Mart up in Superior, and she obviously wasn't too thrilled to be crawling in it now.

Behind Turner at the window, she could hear Mr. Johnson's tinny voice through the speaker. "Can I have that in fives? No, better make it ones. And I need some quarters, too, for the washing machines up at the Spin 'n' Go. Make sure they're nice new ones. Last time you people gave me a bunch of sticky change."

Those inside the bank were all out in the lobby now. Turner lay on her belly and contemplated the manure-brown floor tiles. They needed mopping. Typical. Calvin Hyman, the bank president, who naturally wasn't working on a Saturday and thus wasn't in danger of having his head blown off—more's the pity—had saved money by cutting the cleaning to once a week.

"Here." A black plastic garbage bag was thrust in front of Turner's nose. "Fill this with, like, money."

She squinted over her glasses at SpongeBob. Did he realize that in order to ...?

"We're going to have to get back up to fill those," Ashley said, loud, exasperated, and nasal. "Why'd you make us come on out here and get down on the dirty floor if—ow!"

Ashley stopped talking to glare at Turner, who'd just kicked her in the ankle.

"Shut. Up," Turner hissed.

"Don't you go telling me to shut up, Turner Hastings. If you think—"

"Ashley, honey," Marge interrupted from her spot on the floor next to Turner, "just get the nice bank robbers their money."

Good idea. "I'm going to stand up and go get the money, okay?" Turner said to the robbers to give them plenty of warning. She didn't want to make them any more nervous than they already were.

"Yeah, yeah, okay. Hurry up," Yoda answered. She noticed for the first time that the mask's right ear had a tear in it. It'd been Scotch-taped back together.

Turner stood. She took the garbage bag gingerly and walked back behind the counter with Ashley. Behind them, Marge stayed on the floor. It sounded like she was muttering about dirt and men. Turner hit the release on her teller drawer.

Mr. Johnson's scratchy voice was still complaining. "Hello? Hellloooo? What's taking so long? I ain't got all day here, you know—some people have work to do."

Ashley huffed at her counter teller station and pulled out wads of cash.

Turner put a bundle of twenties into her bag and glanced carefully at the big round wall clock—11:56. Fudge. Ashley's boyfriend, Doug, came to pick her up for lunch every Saturday. And Ashley's boyfriend just happened to be a—

"Cop!" SpongeBob squeaked.

"What? Where?" Yoda swung around to look, his shotgun going with him.

Sheriff's Deputy Doug Larson pushed open the tinted glass doors of the bank and paused. The little silver star on his khaki uniform winked in the sunbeam streaming in from the big skylight. His Smokey-the-Bear hat had always seemed a little too big on him to Turner's eye, but that might've been because Doug had such a little pin-head. If you looked at him sideways, the back of his skull was totally flat. Something had to be wrong about that. A ludicrous expression of horror flooded Doug's face, and Turner could almost hear the *Oh, shit.*

Then Doug drew his gun.

Turner decided to duck behind the counter at that point, so she didn't actually see Yoda shoot out the sky-light, but she did hear the *BOOM!* of the shotgun and the subsequent tinkling as glass rained down on them all.

Beside her, Ashley was whimpering, but that soon turned to a shriek. "Doug!"

Oh, Lord, thought Turner. *Please don't let Doug be dead.*

Then Ashley's hollering continued. "Doug! Dougy! Don't leave me! Goddamnit, Doug Larson, see if I ever let you take me out to the Ridge again!"

Turner blinked at that information slip. The Ridge was the local makeout spot. She chanced a look over the counter. Doug, as Ashley had already indicated, was nowhere to be seen. Smart man. He'd probably calculated the odds and gone looking for some backup. Or at the very least, a bigger gun. Meanwhile, Yoda and SpongeBob were still milling in the lobby. Yoda's right ear was dangling from the mask now. Evidently, the Scotch tape hadn't survived the excitement.

"What the hell did you do that for, you douchebag?" SpongeBob yelled. "Why didn't you shoot at the cop instead of the ceiling?"

"Hey, I was trying," Yoda said. "It's not as easy as it looks to aim a sawed-off shotgun—"

"Yes, it is!" SpongeBob retorted. And *BOOM!,* he shot out the front doors.

My, wouldn't Calvin just be miffed when he saw that? Turner's ears were ringing, and the bank filled with the acrid stench of gunpowder.

"Shit," Yoda muttered. "That's not fair. You've had way more practice, dude."

SpongeBob had turned away to shoot the doors. In doing so, he'd revealed a stunningly lush growth of back hair.

"Ew," Marge said from the floor, which pretty much summed it up.

"Fish!" Ashley yelled.

SpongeBob jumped as if someone had poked him in the butt. He swung around to stare at Ashley.

"You're Fish!" Ashley was waving a bubble-gum-pink fingernail at him, apparently unaware that it wasn't a good idea to identify a bank robber when he was actually in the process of robbing the bank. "I'd know that hairy back anywhere. I spent an entire year sitting behind it in sophomore social science. You're Fish."

"Am not!" SpongeBob said, confirming for everyone present that he was indeed Fish.

Wonderful. Turner grabbed Ashley's plastic garbage bag from her.

"Hey—!" Ashley started.

Turner shoved both bags at Yoda and SpongeBob. "Here."

"What are you doing?" Ashley shrieked.

Turner ignored her. She enunciated very carefully to the robbers. "Take the money. Run away."

Yoda lunged convulsively, grabbed the bags of money, and galloped out what was left of the front door. He was followed closely by SpongeBob.

"Can I get off the floor now?" Marge asked plaintively.

Outside, a car with a bad muffler roared away.

"I guess so," Turner replied. She looked around the little bank. Calvin's manure-brown floor was covered in sparkling glass, and a hot August breeze was blowing through the skylight and doors. Hard to believe that ten minutes ago it had been a normal Saturday.

"What'd you do that for?" Ashley demanded, fists on discount Wal-Mart hips. "You just handed them the cash. What kind of First Wisconsin Bank employee are you?"

"A live one," Turner replied.

Ashley looked disgusted. "At least I got one of those ink bundles into my bag."

Turner stared. "You did?"

"Yeah, why?" Ashley asked aggressively.

Turner just shook her head and went to the drive-through window. "I'm sorry, Mr. Johnson, the bank's closed now."

Sirens wailed in the distance, getting closer.

"Why, of all the—" Mr. Johnson began, but Turner switched off the speaker.

There was a squeal of tires from out in front and then the rapid slamming of car doors.

"Looks like the cavalry's arrived," Marge said to no one in particular.

"Come out with your hands in plain sight!" Sheriff Dick Clemmons's voice bellowed, amplified by the speaker on his squad car.

"Oh, for Pete's sake," Turner muttered. It hadn't been

a good day so far, and she was getting a little cranky. She walked to the doors and peeked through broken glass. Outside, two Washburn County sheriff's cars were skewed dramatically across Main Street. Predictably, a crowd had begun to gather behind them.

"They're gone," she said.

"What?" Sheriff Clemmons boomed, still using the speaker.

"They're gone!" Turner yelled.

"Oh." There was a crackle from the speaker, and then Dick stood, hitching up his black utility belt. The sheriff was a tall man with a sloping belly, and the belt had a tendency to slide below it. He looked a little disappointed. "Anyone hurt?"

"No," Turner replied in her best repressive librarian voice. She held open what remained of the shot-out bank door.

Dick strode up the walk in an I'm-in-charge kind of way, trailed by Doug, who still looked a little spooked. Turner couldn't blame him. It wasn't every day that a man got shot at by a Jedi Master.

The sheriff stepped inside the bank and squinted around. "Okay, now—"

"Doug Larson!" Ashley had caught sight of her boyfriend. Doug sort of hunched his shoulders.

"Of all the low-down, ratty things to do," Ashley began.

"Now, honey," Marge interrupted. "You can't go blaming the boy for not wanting to be shot just so you wouldn't ruin a pantsuit from Wal-Mart."

"But he left me!" Ashley wailed, tears running down her cheeks along with a bunch of black mascara.

Marge began patting, Doug started explaining, and

Sheriff Clemmons became authoritative. Then the paramedics arrived, crunching over the floor with equipment nobody needed. Two more deputies appeared, as did the volunteer fire department, most of whom had probably heard about the robbery over their scanners and wanted in on the action.

Turner watched all the people running around, talking, arguing, taking notes, getting in each other's way, and generally trying to look important. She thought about how easy it would be to rob the bank right at that moment when everyone was so very busy. She glanced at the surveillance camera in the corner, dumbly taping everything within the bank. Then she strolled to Calvin's big fake mahogany desk and pulled out the middle drawer. There, sitting in plain sight, was the red paper envelope that held the key to his safe deposit box. She stared at it. She'd never have another chance like this one. She knew because she'd been waiting for this moment for four years. Turner smiled a small, secret smile and palmed the key.

It was time for her own heist.

When free-spirited Zoey Addler hijacks Special Agent Dante Torelli, she doesn't expect to be dodging bullets *and* an inconvenient attraction to the sinfully sexy federal agent.

A PREVIEW FOLLOWS OF

For the Love of Pete

Chapter One

Things finally came to a head between Zoey Addler and Lips of Sin the afternoon he tried to steal her parking space.

Okay, *technically,* her upstairs neighbor's name wasn't really Lips of Sin. She knew the guy's occupation but not his name. Since the man was drop-dead gorgeous, Zoey had taken to calling him "Lips of Sin" in her mind. And yes, *technically,* the parking spot in question might not legally have been hers—she hadn't paid for it or anything—but she *had* shoveled it. This was January in Chicago. In Chicago in winter, shoveling out a parking spot made it yours. Everyone knew that.

Everyone but Lips of Sin, that is.

"What the hell are you doing?" Zoey screamed at him. She body slammed the hood of his black Beemer convertible, which was sitting in her stolen parking spot.

Lips of Sin, behind the wheel of said Beemer, mouthed something she couldn't hear. He rolled down his window. "Are you insane? I could've hit you. Never get in front of a moving vehicle."

Oh, like he had the right to lecture *her*. Zoey straightened, planted both Sorel-booted feet firmly, and crossed her arms. "I shoveled this parking spot. This is *my* parking spot. You can't take it."

Her words emerged in white puffs into the frosty late-afternoon air. They'd already had eight inches of snow the night before, and it looked like it might very well snow again. All the more reason to keep this spot.

The Beemer was at an angle, half in, half out of the parking place, which was almost directly in front of their apartment building. Every other parking space on the block was filled. There was a yellow Humvee, hulking in front of the Beemer, and a red Jeep to the back. Her own little blue Prius was double-parked next to the red Jeep. It was a sweet parking spot. Zoey had gotten up at five freaking a.m. to shovel it before she went to work at the co-op grocery. She'd marked the spot with two lawn chairs and a broken plastic milk crate in time-honored Chicago tradition. Now, returning after a long day of work, it was too much to find Lips in the act of stealing her space.

"Jesus," Lips said. "Look, I'm running a little late here. I promise to shovel you another parking place tonight. Just get out of my way. Please?"

Obviously he wasn't used to begging. Gorgeous guys didn't beg. He had smooth, tea-with-milk brown skin, curly black hair, and bitter-chocolate eyes, framed by lush girly eyelashes. Except the girly eyelashes helped emphasize the hard masculine edges of his face. In fact, the only soft things on his face were the eyelashes and his lips of sin. Deep lines bracketed those lips, framing the cynical corners and the little indent on the bottom lip that made a woman wonder what, exactly, the man could do with that mouth.

Perfect.

He was perfectly perfect in his masculine beauty, and Zoey had hated him on sight. Gorgeous guys were always so damn full of themselves. They strutted around like they were God's gift to women. *Please.* Add to that the fact that the man was always dressed for corporate raiding in suit and tie and black leather trench coat, and he just was not her type.

Lips was getting out of the car now, looking pretty pissed, his black trench coat swirling dramatically around his legs.

Zoey leaned forward, about to give him what-for, when the front doors to their apartment building burst open and a middle-aged guy in a red puffy jacket came running out. He had a baby under his left arm like a football. Zoey froze, her heart paralyzed at the sight. In his right fist was a gun. His bald head swiveled as he caught sight of them, and his gun hand swiveled with it. Zoey's eyes widened, and then a ton of bricks hit her from the side. She went down into the frozen gray slush on the street, and the ton of bricks landed on top of her. An expensive black leather sleeve shielded her face.

BANG!

The shot sounded like it was right in her ear. Zoey contracted her body in animal reaction, trying to make herself smaller beneath the heavy bulk of the man on top of her.

"Get behind the car," Lips breathed in her ear, and she had the incongruous thought that his breath smelled like fresh mint.

Then a flurry of shots rang out, one right after the other, in a wall of sound that scared her witless. The weight lifted from her body, and she felt Lips grab the back of her jacket and haul. She was on hands and knees, but she barely touched the ground before she was behind the Beemer on the driver's side. She looked up and saw Lips crouched over her, a black gun in his hand.

"Don't shoot," she gasped. "He's got the baby!"

"I know." His gaze was fixed over the roof of the car. "Shit."

The word was drowned out by the sound of a revving engine. Zoey looked around in time to see the yellow Hummer accelerate away from the curb, the bald man at the wheel.

"Come on!" She grabbed the door handle of the Beemer and pulled, scrambling ungracefully inside. There was a moment when she thought she might be seriously tangled in the console between the seats, and then she was on the other side, pulling out the passenger-side seat belt. She looked back, and Lips was still standing outside the car, staring at her. "What're you waiting for? We'll lose him."

He narrowed his eyes at her but thankfully didn't argue. Instead he threw back his coat and suit jacket, holstered his gun in a graceful movement Jack Bauer would've envied, and got in the car. He released the emergency brake and shifted into first.

He glanced at her once assessingly and said, "Hold on."

The force of his acceleration slammed her against the Beemer's lush leather seat. Then they were flying, the car eerily quiet as they sped through Evanston.

"Do you think he's a pedophile?" She clutched at the car armrest anxiously.

"No."

The yellow Hummer had turned at the corner onto a medium-sized boulevard lined with small businesses and shops. Zoey was afraid they would've already lost him by now, but two stoplights ahead, the Hummer idled at a red light.

She leaned forward. "There he is. Up ahead at the stoplight."

"I see him." The words were quiet, but they had an edge.

Well, too bad. "Can't you go any faster?"

He sped past a forest green minivan.

"The light changed. He's moving again." Zoey bit her lip, trying to still the panic in her chest. "We can't lose him. We just can't. You need to go faster."

Lips glanced at her. He didn't say anything, but Zoey heard a kind of scraping sound, like he was grinding his teeth. She rolled her eyes. Men had such delicate egos. She hauled her cell out of her jacket pocket and began punching numbers.

"What're you doing?" he asked. The Beemer swerved around a Volkswagen Beetle in the left lane, briefly jumping the concrete divider before thumping down again in front of the Beetle.

Zoey righted herself from where she'd slid against the passenger door. "Calling 911."

He grunted, and she wasn't sure whether that was an approving sound or not. Not that it mattered.

There was a click in her ear and a bored voice said, "911. What is the nature of your emergency?"

The Hummer had turned right at the light onto Demp-ster. Lips steered the Beemer into the turn going maybe forty mph. The Beemer's tires screeched but didn't skid. Points to BMW engineering.

"A baby's been kidnapped," Zoey said to the 911 operator. "We're chasing the kidnapper."

The operator's voice perked up. "Where are you now?"

"On Dempster, near uh…" She craned her neck just as Lips swerved again, nearly sending her nose into the passenger-side window. "Shit."

"I beg your pardon," the operator said, sounding offended.

"Not you. I know we've passed Skokie Boulevard—"

"We're on Dempster and Le Claire," Lips said tightly.

Zoey repeated the information.

"Tell 911 that it's a yellow Hummer," Lips said as he accelerated around a postal truck, imperiling the paint on the Beemer's side. "The license plate's obscured by mud, but there's a dent in the back left panel over the wheel."

The Hummer suddenly swerved into the right lane and took a ramp onto the Edens Expressway.

Zoey gasped in the middle of her recitation. "He's gotten onto the Edens going north."

The Beemer barreled up the ramp and abruptly slowed. In either direction on the freeway, as far as the eye could see, was a four-lane-wide trail of cars.

"Shit," Zoey muttered.

"I beg your pardon," the operator said again. Must get sworn at a lot in her job.

"Not you," Zoey replied and then said to no one in particular, "This is why I never take the Edens after three. They've been doing road construction for, like, ten years here."

"I'll be sure and tell the guy that when we catch up with him," Lips ground out.

If they caught up with him, Zoey thought and bit her bottom lip. The Hummer was already several cars ahead and moving, whereas their part of the traffic jam was stopped dead. There was a good possibility that they'd lose the Hummer in the traffic. She kept her eyes firmly fixed on the massive lump of yellow steel. She wasn't letting it out of her sight. That truck contained a kidnapper with a gun and a very important little piece of humanity. 'Cause the kidnapper hadn't taken just any baby.

He'd taken Pete.

Fall in Love with Forever Romance

Fall in Love with Forever Romance

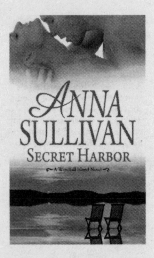

SECRET HARBOR
by Anna Sullivan

Fans of *New York Times* best-selling authors JoAnn Ross, Jill Shalvis, and Bella Andre will love the last book in Anna Sullivan's witty contemporary romance trilogy about a young woman who left her beloved home in Maine to become an actress in Hollywood. Now a star, and beset by scandal, she wants nothing more than to surround herself with old friends... until she meets an infuriating—and sexy—stranger.

MEET ME AT THE BEACH
by V. K. Sykes

Gorgeous Lily Doyle was the only thing Aiden Flynn missed after he escaped from Seashell Bay to play pro baseball. Now that he's back on the island, memories rush in about the night of passion they shared long ago, and everything else washes right out to sea—everything except the desire that still burns between them.

Fall in Love with Forever Romance

HOT
by Elizabeth Hoyt
writing as Julia Harper

For Turner Hastings, being held at gunpoint during a back robbery is an opportunity in disguise. After seeing her little heist on tape, FBI Special Agent John MacKinnon knows it's going to be an interesting case. But he doesn't expect to develop feelings for Turner, and when bullets start flying in her direction, John finds he'll do anything to save her.

FOR THE LOVE OF PETE
by Elizabeth Hoyt
writing as Julia Harper

Dodging bullets with a loopy redhead in the passenger seat is not how Special Agent Dante Torelli imagined his day going. But Zoey Addler is determined to get her baby niece back, and no one—not even a henpecked hit man, cooking-obsessed matrons, or a relentless killer—will stand in her way.

Fall in Love with Forever Romance

ONCE AND ALWAYS
by Elizabeth Hoyt writing as Julia Harper

The newest contemporary from *New York Times* bestselling author Elizabeth Hoyt writing as Julia Harper! Small-town cop Sam West certainly doesn't mind a routine traffic stop. But Maisa Bradley is like nothing he has ever seen, and she's about to take Sam on the ride of his life!